Godspeed
by Alan C. Lyons

Godspeed

ISBN: 098472981X
ISBN-13: 978-0-9847298-1-4

DEDICATION

This book is dedicated to those living avatars who are leading us into creating a shift in consciousness toward the "knowing" of our Universal connection.

"Science without religion is lame, religion without science is blind." ~ Albert Einstein
"Science, Philosophy and Religion: a Symposium", 1941

1

Dawn Sky drifted. Above her, the shimmering surface of the ocean quivered unbroken, flowing from deep distant royal blue, aquamarine and into bright turquoise around the sparkling white center created by the diffused sun. She glided over the bony, brilliant coral that resembled fossilized flowers and petrified plants. Her eyes were dizzied by the hot colors of reds, oranges, purples, yellows and pinks. Schools of shimmering fish parted around her as she swam onwards. Golden damsels scurried by; their little fins flashing yellow, when Dawn suddenly burst through a cloud of blue-and-white striped clownfish, tipped with yellow.

As her slight form sank down towards the sand, she saw translucent blue fish whisking away from her into a darkened arch. Slowly propelling herself with her flippers, she followed them downwards and peered into the shadows. She saw a smooth grey shape, undecorated by the clusters of coral that clung to all the other rocks – then saw it whirl towards her and the mouth of the arch. Its tail swung heavily to each side, the clean sharp fin cutting through the water. Before she had time to register the shark's fatal streamlined jaw, it was opening to show rows of serrated teeth...

Everything snapped out of existence.

She opened her eyes.

"If you don't mind, *miss,* there's other people who want to try the VEC2020 – people who might actually want to purchase it."

The pimply salesman sneered at Dawn from the safe

confines of his synthetic suit and plastic counter. She glanced at her newly-imposed surroundings, still dizzy from shock. The showroom had filled with the lunchtime rush, which now stood in lines three-deep around every stand. RUSH and PURE dominated the exhibition. Their illumined names darted on spotlights around the hall while holograms projected teasers on the wealth of experiences they offered. The RUSH extracts were restricted to extreme sports, given the number of children milling about, but the display stand stood surrounded by black-and-purple booths to allow adults a sampling of the company's more explicit offerings.

"Umm – yeah," she said, flashing him her most charming smile. "I'm gonna come back with my brother to actually buy it, I just thought I'd pick one out first…"

"So have a look," he said curtly, waving at the plastic-wrapped VECs hanging on display. "They come in pink, silver, black and green. We also carry fashion snap-on covers, located over there." His thumb gestured to the other side. "But *this*," he lifted the headset off her, "is going to the next *paying* customer."

Dawn sighed and pretended to examine the display. While her brother could certainly afford a Virtual Experience Creator, it didn't necessarily mean she would get one. She glanced at her cell phone to check the time and swore violently, earning a nasty look from a woman herding three kids through the crowded showroom as she dashed by. Dawn's fascination with the latest technology made her late for this afternoon's political demonstration. She chided herself for her lack of focus as she burst through the showroom doors and out into the street. No more dawdling…the Afghani women needed her voice!

Marianne Summers peered at the thick package messengered over from her publisher and dropped it on the low carved wood of the living room table while she chose a bottle of wine from the rack. At this point, she would typically open a bottle of French champagne in tribute to her first, ecstatic experience of receiving a bound copy of a book with her own name on it. Regardless of how many were lined up on her shelves now, she always tried to remember her initial excitement. She lit a stick of incense and muttered "Evening ambiance." to the control switch. The overhead light slowly dimmed as the panel's LED lights brightened and the music system flipped on. With the volume of her evening playlist rising steadily, Marianne lit a candle and curled up on the sofa, the book in front of her.

"Music off," she snapped irritably. "TV on – film list. Select 2Ds. Down… down…" She scrolled through her collection of old 2-dimensional classics, looking for one to pass the slow evening alone and settled on "*The Da Vinci Code.*"

She was old enough to remember the old, flat films, of which the infants who ran the publishing house found incredibly bland. Marianne found them soothing – the way they stayed on the other side of the room, but forced you to imagine your way inside them with clever angles and lighting techniques. This time, the usual allure failed her, and while Sophie Neveu was unraveling great swathes of plot to the hero, Marianne lifted her package and slit it open. Her own face beamed at her from the cover, alongside the strong, lined face and grey hair of everyone's childhood hero, the astronaut Jack Firestone. The graphics team had played with the hologram, so that the dusty golden light behind them seemed to spin and their eyes changed when you angled the book in various directions. *Godspeed: Breaking the Metaphysical Plane* it declared, in letters only a little larger than her own prominent name. She stared hard at his face, her mouth quivering, and flung the book back on the table as her tears broke. Since Marianne passed the age of 25; however, tears lost their venting quality along with their ability to ease heartache. She stopped crying, refilled her glass and reached for her VEC. Now *this* was immersion.

"Activate *Massage Parlor Pleasure*," she choked out, and then lay full-length on the sofa, closing her eyes. Within the world of the VEC, her eyes fluttered open to see Henrik's long blonde hair and barrel-chest approaching her. His powerful hands began to glide over her shoulder muscles and she sighed in surrender.

While she rushed to get to her protest, Dawn's older brother Ray spun slowly in NASA's zero gravity chamber, his legs drifting in the direction that his vision told him was up, and his head – by the same logic – pointing downwards. His inner-ear, usually responsible for such decisions, did nothing but make him feel sick. He breathed slowly and deeply, controlling the nausea, while he mentally reoriented himself. Gradually he came to believe that the doorlock he'd come through was at an angle on the "ceiling" of his capsule and that his feet hovered a little above the "floor." Using the handholds, he began to turn himself around slowly, carefully maintaining the idea that wherever his head pointed was up.

He'd played a similar game as a child. With his mother's dressing room mirror held against his waist, he'd walk around the house, looking intently at the reflected ceiling, pretending it was the floor. He persuaded himself to step over the ledges as he passed through doorways and to carefully circumvent light fixtures, though he bumped his knees on the furniture. When he walked out onto the porch, he imagined himself carefully balancing on the struts of the overhang, while the blue sky of the heavens came into view. He'd sit on the steps, staring at the mirror, wondering if he had the courage to leap into that blue beyond. If he did, would he discover the ability to fly, or would he just fall off the earth? Both appealed.

Now he could do both. He allowed himself a few more lazy turns, lost in meditation beyond the nausea, and then slowly settled in front of the doorlock, telling himself it was upright and so was he. He pressed a button on his suit and gravity slowly returned.

Les Hamilton hovered underneath the glass pyramid at the Louvre, lost in happy wonder at its cleverness. A true pyramid, the relationship between its square base and its altitude respected the golden ratio. This made a slope of about 51 degrees – pretty much what a pile of salt achieved naturally. His eyes flashed happily over the diamonds and triangles of glass so neatly slotted into space, taking in the simple beauty of its geometric panes. Through these refracting panels, he could just see the pale blue sky of a Parisian spring. While Les could understand the mathematical beauty of it, its visual beauty caught his heart and squeezed it strangely. How did this work – that through his eyes, just cornea, he absorbed something that made him want to cry with love? No one paid much attention to the gangling young man with prematurely thinning hair who stood staring upwards, except for an older Italian woman with striking, albeit waning good looks.

"Les," she called impatiently, folding her arms over her wide bosom. She'd been brought up in a time when the sun was not so terrifying and her already olive skin was permanently stained with gold, her cleavage overlaid with a fine net of wrinkles. Her wide mouth was painted dark red, bleeding a little into the skin around her lips.

"Coming, Mamma…" With a last lingering look, he walked after her.

Les stopped again, dumbfounded, in the foyer. A headless angel, its wings flung behind and its bust thrust forward, dominated the staircase. The massive marble figure seemed to stand at the gates of the Garden of Eden for him, forbidding him to come further until he could come to terms with its beauty.

"*Les,*" his mother called again, already at the top of the staircase. "Will you come on? I want to see the Mona Lisa this time and I left supper on the stove!"

"Yes, Mamma," he replied, and hurried on, only to be stopped by another architectural detail. "I don't get it," he said, as they made their way down the wood-paneled corridor hung with priceless works. "If I'm so clever, why can't I *understand* all of this?"

"What's to understand?" his mother shrugged.

"Why it's so beautiful – why I feel like I'm seeing more than is there – why I want to cry and jump and eat it…"

She laughed and batted him over the head. "Stupid boy. You don't feel beauty with your head, it's *here*." She thumped her chest. "You can't think your way through everything, you know. Sometimes you must just stop thinking and *feel*."

Perhaps that, reasoned Les, was the problem – his sheer inability to stop thinking. His virtual hand reached to grasp his mother's, as his own hand did the same.

"Thomas?" A voice drifted down the stairs of a stately home in the Orlando suburbs.

"Hey honey," Thomas Goodman called back. "I'm not so sleepy yet – I'm going to watch a film in the den, okay?"

"Sure thing. Love you!"

"Love you too," he yelled back automatically, opening the basement door. On his faded couch, banished from the living room some years back, he cracked open a beer and settled his headset into position. He pulled out a slim jewel case that held a picture of a nurse in an outfit that would give most patients an instant coronary. *Naughty Nurse*, it read, and at the bottom the usual strapline – "Experience the RUSH." He grinned as he slid the disc into the machine. It began to play automatically and his scruffy den was instantaneously replaced by the sanitized purity of a 1950s style hospital. He was lying in bed wearing old-fashioned pajamas, his window overlooking a porch where a few nurses wheeled around other handsome, young patients. The stunning nurse from the cover picture stood in the doorway, her hair cut in a post-war bob with a bright smile on her fresh face. Her tight uniform came halfway down her thighs and was cut to let her full breasts almost spill over the top, but she walked towards him with demure prettiness.

"Oh, baby…" he muttered, as she took his rising pulse from a rather unconventional place.

Upstairs, his wife Cathy glanced at the door and her VEC set. Her collection of programs stood neatly piled next to it, the PURE logo visible on the spine of each. She slid a different jewel case out from under the mattress. Thomas never made the bed, so it was the safest hiding place in the house. *Moonlit Meanders* bore the byline "Purest RUSH." PURE's original *Moonlit Meanders* stood on her bedside table, offering a very romantic coach-journey around Hyde Park, vaguely nineteenth century or maybe earlier, with a heart-meltingly charming driver. In RUSH's copycat version, the driver was a bit more attentive… She slid on her headset. A period-drama version of herself was soon protesting, *very* ineffectually, against the approaches of the roguish driver. Inside and outside the program, her bosom heaved.

Ray was leaving NASA's Kennedy Space Center when the receptionist beckoned him back. "Your sister called from the police station again."

"Oh, Christ!" he said irritably. "What now?"

"Hey, don't shoot the messenger…" The receptionist held up his hands in mock surrender. "She needs bailing out, of course. I think she said…" He glanced at the note, "Yes, that's right – the Free Afghanistan protest. She didn't say why they took her in, though."

Ray sighed heavily and called his thanks over his shoulder as he strode towards the door.

"So what was it for this time?" said Ray, as he and Dawn slid into the car. "For someone who cares so much about the planet, you make me consume an awful lot of gas getting to and from the police station to bail you out."

"It was a Free Afghanistan Women *peaceful* demonstration," said Dawn.

"I mean what did you do wrong?"

"Why do you always assume it's my fault?" she flared up. "I was falsely imprisoned because the establishment doesn't support the right to free speech!"

"Or the right to assault officers?"

Dawn opened her mouth and closed it again.

"I had a chat with the guy on duty," her brother went on. "I'm getting to know him quite well, actually."

"Radio on," Dawn instructed the car.

"Radio off," said her brother, as the first twang of a guitar note hit the speakers. "We agreed on this: I bail, you listen to the lecture. Dawn – it's just the same as that time with Save the Rain Forest …"

"*That* was not my fault!" she said. "They threw an egg at me – I just happen to be a good catch and lobbed it back."

"Okay, then – what was the other one? The know-what-you-eat party…"

"The Food Labeling Movement," corrected Dawn.

"Whatever." He shrugged and took the next turn. The route was so familiar by now he hadn't bothered to start the GPS. "But why do you do it?"

"After over ten years of intense struggle, Afghani women are still being persecuted for demanding that their basic human rights are upheld! Whatever the media may say about the U.S. involvement in restoring order, the stories that come out are appalling – corruption, disappearances, bribes…"

"So you did it for the women of Afghanistan?"

"Yes." She folded her arms and looked moodily out the window.

"Well, then. I assume that's okay."

"Really?" She spun on her seat to look at him. "You support me?"

"Of course. As a result of your getting another charge to your name, their condition has improved, right? The Afghani women will feel the difference?"

"We-ell…" Her face fell a little. "Not exactly… not immediately, at any rate – but it'll draw attention to the issues, at least…" Her voice petered out and she watched the streetlights flash smoothly through the windshield. "Shit, Ray, I don't know why I bother." She was close to tears. "All we do is draw attention to the cause, then everyone feels sorry for them but doesn't lift a finger to help and secretly thinks it's kind of their fault anyway for being stupid foreigners in a badly-run country and then they get used to the idea and think it's just normal for women in other countries to suffer – and die – and no one sees that it's partially our fault."

"You can't change people's minds overnight, Dawn," her brother said. He felt a little sorry for her now, but didn't think it wise to show that.

"Oh yes, you can," she answered bitterly. "The government does it on a regular basis. Take Iraq – they're our friends, they're our enemies, they're a brave new democratic state, they're an evil corrupt régime, they're extremely secular, and then they're overrun by fanatics… You can change people's minds like that." She snapped her fingers in the air. "What you can't change is their hearts and make them actually give a fuck about the rest of the planet."

They drove on in silence, joining the long line at the gas station.

"Radio on," said Dawn, and this time Ray didn't contradict her. The car edged forwards by minute degrees; Dawn humming tunelessly, Ray tapping his fingers on the wheel and looking out at the traffic around them. He let out a long, slow wolf-whistle.

"Who is *that*?" On a truck up ahead, the lower half obscured by a van, was a massive picture of a woman. Her long dark hair was parted at the center and combed down smooth on either side while strong, slightly witchy features gazed mysteriously from between their curtains. A glowing blue crystal nestled in full cleavage, shown off by a tight white gown.

Dawn glanced up at the image and then in disbelief at her brother. "You don't know?"

"Nope. Some actress or something?" He kept his eyes happily on the picture as the truck and van ahead of them nudged forward.

"Marianne Summers? The author? She wrote *The Spiritual Seduction*?" He showed no signs of recognition. "*Crystal Being*? *The Missing Commandments*? *How To Unblock Your Soul*? Jeez, Ray, you really do live under a rock, don't you?"

"Us *working* people don't have as much time to read as *students*," he said pointedly.

"No excuse. Everyone in the country has this woman's books…"

"We don't."

"*I* do. I've got *Crystal Being* and *The Soulful Life*."

"Do they have cover pictures? Can I borrow them?" He was grinning.

Dawn slapped his arm with the back of her hand. "You're disgusting."

"Hey – at least I don't use a VEC! I take the trouble to

fantasize manually…"

"Ewww! I do *not* want to know that!"

"So I'm lying naked on my stomach," Harry Woodhouse, NASA's rough and ready chief flight surgeon was saying, "blindfolded – my wrists and ankles are tied to the bedposts – and she starts spanking me. How erotic is *that*?"

Thomas wrinkled his nose and looked with less appetite at his macaroni & cheese. "I'm pretty sure erotic is not the word that comes to mind at the moment."

Harry, and Thomas, the head of NASA, were having lunch together in the cafeteria.

"All I'm saying is, the RUSH programming is improving all the time. I don't even want to imagine what they'll come up with next."

Thomas stirred the pale pasta sauce unenthusiastically. 'Trust me, neither do I. You know, Harry – the visual inspired by that story does not go well with this food. Or its digestion. You're the doctor, so please try to bear that in mind when you're relaying your next RUSH experience."

Les, NASA's lead engineer, set his tray down next to Thomas's and slid into his seat.

"What are you guys chatting about?"

"Nothing," said Harry quickly.

"Come on – tell me."

Harry looked condescendingly at him as Les began to take his food off the tray, arranging it neatly. "We're just two guys chatting. Why does Mr. Know-It-All have to know it all?'

"Were you talking about me?" Les looked between the two men anxiously. "Were you saying stuff at my expense?"

"Settle down, Les." Thomas patted him on the back. "Harry was just telling me about some of the new RUSH programs he's got. And trust me, for the sake of my newly dry-cleaned clothes, it's not worth repeating."

Harry shot Thomas a dirty look and started stacking his dishes.

"Then why couldn't you just say so?" said Les, tucking into his food. "I enjoy my VEC as much as the next guy."

"Oh yeah?" said Harry. "Tell us, Les, what kind of programs are you into?"

"Well, just this weekend," the engineer replied through a mouthful of pasta, "my mother and I toured the Louvre museum and it was a tremendous and educational experience."

Harry rolled his eyes. "Adult programming, Les. *ADULT.* I want to hear about your favorite *adult* program. And please, leave out the phrase 'my mother and I' from that particular description, okay?"

Les shifted uncomfortably. He knew the other men enjoyed comparing notes on their sexual explorations in the VEC. It was just like the locker-room at school, except the girls were virtual sluts and could be passed around in a jewel case. "I do like the moonlit carriage rides," he said hesitantly, "they're very – romantic. And of course," he happily remembered, "I've become an excellent ballroom dancer with help of the *very* sexy Alexandria."

Harry gaped at the young brainiac from across the table. "What program provider do you *have?*"

"PURE – why?"

"*PURE?* Seriously, are you a guy or a girl?"

"Come on, Harry," Thomas broke in; "take it easy on Les."

"What's wrong with PURE?" asked Les, bewildered. "I think it's very tasteful, educational and romantic. What do you and your wife use, Thomas?"

Thomas was torn between not showing Les up and not embarrassing himself in front of Harry. "I have RUSH in the basement," he admitted.

"Your *wife* enjoys *RUSH?*" Asked Les, wide-eyed and gaping at his superior.

"No, no – she's got PURE in the bedroom – and we've developed this understanding between us not to ask what the other is simulating."

An uncomfortable silence fell across the table. "Hey," said Thomas jokingly, "it helps make the marriage work!"

"Okay, Les," said Harry, leaning across the table. "It's time we took your education in hand – no…" He silenced him with a gesture. *"Not* your formal education which we all know way outstrips the rest of us – Thomas and me, we're going to club together, *aren't we Thomas?* And lend you some…"

"Hi guys." Ray set down his tray. The other men looked at each other, Harry's unfinished sentence hanging in the air. "What's with the silence?"

"We were just discussing PURE versus RUSH," said Thomas.

"And getting enlightened," added Harry, "about Les' *softer side.*"

Les flushed red and Thomas glared at Harry. "And I," Thomas said, "just had the misfortune of finding out that Harry likes to be handcuffed and spanked while setting his pain-simulator to 8."

Les laughed, pointing at Harry. "You're one of those no pain no gain guys! I love it!"

"That was just between us, Thomas," snarled Harry.

"Then lay off Les next time."

"Whereas Mr. Purity here has never tried one before, I suppose." Harry offered, attempting to shift the spotlight onto NASA's top astronaut.

"No, I haven't," Ray answered calmly, cutting his food. "I disapprove of them one hundred percent."

"Remind me…" Harry said, leaning back, "How exactly can something that gives so much pleasure bring hell on earth?"

"Because the mind can be imprisoned by pleasure just as much as by pain," answered Ray unsmiling.

Les burst into a loud donkey laugh. "Then Harry's mind's in double-hell, because pain *is* his pleasure!"

Thomas cracked up and even Ray started laughing despite himself. Harry, fighting to keep a straight face, finally caved and burst out laughing in spite of himself.

Dawn wiped off the marble counters and pulled the stew out of the oven, setting it down on in the center of the island. The kitchen was one of her favorite rooms in the house and its renovation was one of the few times she and Ray had agreed on how to spend his salary. Whatever else their parents had or hadn't given them, they'd both gained a love of good food made from first principles. It wasn't always easy to find fresh vegetables or meat outside a ready-made meal, but the effort was worth it. She opened the lid, letting the smell seep through the house, and began to tear mushrooms in thirds, chucking them in as she went. Cooking was a good study-break, too. The slow, repetitive process of chopping and stirring shifted her mind away from the anxious hyper-analysis that characterized her Media Politics studies. With a shock, she remembered she was supposed to be watching the news for tomorrow's tutorial and yelped, "TV *on!*" She must have slurred the words, because the screen on the fridge opposite her remained obstinately black. "TV on," she repeated more clearly and returned to ripping up mushrooms while it flickered to life.

It was the usual fare, and she didn't need to even look at the visuals: long lines outside gas-stations, interviews with panic-buyers, reports on garage or house explosions from people stockpiling gasoline. *Discouraging bulk-buying to preserve supplies*, Dawn noted to herself. All this was juxtaposed with sheiks getting into jets or expensive, gas-guzzling cars, while their own President was shown walking across his lawn. *Suggesting they don't have a right to their own oil because they'll only waste it.*

15

"…negotiations with the coalition of Iran, Iraq and Saudi Arabia," the presenter was continuing, "or as the pundits are now calling it, 'the Axis of Oil'…"

Dawn replaced the heavy ceramic lid and returned the stew to the oven.

"…oil sanctions to the United States until their demands that the US withdraw its military presence in the region are met. Alongside the ever-increasing energy demands of China and India…" *What's sauce for the goose is not sauce for the gander,* thought Dawn. *Our consumption is still double theirs,* "…gas prices have sky-rocketed to an all-time record high at $6.66 per gallon, which economists are saying is the main cause of the country's current recession…"

The news finished on a human-interest piece: RUSH's new contract with the latest basketball sensation, the story evidently geared to keep the channel's sponsors happy. The screeching, razzmatazz jingle of a talk show began, and the host, cheerful and orange from a spray-on tan, walked on waving at his adoring crowd. Dawn turned her back on the scene to load the last chopping knives into the dishwasher, but swung around again at a familiar name.

"…welcome Marianne Summers, author of *Godspeed: Breaking the Metaphysical Plain!*"

"Ray!" bellowed Dawn at the top of her voice. "RA-A-AY!"

"What!" came his muffled reply. "I'm in the shower!"

"It's your wet-dream on TV!"

He came through to the kitchen, still soaked, his towel wrapped around his waist.

"Oh, it's the nut-job," he said dismissively, opening the fridge.

"I thought you liked her."

He shrugged, his powerful shoulder blades shifting. "She's hot…" His eyes wandered to the screen appreciatively. "But I flipped through your books and she's a fruitcake with fruit toppings."

He sat on a stool anyway, poured himself a glass of milk and peeled a banana.

"Supper's almost ready," said Dawn reproachfully.

"Hang on here – she's written a book with Jack!"

"Jack?" asked Dawn.

"Firestone – the astronaut? The speed-of-light guy."

"Oh yeah," Dawn shrugged. "Didn't you used to work with him?"

"Shh – I want to hear this."

Marianne's wistful smile was filling the screen as the host's question continued in voice-over, asking about Jack Firestone's experiences.

"What Jack – excuse me, Senator Firestone – underwent at the speed of light forms the basis of the whole book. Without his confirmation, the concept of the speed of light's spiritual nature would never have been able to develop beyond mere conjecture. His experience was that of a connection to a greater source. It generated in him a feeling of understanding and inner peace with himself and the universe around him and – in his own words – "a feeling of oneness and enlightenment."' Her voice was low and well-modulated, using the language of a mystic with matter-of-fact precision.

Prompted by the interviewer's carefully-scripted questions, Marianne went on to explain the metaphysical reasoning behind the book. Einstein, she explained, believed that time didn't exist at the speed of light – in that sense; the speed of light was closely related to a singularity, or "black hole."

"Whoa!" laughed the interviewer. "You've lost me there."

Marianne smiled, her eyes narrowing sensuously, as she backed up a bit in her argument. "We have this idea that time is absolutely fixed – a second will always be a second. Most of the time that theory works out for us. But in reality, Einstein showed that absolute time is a myth. Imagine two completely accurate clocks – one on top of a mountain, the other at the bottom. Now the clock on top of the mountain will actually *keep slower time* than the clock in the valley. It'll only be a tiny discrepancy in this case, but the faster something moves, the more difference you can measure. Again, imagine two twins. One is in a spaceship traveling near the speed of light, while the other is living on the ground. When the spaceship comes back, the twin inside it will be significantly younger than the twin on earth. In other words, the nearer the speed of light one travels, the slower time passes for them."

"But speed means distance over time, doesn't it?" said the interviewer. "So if time isn't fixed, how can you talk about the speed of light?"

"Well, time and space are the same, so neither are fixed - but for a further exploration into *that*, you'll have to read the book," replied Marianne flirtatiously. "I'm not sure I can do justice to the theory of relativity during a live interview."

Her host chuckled appreciatively. "Okay – so back to the idea that speed-of-light travel has a spiritual dimension."

Marianne took up her main thread again. She explained that the human concept of time and space is the boundary that separates us from the metaphysical world – in other words, Heaven. It defines our individuality, which prevents us from experiencing the oneness of all things. Heaven, at the speed of light, resonates at such a high vibration that our five senses aren't able to detect it. In order to move at the speed of light, the traveler's vibration has to rise to the same frequency as Heaven. Ray was shaking his head in irritation. "Pseudo-science bullshit," he muttered, his eyes still glued to the screen.

"Okay," the interviewer summarized, "when someone travels at the speed of light, time and space cease to exist for them. At that point, they enter into the metaphysical world, or Heaven, and experience enlightenment."

"Exactly," confirmed Marianne.

"And this is what Senator Firestone actually experienced on his trip?"

"It is." The camera zoomed in on Marianne's face, so that her large, soulful eyes seemed to be gazing directly into Ray's. "And I believe *anyone* who travels at the speed of light will experience the same."

2

Robert Priest, the U.S. President, poured himself a cup of coffee, retreating momentarily from the chatter of voices filling his office. The meeting was officially over; the secretaries and administrators were long dismissed to type up the minutes, take action points and make phone calls. As usual, the key players lingered awhile to argue their cases. And, as usual, Warren Christian, the Vice-President, and Neal Crossing, the Secretary of State, were allied against the President's Chief of Staff, Helen Cross.

"What pisses me off the most," Warren was saying, "is we liberated their sorry asses and now they're embargoing oil from us. What kind of fucking thank you is that?" His thick, southern accent spun the words out in a long drawl while he paced. With his pared body, knotted muscles and aggressive stance, he would have looked more in place having a show-down with Clint Eastwood. His hand hovered at his belt as though he expected to whip out a gun from underneath his tailored suit.

"What did you expect?" said Helen, "a bunch of flowers and a big card saying thanks for the pile of rubble we used to call our infrastructure?"

"It's called bend-over-infidel, you're taking a large flaming shish-kebab up the ass," chimed in Neal, ignoring Helen.

"You're right, Neal." Warren stood with his thumbs in his belt, facing the windows, as if surveying his kingdom. "We bent over backwards to give them democracy and now they're bending *us* over an oil barrel and giving us the high hard one."

President Priest stirred his coffee thoughtfully. Being a Christian man, he disapproved of Warren's colorful speech, but beneath the bad language and ugly metaphors he had a point, as usual.

"Okay, what are you suggesting we do about it?" interjected Helen. "It's their democratically-elected government and it's their oil. They can choose what to do with it. After all, democracy means letting the people decide what they want, even if it's not what you want."

Warren gave a short bark of laughter. "The hell it is."

"We have to negotiate with them as a recognized government," Helen persisted.

"I'll tell you what we can do about it," said Neal. "We can nuke the fucks off the face of the earth, change the name to Middle East America and add three new oil-rich states to our union. Now *that's* what the fuck we can do about it."

"And send some God-fearing Christian missionaries over there to finally civilize the region," added Warren.

"Hey, now *that's* a foreign policy plan!" Neal clapped his hands and rubbed them together. Of course it wasn't possible, he knew that, but it was so damn frustrating to be sitting on all this power and never able to actually use it. These two-bit countries should know who they are dealing with before they try to play with the big boys.

"I know a foreign policy like that would be ideal to all of you," said Helen sarcastically, "but how about we *don't* start World War III and kill a billion innocent people?"

Neal smirked. The supercilious bitch was actually taking them seriously.

"Mr. President," Warren turned to the Commander in Chief, who moved into the center of the room, sipping his coffee. "You know we're going to go to war with that part of the world eventually. It's obvious."

Robert nodded reluctantly. "It's certainly a possibility we can't dismiss."

"So why don't we just blow them off the face of the earth and get it over with? Do it on our terms, instead of waiting for them to strangle us?"

"You cannot be serious!" Helen's voice rose as she stood and crossed her arms over her chest.

"Little girl, I'm totally serious. They're a few years away from getting their own nukes, they're already doing all they can to kill us with this oil embargo, so why not just eliminate them from the equation while we still can?"

"Mr. President, you cannot possibly be taking this discussion seriously…"

Silence fell as all eyes focused upon the President's impassive face. He drained his coffee, stalling to think, and then arranged his features into the serious expression he used for difficult interviews.

"I want some military options," he said at last.

"Mr. President – we are talking about democratically-elected governments. Sovereign countries. They have the freedom to do whatever they want – the freedom we gave them, after all!" Helen's mind raced, attempting to find the right words that would serve to inject reason into a room full of battle-hungry male egos. She felt as though she were watching a ten-ton truck slipping a little at the top of a steep incline – just a few inches – allowing a scant moment of grace when you could still leap in the cab and yank up the handbrake. At any moment, momentum would build up and the monster would be thundering downhill beyond control.

"I want some military *options*," repeated Robert, emphasizing the optional portion of the equation for Helen's benefit. "I don't spend a trillion a year on my military not to have military *options*."

In a classroom several states away, a strong discussion regarding their government's foreign and domestic policies was taking place. "That's a good point, Dawn," said the instructor. Dawn tried to restrict her beam of pleasure to a mere grateful smile. Professor Alice Jennings was her favorite instructor, and Dawn often bent over backwards to do all the recommended reading and viewing for her classes with extra thoroughness. It was easy to fall half in love with Professor Jennings – or Alice, as she insisted her students call her. A comfortably-shaped woman, always draped in fabulous colors, she exuded warm maternal concern. Where the other professors got results by being overly strict and hard to please, Alice made her students long to deserve her smile. The serious frown that came over her face, if one failed to turn in an assignment or submitted shoddy work, was a worse punishment than being taken to task or given low grades. It was like a blanket of love being snatched away. Dawn's soul vibrated to the frequency of her instructor's responses and her marks soared as a result.

"But be careful with your terminology," the professor added. "Terms like 'the government' or 'the media' can so easily homogenize the specific decisions made by individuals and lead us into the notion of a 'conspiracy'." The small group of students chuckled at the idea. They'd been trained out of buying into conspiracy theories in their first year and knew that the best analysis was always more subtle.

As Alice elaborated her suggestions, the warm spring air that cascaded in from the open windows was filled with the quiet rattle of fingers flying over laptop keyboards to take notes. Alice forbade voice-recording in her seminars. She insisted that she'd never found a student who actually listened to them again and she'd rather they used their own judgment in what they wanted to take down. Dawn – always inclined to conspiracy theories, despite her best efforts – wondered if Alice didn't want such absolute evidence of everything she said in the classroom. The Anti-Liberalist Preaching society was increasingly active on a lot of campuses.

"Alice?" Geoff lifted his hand off his keyboard a moment to catch her attention. "When a specific media corps has a set policy on how to portray things – one they don't display to the public – how can we tell its effect, apart from the choices of the program selectors and makers?"

Geoff was lanky, towering over the rest of the class, with a wild Japanese-style haircut. Dawn quite fancied him sometimes, but he looked a little too high-maintenance for anything serious.

"Good question, Geoff. Comparison is everything in the media," answered Alice. "We're looking at a general climate of opinion here – the ideas that everyone just assumes are true. Did you all read the essay on *Mythologies* I set you?" Heads nodded around the class. "It's exactly what Barthes describes there – the right-wing assumptions that are so fixed. We see these recurring again and again, even on channels with opposing political opinions. That's your baseline. We're going to do a lot of work on baselines this semester; watching various television programs, checking for repetitive sound bites and trying to determine mass assumptions based on what we are provoked into thinking. In other words, what are our overall baseline assumptions?

"Then using our insights, we can compare the individual differences – for example, Dawn's point about how Channel 7 always draws attention to the danger of stockpiling gas. But don't assume that the baseline you discover is fixed. Remember, the tide of opinion fluctuates constantly, which is one of the things that make Media Politics such a dynamic study. Okay – your assignment for next week: I want everyone to do a comparative study of at least five different television channels and bring at least *one* baseline trend for discussion to our next lecture."

"Alice?" It was Geoff again. "If no one's actually watching the news because they're all absorbed in their VECs, shouldn't we be studying the VEC programs instead?"

The whole class laughed. Nothing would be more fun than to spend hours immersed in a VEC, succumbing to all the charms of PURE or RUSH and call it "work." Alice smiled.

"I think we can safely assume most people still watch the news. And I'm not sure I trust this class to keep their analytic sensibilities while romping around inside a VEC. Okay – class dismissed."

During the course of the two-hour class, the sky outside had faded from brilliant azure to pale robin's-egg blue. The air that drifted through the open windows was tinged with a light chill, carrying with it the smells of ivy cooling and soil releasing its heat. Dawn hung back until the small clutch of students had completed their last questions.

"Alice, I wanted to ask you," Dawn began hesitantly, as Geoff hovered just outside the door. "I don't want to sound like a conspiracy theorist or anything, but it's – the government. I can see how media is a collection of individuals," she rushed on, "I get that, but the government is surely more controlled? I mean, there you do have basically one man…"

Alice raised a skeptical eyebrow and Dawn winced inwardly. She wanted to keep Alice's high opinion, but she needed to understand.

"I mean…I know it's not just one man, but an entire administration – and it is hierarchical, there is one president at the top…"

"Yes, that is true. But there's a mass of decision-making that goes all the way through government. Every politician has their own agenda, to further their own career, as well as the agenda of their party. In addition, the views of the electorate must also be considered. It's easy, when we disagree with government policy, to think there's one evil person with some terrible plan to ruin the world, but that's just not accurate. It's a much bigger machine, with many more levels and safeguards than you can imagine. The very complexity of the whole system of checks and balances is precisely what keeps any one person from accruing that much power. And let's not forget the question of motivation, either. That's what conspiracy theories always leave out – the rationale."

Dawn nodded, her eyes fixed on Alice as she tried to

memorize the argument.

"Okay?" said Alice, holding her laptop against her chest, ready to leave.

"Yeah – thanks."

Geoff was lingering outside the door when Dawn came out.

"Still convinced the President's Satan?" He teased.

"Go play with your VEC," retorted Dawn childishly.

"I will if you'll join me." He slid his arm through hers as they walked down the corridor and out into the fresh pale blue-pinks of the evening.

"What, the RUSH-sluts don't quite do it for you?"

He dropped her arm and turned, a wounded expression adorning his usually placid face. "What kind of guy do you think I am?"

Dawn shrugged. "Sorry. Just kidding." She was tempted by his offer, even if she wasn't necessarily drawn to him. Sometimes it felt like she was the only one in the world who didn't have a VEC and by now all the salesmen at the showroom were onto her. In any case, a freebie trial-run, pretending to be a buyer, just didn't compare with being able to choose whatever program you wanted and relax on the sofa, safe in the knowledge that no irritable salesman would hit the "off" button. Her brother probably would, though.

"So, you want to?"

"Yeah, okay. But no adult stuff."

"On a first date? Never!"

"And this is *not* a date," said Dawn.

Geoff laughed and took her arm again as they meandered through the campus. Alice watched her two top students from the window of her study and smiled to herself. That girl could use a bit of fun, she mused. From what she'd been able to pick up, that brother of hers was far too strict. It was a common result of someone having to play the parent without a true parent's loving guidance to check them. She clicked her tongue at the thought and returned to her desk.

Even after twenty years of teaching, she couldn't help getting emotionally involved in her students' lives – not all of them, but when she glimpsed bright young flames such as these in her classroom, her heart constricted with tenderness. She picked up her pile of assignments and slid Geoff and Dawn's to the bottom of the pile. She liked to save the best for last.

"For a long time, the best minds all followed Einstein's assumption that we could never travel at the speed of light – theorizing that, when one had enough energy to travel that fast, the mass would shoot up as well. Trapped within our assumptions, we dismiss so many potentials as mere impossibilities. We are afraid to part with our established views because they are so safe and, more than anything, we all need to feel safe."

Marianne Summers was appearing at Barnes & Noble, reading a section from her newly-published book. An impressively large crowd gathered in anticipation; spilling over into the cafe, leaning against shelves, squatting on the floor, all of them clutching their copies of *Godspeed*. Every eye was fixed on her clear, calm features as her hypnotic voice resonated throughout the room. Ray and Dawn had arrived early and annexed a plush chair – or rather, Dawn had annexed the chair and Ray perched on the edge. He was pleasantly surprised that Marianne's beauty wasn't just air-brushing and TV-makeup. In person, her serene appearance made her even easier on the eyes. He was only half-listening to her words, becoming more absorbed in the shape of her moving lips and downcast eyes. Dawn, hugging her knees, was captivated by every word. The need to feel safe… Since their parents had died, only Ray stood between her and a terrifying world that she was not yet equipped to face.

She was only six at her mother's funeral, which followed her father's by a mere three weeks. She cried, not because

27

her mother was being cremated – she hardly understood that – but because she wanted her mother *now* and couldn't find her. All she saw were these sad, scary people in their black clothes, resembling tragic crows. Ray picked her up – he was eighteen, old enough to understand death, and to know that the entire responsibility for his sister's well-being now rested on his young shoulders. He pressed his own teary face into her hair and whispered in her ear, "I'm here, I'm here… I will look after you, Dawn. I'll keep you safe. And I will never, *never* let myself die while you need me." She clung to him, aware that this was her only safe place and where once there had been three giants to look after her, now there was only one.

Tears sprang into her eyes as Marianne continued to read.

"We don't want people to think we're foolish – that would make us unsafe. We don't want to take risks with the new – that would make us unsafe. We cling to our own, tiny, precious selves, in a universe that we perceive to be bearing down on us in all its complexity. We look at the size of ourselves in comparison with the world, with our galaxy, with the universe. In our hearts, we see vast stretches of space and a tiny labeled dot saying 'You are here.' With that perception of the self, who can blame us for wanting so desperately to be safe?

"The irony is, if we continue along this path, we will never be safe. We must part with our false perceptions of time and space, learn to vibrate at a higher frequency, and understand that we exist as the whole of the universe and it exists as us. There is no boundary between self and other. That boundary of '*I* am *me,* and *you* are *you*,' is instilled in us from our earliest years; during what Lacanians and Freudians call 'the mirror phase.' We are not born that way; it's something we learn. And the rest of our lives, we carry the vague memory of the years before we made this all-important false realization. We dimly remember lying in our mother's arms, awash in an ocean of love with no differentiation. We recall the absolute safety we experienced in that oneness with the universe. And we so long to be safe again, that we are afraid to take the leap towards a consciousness which is the only way back into absolute safety.

"For some, it is possible. Fearless, spiritual people have been able to surrender their sense of self throughout history. But most people turn away, sadly, too scared to try, or too angry to believe that it might be true – that we've been lied to, and that all these years of pain and loneliness have been unnecessary."

Dawn blinked away tears, hoping Ray didn't notice.

"Now, we have found a way that it is possible. In the experience of speed-of-light travel, all artificial boundaries of time and space, all the distinctions on which we rely to identify our scared tiny selves, are collapsed and the perfect unity of all things rushes into our consciousness. This is breaking the metaphysical plane – this is stepping into Heaven."

She closed the book. After a sober pause, the audience began to clap and then cheer. A few younger people sprang to their feet, whistling enthusiastically. Ever gracious, Marianne smiled and blushed, nodding her head in acknowledgement, and then tapped the microphone. "If anyone wishes to have me to sign their copy of *Godspeed*, I will be more than happy to oblige."

She seated herself at the table, while the crowd assembled itself into a long, snaking line.

"She has quite a following," said Ray, looking around.

Dawn buried her nose in her handbag, pretending to look for her wallet while she composed herself. What Marianne said about being small and alone had rung such a painful chord within her. She wanted to break down in sobs, return to that six year-old inside her who hadn't understood enough to mourn properly, and wail for her mother. Where was her guiding figure, the stronger woman, the maternal advice?

Who could she go to with her confusion about Geoff and whether or not she actually liked him? Thinking about it only made her want to cry harder.

"Dawn?"

"Mmph?" She didn't trust herself to speak yet.

"C'mon, let's go. Jack's not here, after all."

"I want a signed copy," she managed to say in a reasonably steady voice. She actually wanted to put her head on Marianne Summer's lap and cry in the cradling warmth of that pure understanding wisdom, to feel a motherly hand stroke her hair. However, a signed copy would have to suffice.

Her brother's hand brushed the top of her head and a flicker of warmth stole into her heart. He might not be a mom, but he was a hell of a lot.

Over an hour passed before the back of the line, where they stood, moved its way to Marianne's table. She shook her hand out, before reaching for Dawn's book, and laughed. "Muscle-cramp," she said apologetically.

"You're really patient to sign them all. Your books are incredible!" said Dawn, breathlessly.

The woman smiled. "To...?" She said, glancing between Dawn and Ray.

"Dawn Sky," they said in unison.

"I was hoping Jack might also be here," said Ray as she handed the book back.

"Unfortunately, Senator Firestone had to cancel at the last minute," said Marianne briskly, standing and starting to gather up her things. Ray felt foolish, knowing she assumed he was just another hero-worshipper hoping to get a look at the famous astronaut.

"We used to work together at NASA," he explained. "I was just starting out, then, but it's a small community and we got along quite well. I was just hoping to catch up."

"Oh." Marianne set her bag down again. "Another astronaut. So are you going to travel at the speed of light,

Mr...?"

"Sky. I just might." He grinned. The name of the pilot for the next speed-of-light flight hadn't been announced yet, but he knew he was a likely contender for the seat. No-one worked harder at their training, mentally or physically, and the extra effort he'd put in had brought him up to peak condition.

"What you said about safety..." Dawn launched into her sentence, almost cutting off her brother's last words, and then stopped abruptly.

"Concerned for your husband's safety on the flight?" Asked Marianne.

The siblings blinked at her for a moment, then laughed. "God, no, he's my *brother*," exclaimed Dawn, exactly at the same time that Ray said, "Christ, no, she's my *sister*."

"Anyway – um, that thing about safety..." resumed Dawn. "I just – really liked it." She squirmed at her idiotic, fawning attempt to convey how deeply Marianne had touched her. "It meant a lot," she added lamely.

"Thank you," replied Marianne softly. "Hearing that means a lot to *me*." She put her bag back on her shoulder as the three of them lingered awkwardly. Around them, the store was emptying and being prepared for closing. "You know – writing – mostly it's just sitting at home with a computer. Meeting readers like this," she waved her hand around, taking in the emptied scene of the book reading, "is rare. And knowing your writing touches someone that deeply is even rarer."

The trio fell quiet as the sound of a Hoover started up on the far side of the shop. Marianne sighed, and then laughed in embarrassment.

"But these things are tiring and I need a drink. Would you two care to join me?" She smiled at Dawn, missing Ray's scowl of disapproval at her words.

"We'd love to," said Dawn happily.

"A bloody mary, please." said Dawn.

"Dawn…" began Ray.

"Back off, Ray," said Dawn ominously. "I'm having a drink. *A* Drink."

Marianne raised an eyebrow. "Are you her father or her brother?" She murmured.

"In a way, both." Ray's expression brooked no further comment. Marianne glanced at Dawn, who lifted her shoulders and nodded.

"I'll have an orange juice." Ray said to the barmaid.

"It's probably better if you don't drink anyway," said Marianne as their drinks arrived. She leaned over the table; her eyes flicking to the arm of Ray's t-shirt, which stretched tightly around his muscles. "The more fit you are, the harder it hits."

"He'd fall over after one, then," giggled Dawn.

"Cheap date," added Marianne.

"I don't need to drink in order to have a good time," said Ray stiffly. He was sitting bolt upright, holding his orange juice tightly, frowning at Dawn. His sister mashed the celery in her drink, as happy as a child with a treat. To him, she wasn't so far past the age when she'd sat, legs swinging, the same silly grin on her face, elated because her big brother had bought her a hot chocolate.

"No," said Dawn smirking. "Just a personality transplant."

Marianne lifted her wine thoughtfully, watching the exchange between the siblings. Tension lay between them, but not in what was being said. She could tell, from Ray's reaction, that Dawn's snipe was an old joke. They circled each other's sore points, but didn't poke them like most siblings would. She'd studied psychology before she was a writer, and these two reminded her of the survivors of a dysfunctional home. Such children would wrangle, but never risk an open fight. The need to cling was stronger than the need to bicker.

"So you're in training, then?" asked Marianne.

"An astronaut's always in training," answered Ray, like a NASA motivational video.

"And was it always your dream, to be an astronaut?"

"Yes…" His expression softened a little. "I'm lucky that way, I guess. There's not many kids who can find a dream, hold onto it, and make it come true."

Marianne nodded, smiling gently, and he continued.

"I used to play a game, when I was little…" He told her the story of the mirror-game, how the mirror turned the world upside down, so he could walk on the ceiling. He described to her the feeling of stepping outside and imagining plunging into the blue, or starry, sky. He kept the backstory to himself, however. The part about when he dreamt of leaping into the stars, it was because his great, big, wild bear of a father was staggering into the furniture, slurring obscenely, while his mother flapped around uselessly squeaking, "Honey, now I know you don't wanna do that…" When he fantasized about flying into the blue, he wanted to escape the sour stink of his father, collapsed and groaning in the TV-room.

"So I worked like hell to become an astronaut. Anyone can make their dreams come true, if they just try hard enough."

"Sometimes," allowed Marianne. "If they don't depend too much on other people… if one has the ability…"

"Everything depends on the individual," Ray insisted. "A person's own determination, I mean. And if someone doesn't have the ability – well, they just try harder, train harder. It all comes down to the individual."

That's not exactly what I say in my book…" She raised a hand. "But I do half-agree with you. I couldn't be a writer without discipline."

He nodded approvingly. Dawn sat quietly, her head lowering to her straw from time to time. She was still too awed by Marianne to speak much and her brother's confession had surprised her. He'd never even told *her* about that game, and he never told strangers such private details about himself.

"And when you're not writing, what do you do?" He was enjoying her company and wanted to steer clear of the subject of her books. His belief in honesty was too strong for polite lies and he didn't want to say he thought they were pablum, based on pseudo-science, and full of meaningless, comforting pap.

"Oh…" she cast around vaguely, wondering which of her arbitrary pastimes she dared confess to this unbending man. "Try to relax, I guess… I walk a lot; it's a good way to think things through. I swim… and I have an embarrassingly large collection of 2Ds," she admitted.

"Really?" His eyes sparked. "You like those?"

"They remind me of my childhood. I'm not as young as I look," she said dryly. "I'm a bit old-fashioned. I think they're less passive than the 3Ds – you have to involve yourself so much more, deliberately think yourself into the film, stretch your imagination."

They started comparing their favorites. Marianne leaned towards the old dramas and forgotten art house classics, while Ray confessed a preference for outdated sci-fi and war films. They both agreed that the original *Lord of the Rings* was far superior to the 3D version, even if some of the effects were a bit antiquated by now. From there, their conversation progressed to music. They were near enough in age for their tastes to coincide – after all, everyone loved to hate the music they listened to when they were fourteen, and was forever attached to what they'd heard at twenty.

"It's alright, it's alright, it's alright," they chanted in unison, "She moves in mysterious ways'"

"Wow…I can't believe I still remember the words! I had the whole thing down pat in fourth grade." Marianne collapsed in giggles. "Do you remember the rest? How did it go…" She snapped her fingers in the air to conjure the lyrics. Her usual poise was replaced with shining enthusiasm. "Something about – mysterious love – that's it!" She began to swing in her seat, snapping her fingers to the beat while she sang. "Johnny take a dive with your sister in the rain, let her talk about the things you can't explain; to touch is to heal, to hurt is to steal. If you want to kiss the sky, better learn how to kneel (on your knees boy)"

Ray gaped at her over his orange juice, cracking up. "I can't believe you just said that! Everyone – come see – Marianne Summers is getting down and dirty!"

"You guys have the grossest taste in music," said Dawn. "You say the stuff *I* listen to is weird, Ray?"

"Ah, Dawn, you don't get it," said Marianne. "Bono was like this – Twentieth Century poet for the masses – he was the John Keats of the nineties, man. He sang about social unity and brotherhood while crossing political lines in an effort to create global change…using his voice for the greater good."

"You were more of a fan than I was, clearly," said Ray.

"Okay, I have just a teensy-weensy little thing for political/spiritual activists…"

"Then I must leave you stone cold."

"On the contrary." Her eyes lingered on his face seductively while she twisted her glass in the air. "I would say you're a spiritual diamond in the rough."

"Still think she's a fruitcake?" asked Dawn slyly, on the way home.

"She's better in person," admitted Ray. "Less touchy-feely-precious than I expected. But her books are still bull."

"You can't *say* that!" snapped Dawn. "You've what – flipped through two? You're always carrying on about the importance of informed decisions, so get some information before you make a decision." She slammed irritably back into her car seat. After two hours with this extraordinary woman, while Dawn was soaking up every moment, Ray could still be cold and critical.

"Okay," said Ray. "I'll read her book. With an open mind. And if I still think the science is bunk afterwards, I'm allowed to say so. Deal?"

"Deal."

When he walked into the cafeteria the next day, the room instantly filled with claps, cheers, whistles and catcalls. Ray's face split into its biggest smile in the last eighteen years.

"Everyone knows then?" he said as Harry smacked him across the back.

"Everyone in the whole world will know by tomorrow," said Thomas. "Hope you've got a stick to beat the ladies off – you're going to be the World's Most Eligible Bachelor. And you'll need *all* – I mean *all* – your time and energy to prepare for this one." He was suddenly serious. "We're not talking your usual SST and buoyancy and vomit-comet practice. We have a whole new Shuttle Mission Simulator for your use, boy, and you are going to practically *live* in that thing."

"You will *live* in it!" barked Harry. "You will *eat* it! You will *sleep* with it!"

"I know guys, I know." Ray held up his hands. "We've been through all this, remember? In the selection process?" Ray picked up his tray and made for the food counter, his euphoria fading a little. "Have I ever let you guys down?" he said. "Have I ever shirked practice, failed to study, done badly, or not tried hard enough at *anything*? Have I ever put anything ahead of my training?"

"Of course not," said Thomas reassuringly. "That's why we picked you. But there's a lot riding on this, Ray. It's the single most expensive mission we've ever undertaken and we have no idea what kind of stress your body is going to go through." He glanced at Harry and the doctor took over.

"We need to prepare you for vibrating at that frequency, Ray. We know from the selection tests that you're the most likely to withstand it – but we've gotta make sure this doesn't kill you. Your molecules..."

"I know the theory," interrupted Ray. "But Jack's still alive."

"Jack only touched the speed of light, Ray, you know that." The NASA Head frowned in concern. "You're going to actually *travel* at it."

3

If Ray had worked hard before, he was obsessive now. An additional zero-g simulator had been installed for his sole use, with a wider range of controls. Theoretically, he should have no mass at the speed of light, but what he would actually experience was a different matter. His trainer put him through a grueling series of changes, shifting the gravity from zero to high repeatedly. One moment light as a feather, Ray would be slammed to the side of the orb at the next moment, using all his strength to lift one arm. At those times, half of him longed for the old neutral buoyancy tank – a clumsier way of experiencing zero-g, but at least no maniac could stand on the other side and play with the dial at random.

His heart and blood pressure were measured several times a day, along with all the other vital signs. The fear that the trial flight might kill him remained unspoken, but anxiety hung heavy in the air. At least they could make sure they didn't kill him themselves, during the preparations.

If all went well, his route would be a quick circle that took him halfway to Venus and back again. The worst-case-scenario was the potential for damage at the furthest point of his arc, which would force him to face a 20 million kilometer trip home alone, without even the radio for company. Other worst-case-scenarios included the possibility of blowing up or the pressure causing him to disintegrate and disperse, but no prior preparation or particular expertise could reduce that risk. Ray spent several hours a day in the simulator while his instructors presented every malfunction possible for him to solve.

Les, their boy-wonder engineer, took him through every aspect of the spaceship's design. If anything went wrong out there, Ray would need to know what every wire and every chip was for. He'd already studied the manuals for the basics, was now being drilled into him until he was as lovingly familiar with this machine as a soldier is with his rifle.

"*No*" yelled Les. "you *cannot* remove that panel without disengaging the throttle! It's elementary! Christ, Ray, I am *never* letting you near the real Solar if this is what you do to the sim!"

"I am *learning*, Les," said Ray through gritted teeth. Every muscle in his perfectly honed body ached with the strains of his training and his mind swam with new information. "I've got the physics, I've got the training, I've got the fucking electronics, but I am not a technical specialist of your level, which is why you built this thing and I am flying it." He sighed, rubbing his hand. "Sorry. Again. Disengage the throttle..."

"Wait – look at your readouts. You're still at near light-speed. You'll be blown into a thousand bits. Bring it down first. Navigate the debris... Okay, now before you disengage, transfer life-support systems – no, that power source is corrupt, remember?"

They were simulating a maximum crisis situation, using the most damage the spaceship could take while keeping Ray minimally alive as a springboard.

"What are you doing now?"

"I'm wiping simulated blood out of my simulated eyes," retorted Ray. "Jeez, I don't know what would be worse; losing radio and doing this on my own, or having radio and you bitching at me over it."

"You won't have radio, Ray. Radio waves that have to travel through the atmosphere are slower than..."

"Look at my readouts," Ray replied smugly. He'd brought the sim ship's speed right down, using expertly-angled power thrusts against the clouds of debris through which he was picking his way – simultaneously clearing his path.

"No one said you weren't the best man for the job," said Les admiringly. He might have a brain the size of a planet himself, but Ray was no slouch – and way, way cooler than Les could ever dream of being. "Okay, let's start disassembling and fixing this thing. *Do not touch that panel without disengaging throttle!*" Ray's virtual hands had moved unthinkingly. Both men held their breath and let out a deep sigh at the narrowly-avoided disaster. It wasn't real now, but it would be – it could be. Or Ray could have a smooth trip and just pop back two minutes later, grinning and giving a thumbs-up to universal fame and adoration. Everything hinged on the success of Ray's training.

From the gravity orb to the shower, from the Shuttle Mission Simulator to more study, from the gyms to the shower again, to the sim and back into the showers, Ray spent his days cranking up his body and mind to their utmost.

"You go through more soap than anyone I've ever met," said Harry as he waited to run through tests while Ray dried himself off. He felt a flicker of envy at the astronaut's perfect physique. All the men were in great condition, but it didn't suit them all equally. Ray wore his with the unselfconscious splendor of Adonis. Already past fifty, Harry knew he'd never look like that. In fact, the only time Harry had ever looked anywhere near that good was inside his VEC2020.

"If you'd rather I stank all day, just say the word," replied Ray cheerfully. "If the doctor prescribes the natural grease of skin oils…"

"Just hurry up, I've got other jobs on the agenda besides attending to your invaluable heart."

Ray sat down on the bench while Harry took a few quick measurements.

"If I crumble into my constituent atoms, a healthy heart won't be much consolation. What accounts for a body staying together anyway?"

"Skin, usually. Deep breath…" said Harry, listening carefully. "Uh-huh. Fine."

"I'm serious, Harry." Ray's eyes met his. "What's the medical reason that our atoms don't just fly apart? Just curious, y'know, in case mine do."

"We don't usually practice medicine at the sub-atomic level," said Harry dismissively. "But okay, if you're so worried about it – we don't know. There is some research into it going on. I can get you the papers if you want…"

"As if I don't have enough to learn," muttered Ray.

"But essentially, it's a theory called 'liking'. Well, that's the medical term, anyway. It's a bit like calling a quark chocolate-flavored. It doesn't mean anything except that we don't know what else to call it, so we figure the atoms *like* each other enough to hang around. But that's not really my field. Anyway," he glanced at his watch, "you're due in the SMS."

"The world is my minder," sighed Ray, pulling his clothes on.

As the weeks went by, the rest of the team gradually eased up with their pressure on Ray; the pace and demands he set on himself were higher than what they demanded of him. After a couple weeks of this, Harry had a word with him about resting a bit more. In response, Ray adjusted his schedule to allow for a quick jog down to the beach after lunch. Gazing at that boundless horizon of blue Atlantic meeting blue sky, listening to the soft rhythmic rush of water, he could sit still for a bit and just breathe. He was too wired by his tight schedule to fully relax, and since Harry insisted he sit there for at least ten minutes, Ray took Marianne's book with him. Its subject matter was a lot closer to home than it had seemed at the book signing.

He read with his usual swiftness; his mental framework tuned into the scientific papers and engineering manuals that were filling his study hours. In Marianne's book, the occasional nod to a scientific concept would be extrapolated into pages of what Ray felt was nebulous self-help nonsense; spiritual lessons drawn from everything, as if the extreme quantum conditions of these ideas actually applied to the every day. With a vast complex of unbelievably sophisticated machinery behind him and titanic minds like Les' straining just to simulate such conditions, he could only chuckle at her naivety. It made the rest of her subject matter easier to bear.

With her scientific grounding so shaky, he could laugh off the notions of stepping into Heaven at the speed of light. The only thing that really bothered Ray about the book was Jack Firestone's own testimonies. Ray had worshipped Jack as a boy, grew to admire him as a young man, and now it pained him that someone whose scientific understanding *was* valid could actually buy into such absurdities. It appeared that no one was immune to self-delusion. Some found it in alcohol, some in pharmaceuticals, some in their VECs, and some in nonsensical mumbo-jumbo. So his idol had clay feet – that didn't mean Ray needed to go the same way.

Paris bustled around the pair on a late spring evening just before twilight. A soft breeze off the Seine River brought the scent of blooming magnolia and horse-chestnut trees to intermingle among the somewhat acrid scents of a modern European city. Dawn leaned back on a wrought-iron park bench, savoring the myriad sensual delights as the perfumed breeze tickled her arms and ran its delicate fingers through her hair. She craned her neck back to look up at the latticed wonder that towered above them. Somehow, in such close proximity, the Eiffel Tower appeared more enormous and awe-inspiring than it had in any picture she'd ever seen.

Pedestrians strolled by the couple as they took in the towering vista with its iron beams and intricate latticework or strolled in and out of the restaurants and shops located within the tower's concrete feet.

"I can understand why everyone wants to come here," she said. "It's strange…its structure doesn't change, but you feel that if you stop watching it for a second you'll miss something."

"I'm glad you like it." Geoff smiled. His own eyes were on Dawn's shapely limbs and contented profile. He slung an arm casually about her shoulders and hugged her to him. Her body stiffened, but she let him pull her in. They sat awkwardly like that for only a few seconds before she leapt up.

"C'mon, let's go up!" She said, moving toward the entrance to the lifts.

The shift from the soft breeze at the feet of the tower to increasing gusts that filtered through the door as they ascended caused goosebumps to form on their arms. Geoff moved to hug her close for warmth, but Dawn shifted against a wall and peered out the window to watch the ground sink far below. Dawn commented inanely on what she saw in an effort to keep her distance from Geoff's advances. Their conversation soon drifted back to its usual preoccupation: politics and what the government should do about the oil embargo.

She liked Geoff better when he was talking. It was then that he was most insightful and interesting. From the far side of a room or a table, he was even good-looking. Why she didn't warm to his touches or kisses, she couldn't fathom, but if she hung out at his place after they finished this VEC-tour, he'd probably try to kiss her again. Conversely, if she went home, it would be to an empty house. Since Ray began intensive training for his mission, he barely even made it home to sleep. Loneliness or Geoff's kisses, she wondered – which was the lesser evil?

Ray picked up his digi-pen and began to scrawl calculations. His jagged writing appeared on the screen in scribbled digits and symbols. To restart his spaceship, he might need to calculate the negative mass settings himself. In space, he'd have a pencil and paper – the space pen was long since abandoned in favor of its less expensive alternative. Maybe he should practice like that? He was searching in his desk drawer when a rap sounded on the door. Jack Firestone's salt-and-peppered head popped round its edge a second later.

"Have any time for an old astronaut like myself?"

Ray grinned. "You bet." He leapt up to shake hands and hug his friend.

"It's great to see you, son," said Jack, pounding his back affectionately.

"It's always an honor, Senator." Ray gestured towards a chair.

"Now let's not get carried away with formalities – I'm still Jack to you."

"So what brings you to NASA, Jack?" Ray slid his desk drawer shut and resumed his seat.

"I just thought I'd come visit our next national hero and wish him luck on his mission."

"I really appreciate that," Ray replied. "It means a lot – I know your schedule must be pretty booked-up these days. And the way the techs are talking, I'm starting to think I'll need all the luck I can get!" He spun the monitor around to show his efforts. "Did they make you learn all this stuff? They've got me cramming on solutions to every scenario they can dream up – I'm expecting Les to pop in here someday soon and explain how to rebuild the ship if all that's left of me and it is one fingernail and a length of wire."

Jack nodded sympathetically, but didn't speak.

After a few moments' silence, Ray spoke again. "Is there something else on your mind?"

"Yes," said the older man slowly. "There is."

"Then spill it." Ray said, leaning back in his chair.

"I don't want to blow your mind," said Jack, "but I think you're going to break the physical plane and go to the other side."

"The other side of what?" Ray's voice was a little stiff.

Jack's face twitched with embarrassment as he began to pace the room. "Ray – you've read my book, haven't you? You know exactly what I'm talking about. I'm talking about stepping into heaven. I'm talking about actually Meeting God."

The younger astronaut suppressed a wince. He could bring himself to acknowledge that Jack had some unscientific ideas, but had no desire to argue with his childhood hero.

"Come on, Jack," he said with forced jocularity. "You know as a scientist I can't approach this mission in that frame of mind."

"This is not a science project, Ray." Jack spun around. "This is about knocking on heaven's door and getting invited in!"

"It doesn't work like that." Ray tried to keep irritation out of his voice. "I'm on a mission. I must use the logic and scientific reasoning of a scientist – not the spiritual insight of a, a, a Buddhist monk."

Jack put a heavy hand on Ray's shoulder. "Son, the same reasoning tells you that you're going to go past the physical boundaries of your five senses, so much so that scientific observation will be impossible."

"So if I'm not observing, what then?"

"You will first connect – and then you will be."

Ray waited for him to finish, but he'd stopped speaking, staring out the window at his private thoughts. "I'll be?" Ray prompted Jack to continue. "What will I be?"

"You'll *be*," emphasized Jack. "Dammit Ray, you have to take this seriously."

With his every hour devoted to preparing for his mission, the accusation stung Ray.

"What's serious," he retorted, "is that there's a chance I

might get stranded in the middle of space with a battered ship and only me to repair it and I have to know what to do. What's *serious* is that my body might endure a punishment so severe that it cannot possibly survive, and I have to do everything I can to make sure it has the best possible chance, otherwise I might just…well…" He bit back the words "meet God for real," when his instinctive atheism cut in.

"I know you're under pressure, Ray." Jack's voice grew gentle and he sat down again. "But there's even more at stake, I think. I'm chairman of the armed services committee – you know that, correct?" Ray nodded. "Well, like you, I've faced potential death on missions and not flinched, but the rumors I'm hearing from the Pentagon scare me shitless. There would be hell to pay if they found out I'm leaking this to you, but there's word that the White House is actually thinking of using its nuclear arsenal to end the war on terror, once and for all."

"That's absurd," exclaimed Ray. "No one ever actually *uses* nuclear weapons…"

"No one but us," said Jack heavily. "We're the only ones who ever have. And I think we might be getting ready to do it again."

Ray shook his head in disbelief.

"You see the news – all the talk of attempts at diplomatic solutions, failed negotiations – it's all bullshit, you must know that. It's press-release, first-grade bull. They don't negotiate, though they might pretend to. Really, they're just saying, 'do as we say or else.' And it looks like 'else' is 'we'll blow you off the face of the earth.'"

"But…"

"Of course the Arab nations don't believe it, even if they assume we might have a hundredth of the morality we preach. No one *will* believe it till it happens. I'm not saying the launch codes are out yet, but it's heading that way."

"The senate would never allow that!"

"The senate's not the Commander-in-Chief."

"That's... But... How... So why are you telling me?" A suspicion began to form in Ray's mind and he sank slowly against his chair seat. "Oh no, Jack. No. You want me to meet God when I'm at the speed-of-light, get enlightened and come back and save the human race from itself?"

"Just saving it from the good ol" US of A will do for now," said Jack, "but basically, yes. You always were a fast learner. And that's what I mean – there's more at stake here."

The Commander-in-Chief was meeting with his Vice-President, Chief of Staff, Economic Advisor, and Political Advisor. Rich Caseman, the Economic Advisor, was advising the President on the impact the wide-spread use of VECs was having on the economy. Almost every industry was being badly affected: travel, entertainment, sport and fashion were hit the directly, but the residual effect was hurting everyone.

"All people want to do anymore," he explained, "is sit in their pajamas and simulate their greatest fantasy in the comfort of their homes. The idea of actually *leaving* one's house to experience life is disappearing."

The President frowned. "Is there any way we can outlaw these things in the best interest of the country?"

Reed Polman, the Presidential Political Advisor, took up the bat. "I'm afraid that's not an option, Mr. President. Your impeachment process would be underway before your signature dried on the bill. We're looking at an addict mentality and the voters will crucify anyone who even thinks about taking their precious VECs away from them."

"But don't they see what it's doing to the economy – to the moral *clarity* – of the nation?" asked Helen.

"Economically speaking," said Caseman, "the only thing the American people are worried about is making their next monthly installment on their simulator programming. Anything else is inconsequential to them."

"And when it comes to the issue of moral clarity," Polman continued, "many people actually see their VEC as a gift from God Himself."

He spoke lightly, but the President's attention was instantly snared.

"Really?"

"Yes, Mr. President, in a way, they do. These simulations are like a little slice of heaven for most people, and an escape from their perceived reality of a living hell.

Robert shook his head gravely. 'That's what scares me the most. When the weak-minded interpret a meaningless, non-Christian event like a VEC simulation as a gift from God, we are in big trouble. We need to do something about this. And we need to petition God about it in our prayers."

Warren held in a sigh of irritation and nodded sagely. His personal heaven took the form of RUSH's Madam Raven at her strictest, where the only petitioning was for permission to lick her heels, but he wasn't yet lost to reality. He still occasionally hired real-life services of the same kind.

As the day of his lift-off approached, Ray began to step up his training and study. Unlike most flights, where he would be pilot with the support of whatever mission or payload specialists were required, he was alone in this one. Due the complexity of what they were doing, allowing for only one person greatly simplified things. Another reason for a solo mission, inadmissible but just as real, was minimizing collateral damage. In other words, better to lose one man than three or more. Ray had always studied hard, but never before had he tormented his mind to the limits of its abilities like this. Throughout his studies at Yale, the only challenge had been to study enough to remain top of the class. Now, he felt his way to the edge of his brain and forced it to conceptualize everything Les presented to him. It was humbling. Everyone knew Les had the highest IQ in recorded history, and if they didn't, Les told them. Nevertheless, Ray had never before appreciated what that meant – that there was a limit to how elegant or sophisticated his thinking. No matter how hard he worked, Les easily overflew those limits. He realized that, like so many other people at NASA, he'd dismissed Les as a geeky misfit who was tethered to his mother's apron-strings. Yet all the while, they'd all happily drawn on the boy's brilliance. During a break on the simulator, he asked Les about it.

"Do you ever reach a point where you think, 'I just can't think my way around this concept?' or, 'I can't hold all this in my head?' and that, 'Anything I think now is far beyond the edge of what I can naturally do?"

Les reflected a moment and shrugged. "Not really," he admitted. "Not with this stuff. Lack of information, sure…"

"But when everything loops into something else and you can't hold it all at the same time?"

Les shook his head, and then stopped. "Actually…" he began. "There is something. It's stupid, because everyone tells me there's nothing to get, but I don't really get beauty. I see it – I feel it – but I can't figure it out. I've studied it intensely in my spare time and there are lots of theories; the golden ratio, symmetry, stuff like that, but nothing explains the way art makes me *feel*."

Ray's face softened as he looked at the younger man. "Well, that's the difference between you and me for a start," he said. "I've never even thought about it enough to wonder."

Every session that made up Ray's day was starting to extend. He timed his work now not by hours, but by how much he needed to achieve. He went from an extended session in the sim to the gym, then on to the SMS, where the technician – regretting his dinner – huffed grumpily about the time. Ray ignored him, buckled in, checked his instruments and signed on to the "Malfunction" sim program. Hidden speakers instantly began to deafen him with the simulated thump, roar and grind of a regular shuttle. This background concerto, so startling to beginners, was to Ray the music of flying. The sim skipped take-off and flight procedures, setting him down straight into crisis point. His console flashed, reporting damage. The motion simulator swung him sickeningly while the visuals for his windows showed spinning stars.

Ray flew into his reflexive motions of recovery: stabilization first, assessment of situation when immediate danger was bypassed. As soon as he steadied the ship and brought his power-usage into line, he looked more closely at the stars, and then glanced again at the panels. The sim had given him one of his own nightmare scenarios. He was dangling in empty space, as far from Earth as this flight could take him, and the spaceship was seriously damaged. He'd probably need to spacewalk to fix some of it… First, he'd sort out what he could inside. He began to work at the repairs, when suddenly the speakers reported an almighty blast. His eyes flew to the windows, but the screens were blank, showing only the red flashing words:

"Your spaceship has exploded."

With no one to witness him, Ray succumbed to his feelings. He swore, kicked whatever wasn't delicate instrumentation, and flung his head down on his hands over the console. "I can't fucking do this, I can't *fucking* do this," he groaned to himself. "I'm too damn stupid and I'm going to kill myself out there in space."

Harry was waiting for him when he emerged. "That was a nice little display of feeling," he said, gesturing to the tech's CCTV screen. "Glad you're not bottling it up inside yourself."

"So you saw me screw up," said Ray shortly.

"I see you screwed-up," answered Harry. "How do you expect to function in this state? Look at you – your muscles are shaking from everything you've been putting yourself

50

through. Your eyeballs are starting to spin in their sockets. You have to take it easier."

"I might die if I take it easier," replied Ray through gritted teeth.

"You *will* die if you don't. By the time you climb into that spaceship, you'll be such a ball of nerves we may as well send a kitten."

"Okay – okay." Weariness made it easier for Ray to concede. He flopped onto a bench and rubbed his hand through his hair. "I'll skip the gym – spend the time on the physics instead…"

"No, Ray," insisted Harry. "You are going to rest. This is not a suggestion, this is doctor's fucking orders. One entire day, you will not study, not exercise…"

"C'mon, a jog, at least!"

"Okay – but just to loosen up. No farther than a couple of miles, total. You will *rest*. Catch a movie, put on your VEC, screw your girlfriend, whatever."

Ray didn't rest. Ray paced. He wandered into the kitchen, opened the fridge, studied its contents and shut it again. He loitered in the living room. He checked his email – there wasn't any, because he never emailed anyone. Five minutes later, he checked again and nothing had arrived. He opened up a briefing, remembered he wasn't supposed to work, and closed it. He put some music on and drummed his fingers to it. He meandered back into the kitchen, where Dawn was still glued to the screen, using the central island as a desk while she made notes.

"What's that you're working on?"

"Shh…" She paused the TV and looked up. "Ray – I've missed you, I really have. It's great to know my brother's still alive. But I've got this assignment due and I still have a lot to do. I'm sorry – it is urgent."

"Sure," he said. He switched the kettle on and strolled

aimlessly out to the garden while it boiled, switched off and cooled. *What do people do in their spare time?* He wondered.

Back in the kitchen, he leafed through Marianne's book, which he'd already finished over his coffee in the morning.

"Where are the tools?" He asked Dawn. "I'll fix the gate."

Dawn paused the TV again, in the middle of President Priest's passionate oration that the way of life of America ('cf. high energy consumption,' Dawn had typed) would never be brought low, and that the US would never be diverted from its duties to bring democracy to ('buy up oil sheikdoms in') the Middle East..

"Geoff already fixed it. He was here yesterday."

"Who's Geoff?" Ray's tedium vanished in a flood of fraternal alarm.

"A guy from my class I'm sort of seeing." She returned to the news and her laptop.

"So why haven't I met him?"

"Because you're never *here*!" snapped Dawn, hitting pause again. "Unless, of course, I have an assignment due in two days."

Ray returned to his occupation of spinning *Godspeed* around and around on the counter, so that Marianne's features swam in a swirl of color. Dawn leaned on the island, watching him, the TV still on pause.

"I'm sorry I got mad," she said after a moment. "Look, if you're bored, why don't you give Marianne a call? She's probably the only person we know who isn't at work today."

"That would just be weird," said Ray listlessly.

"No, it *wouldn't*. It's what normal people do – it's what phones are for. Normal. People. Phone. Each other," she spelled out patiently. "Anyway, why'd you think she gave you her card? I think it's because she *likes* you…" She grinned at his sudden discomfort.

Being normal was easier than Ray expected. He and Marianne chatted comfortably as they walked along Cocoa Beach, the evening breeze throwing salty air over them. The sandpipers took to the skies and dived in disorderly flocks, screeching.

"It's a pity we don't get the sunset on this side," he said.

"This is pretty too though, don't you think?"

In the clear air, the horizon was layered with bands of color that diffused gently into each other: pale pink and soft blue, light violet, all the way to the deep Prussian blue overhead. Against that backdrop, Marianne's composed beauty took on the spiritual simplicity of a Madonna.

"So, did you enjoy the book?" she asked.

So much for a romantic stroll, thought Ray regretfully. Lying about his opinion didn't occur to him. "As – um – science fiction, yes," he said truthfully.

"I can see you read it with a closed mind." Marianne's plump lips set in a line.

"I'm an astronaut, Marianne. I read it with a scientific mind."

"And you didn't believe a word I said?"

"You wrote that Jack Firestone is an extraordinary man – I believe that."

"I see." She walked in silence, a slight cloud over her mood. "And even this so-called extraordinary man's testimony isn't enough for you? He believes it whole-heartedly and you can't give it even the slightest possibility of being true?"

Ray sighed. "Jack's the best astronaut I ever met and a very dear friend. Hell, I'd even call him a mentor. Unfortunately, that doesn't stop him being a space cadet."

"A space cadet that is now a Senator from California?"

"Hey," said Ray, trying to lighten the atmosphere, "they elect actors for governor on a regular basis, so a space-cadet for Senator sounds about right!"

"What do you have *against* my ideas, Ray?"

Whatever her delusionary notions, he liked her too much to attack the spiritual side of the book. That, he figured, would be too personal for her to forgive. "The science," he said. "It was – forgive me, but physics was my major and takes up at least half, if not more, my life at the moment. Look, the science was bull."

"Oh, really?" snapped Marianne. "Did I say *anything* scientifically inaccurate?"

"I'm sorry Marianne, but you did." He couldn't understand her anger – things were either true or not true; the science was either right or it was wrong. No grey areas. "The assumption that…" He floundered. Nothing she'd written about physics was actually *wrong*, he had to give her that much credit. The wild conclusions she'd drawn, however, were. "Okay, theoretically time does cease at the speed of light, but we still don't know about subjective time…"

"Is there any other kind?" she cut in.

He grinned. She did know her stuff. "Fair point. But to jump from that to heaven – to say that no time means you're in the presence of God – *that's* unscientific."

"That's spiritual. And forgive me, but spirituality is *my* major, so to speak, and takes up most of my life and I don't think it's a subject on which you're qualified to speak!"

They strolled on in silence through the darkening air. The full moon was cresting the horizon, slipping out of the Atlantic and gilding her silhouette with silver as he snuck a sidelong glance at her.

"Touché," he whispered.

She glanced reluctantly sideways and saw he was smiling.

"Not that I agree with you," he went on, his smirk broadening as he saw her soften again. "But I'm glad we agree spirituality is unscientific."

"I guess you'll just have to reassess your position after *you* travel the speed of light," she said, still unwilling to concede. "And when you go face-to-face with God, please reflect on this conversation and regret your narrow-mindedness."

As they walked along, their arms swung into each other; their fingers brushed and tangled, holding on. When they turned back, they swapped hands unselfconsciously. Her small, cool palm nestling lightly against his gave him a funny, leaping feeling of joy inside which made him notice how the moonlight scattered itself over the waves.

"What I'm more concerned about," he said after a long time, "is whether I'll go face-to-face with God in a more final way, during this mission. At least, that would worry me if I believed in God. The more immediate concern is whether or not my atoms will all blast apart."

Her hand answered him with a gentle squeeze. Scientifically speaking, that gave him no protection from death, but it eased his mind nonetheless.

"I'd like to see you again," Ray said as he dropped her off, "but I've got this mission coming up and lots of preparation to do..."

"That's fine, whenever," Marianne interrupted hastily. She hated hearing men make the usual, polite excuses. "So I'll see you round, then" she said brightly.

"I mean it – I do want to see you again. I don't agree with you, but I like arguing with you." *And looking at you,* he thought. "So if the doctor orders another day off, can I give you a call?"

Her stomach leapt and lodged itself in her throat. Suddenly unable to speak, she smiled and nodded.

Over the next three weeks, Harry ordered Ray off-site on another two occasions. Each time, he spent the free day with Marianne, their minds and mouths arguing while their hands shyly entwined. On their last meeting before the mission, as they said goodbye, she stood on tiptoe and kissed him softly.

"In case your worst nightmare comes true," she whispered.

"You mean in case I die?" Ray winced.

"Nah," she chuckled. "In case you meet God. You can pass that on from me."

The next morning dawned early, and Ray strapped himself in; every movement, flip and switch familiar from his long hours in the SMS. The initial blast-off of a space shuttle flight was standard procedure, but Ray's stomach always fell into his feet as the plumes of orange and white propelled the shuttle upward. He couldn't see the shape of the States taking shape as he soared above them, and then the whole planet shrinking off behind him as he lunged into the great beyond, but he knew how it would look after he finally leveled off.

The first time Ray had ever seen the planet Earth from space, he'd wanted to laugh aloud with surprise – it really was round! It really was a little blue-and-green planet! It hung in space as innocently as a floating brick. Seeing it as this pretty, spinning, mostly oceanic ball put a certain perspective on things.

When he was in position, surfing the atmosphere, he and Thomas spoke.

"Solar - all systems go?"

"All systems go."

With a shimmying feeling in his belly but a steady pulse, Ray began to manipulate his control panel.

"Godspeed, my friend," said Thomas from the ground. "Godspeed."

"Thanks, Thomas." The moment upon him, Ray's pre-flight nerves vanished. He hit the last few buttons as the countdown approached zero.

In the NASA control station, all eyes were fixed on the satellite images. The ship accelerated as planned – and vanished.

4

Calm descended on Ray. There had been times, in a life so heavily burdened with responsibility, that he had felt simply happy. They didn't flash before him, but unspooled simultaneously. Nestling in a cocoon of blankets, the residual feel of his mother's gentle goodnight kisses on his eyelids, hearing the sound of laughter drift from downstairs, he felt utterly at peace. Those were the days before the shock of being the only adult in the house had overtaken the rest of his days.

Years later, he was floating up from sleep into a world still dark and shapeless, dreams of a woman still real in his heart and arms; he hovered in the land between sleep and wakefulness, savoring the sensation of being absolutely loved.

Other fragments of his past unraveled before him. He saw a sunrise so beautiful that his heart couldn't contain its joy and he wanted to scream and jump. He overheard a little Dawn, seven years old, explaining to her friend that instead of a mommy and a daddy she had a Ray, who was like the best daddy in the world, but younger.

The first time he really listened to a piece of classical music – Pachelbel's Canon – he felt how the stately beat slowed his heart and the strings came in layer upon layer, building up to a perfect explosion of joy.

Peaceful joy subsumed him. His heart somehow enlarged to bear that much happiness. The elation that usually threatened to overflow the boundaries of his body swelled, spreading into everything. He was surrounded, not by light but by luminescence, unrefracted and undifferentiated, of which he was also a part.

After all his conviction that the Universe was just unfeeling chaos, and death a final end, he found a sense of understanding here. Something huge and gentle enveloped every atom. It imbued him with its own wisdom. Here, at the vibration of infinity, he was one with the source whose breath made life out of matter.

Every amoeba that divided itself to make another one was alive with this being. Every tree that drew its sap upwards, to make leaves that would fall and fruit that would ripen, had this vitality. Every heart that opened to another person sent out loops of this lifeline. Like a hum whose pitch is too high to hear, but you feel anyway, he had always known this. In the limits of his five senses, bounded by three-dimensional space and linear time, all he had believed in was matter. Now, he felt its spark and recognized it as himself.

The darkness of his pain had been left behind. His icy fury at parents who had chosen death now melted, because he understood. They too had desperately tried to live in a material world, but sensed that there was oneness and peace, erroneously believing it forever out of reach. They'd tried to reach it – by terrible means, but they had tried nonetheless. They had only been attempting to realize what he now had: to be aligned with infinity.

He never believed in souls. He'd always thought that without the five senses, only perception remained. How could you hear without ears? He now knew the answer: better. His physical sense of hearing was like a cheap sound-system playing a low-quality recording. Now he heard without those barriers, and the music of the spheres eddied around – and in him.

Are you God? His question was addressed to everything, because the light was everywhere, but also to the source of knowledge.

At your level of spiritual evolution, I would be God.
Is this Heaven?
It is all one – a state of being at the highest vibration that connects you to the source. A state of Love.

"Come in, Solar – come in, Solar – Ray, are you there? Please respond!" Thomas's voice had a hairline crack of panic in it.

"Yeah, I'm still here," said Ray.

"You did it!" In the background, he heard whoops and cheers.

"Did what? I haven't done anything." He glanced around: nothing had changed.

"You just traveled at the speed-of-light!" exclaimed Thomas. "We can do it – we did it – you did it!"

"We haven't done anything," insisted Ray, bemused. "I've just pressed the button, nothing's happened."

"You pressed that button two minutes and twenty-two seconds ago."

Ray checked his panel, which showed the seconds counting upwards from blast-off time: eleven, twelve…

"My equipment shows something different," he insisted. "There's a fault with the ship – the flight hasn't worked. I haven't moved."

In the base, the ground crew stared at each other and back at the screen. Less than half a minute ago, the ship had blinked back into existence.

"Ray, your ship vanished from the sky for two minutes and ten seconds. We need to check your clock, but the mission was successful. You went, man, and you came back."

On the ground, cameras and journalists were kept at a distance while Ray was taken to the debriefing room. Amelia Jacobson, the PR woman was tearing her hair out – they'd spent a fortune on developing his successful return line, and he hadn't even said it. Instead, a breathless world heard the lines "Did what?" before she'd given the order to cut the broadcast of the conversation. In history would be Neil Armstrong's "One small step for man…," Jack Firestone's "We've touched Heaven,", and Raymond Sky with "Did what?" She groaned at the thought. Her assistant was already hashing out ways to explain it.

In the conference room, Ray perched on the edge of the broad table, his thumb moving over the keypad of his cell phone.

"So you don't remember a thing?" asked Thomas, pacing restlessly.

"One sec…" He held the phone to his ear. "Dawn? Yeah – I'm okay, honey." Through the phone came a squeal of delight and Ray held it away from his ear, his mouth twisting in a little smile. "Fine," he went on. "I dunno – really, I don't know – look, it's a long story and I've got the debriefing. I'll phone you later. Yeah, you too. Bye." He hung up. "Sorry about that. Where were we?"

Thomas sighed theatrically. "What do you *remember*?" He asked.

"Remember? It felt like nothing happened. I hit the button and then you're telling me I vanished, reappeared and traveled at the speed of light.

Thomas stopped in his tracks and looked at the doctor. "Harry – did you find anything that would explain this? Ray passing out, or amnesia, or just not experiencing it?"

Harry shook his head. "We did detect some unusual brain behavior in the seconds between him popping back and when he replied to your hails. The SPECT imaging machine caught this and recorded it.

"So we've got *something*." Thomas sighed heavily. "Let's take a look."

Harry leaned over the laptop and typed in a few commands, projecting a hologram of Ray's brain into the air above the holo-generator. "See this part?" he said, gesturing to the top and the back part. "This is the superior parietal lobe's activity while he was talking to you. And this," he hit a few more keys, "is the instant he arrived back."

They looked at the colorful image, as iridescent as an oil spill with its melting reds, greens and blues.

"Translation?" prompted Thomas. Harry was shaking his head, studying the image and enlarging it.

"Well, there's no activity here. None."

"So this explains my – amnesia?" asked Ray. He was feeling twitchy. A clean bill of mental health was essential if his career was going to continue, and he didn't like this talk of memory-loss. His conviction that no time had passed was so strong that he almost suspected they were all lying to him. Great – I'm an amnesiac *and* paranoid.

"No, this has nothing to do with memory," Harry was saying. "This part processes information about time and space and the orientation of the body in space. Basically, it determines where the body ends and the rest of the world begins."

"Your brain has to *tell* you that?" Ray was surprised.

"Your brain has to tell you that that's your leg," said Harry curtly, gesturing to Ray's foot on the conference table chair. "Your brain has to tell you up is up and that when you see a face it's a face, not a flower." He turned back to the hologram, pointing out the inactive section of Ray's brain again. "That bit's not supposed to go dark. Without it, you have no perception of self – and without that, you can't do anything. You can't control your leg, for example, if there's no concept of 'you' to associate the leg with."

"But it doesn't explain the memory loss?" Thomas pressed.

"Nope. It's not unheard of for activity to decrease here. We've never seen it at zero before – but in certain forms of Buddhist meditation, they deliberately suppress all sense of self – it's supposed to give them this amazing feeling of oneness with the universe. In that case, we see a similar scan."

"Jack said something like that," said Ray thoughtfully. "He was convinced I was going to have this über-spiritual experience – and Marianne Summers, that writer he wrote a book with, thought I was going to meet God. You know what Jack said about his trip."

"Trip" Harry snorted, "being the operative word, in his case. But we didn't have SPECT imaging then, so we don't have a record of his brain activity for comparison."

"I see," said Ray.

Thomas resumed his pacing, while Harry studied the scans in more detail. A soft knock at the door was followed by Les. He took over for Harry at the laptop, bringing up data from the ship's computers.

"Okay," said Thomas, while the engineer tapped away. "There is something we can make of this. We all know Einstein believed time didn't exist at the speed of light and maybe this is why – going the speed of light, your brain shuts down the perception of time. I mean, time clearly passed."

Les glanced up. "I think Einstein would've said it shuts down the illusion of time."

"So," Ray summarized, "I had a supreme Buddhist experience of oneness with the Universe, but thanks to also losing the illusion of time, I don't remember any of it. So what about the ship? The clock?"

Les gestured to the data he'd finished projecting and started to talk them through it. A full diagnostic on the equipment showed no flaws – everything was in perfect working condition and should have registered something during the mission. The clock was functioning normally, but simply lost two minutes and ten seconds during the flight. If Ray had amnesia, the ship apparently shared it. "So that lets you off the hook." He gave Ray a thumbs-up and Ray felt a surge of gratitude.

Thomas had been drumming his fingers anxiously all through Les' explanations and now resumed his pacing around the room. "We're screwed," he muttered.

"Ray's okay," said Les.

"No – we're all screwed. We're scheduled to brief the President in six hours on the results of our four hundred billion dollar mission. I'm not too thrilled about telling him our on-board equipment didn't record any data to work on, my astronaut remembers nothing and it's as if *nothing even happened!"*

For the first time during Alice's class, Dawn was lost in thought. Surreptitiously, she hit a few keys on her laptop to replay Ray's emergence from the spaceship. He wasn't grinning and waving in triumph – he actually looked a little confused. He hadn't even said his successful return line, and they'd practiced it the night before until he was word-perfect. Alice's astute eye noticed that Dawn was lost in her own little world

"Do you have anything to contribute, Dawn?" asked Alice.

Dawn shook herself and attempted to replay the debate in her head. Usually, even distracted, her mind would capture all the words, so she could at least repeat what had been said.

"I'm sorry," she confessed, mortified. "I was miles away."

"We were *discussing*," Alice said heavily, "the baseline assumptions around women's issues. Something I had thought was very close to your heart."

"Oh, okay." She glanced around, embarrassed. A few of her classmates were snickering, glad to see the golden girl put in her place at last. She struggled to recollect what she had worked up on the issue, the day before while Alice eyed her scornfully.

After class ended, Alice asked for a word and Dawn waited nervously, expecting to be told off. Instead, she got something worse – her assignment back, graded at a D.

"I wanted to give this to you privately, because I knew you'd be upset," said Alice.

Dawn stared at the black ink, the down stroke and

semicircle, in disbelief. Tears sprang to her eyes.

"Have a seat," said Alice. "Geoff – stop hanging around the door will you? This is a private conversation."

Dawn sat down and flipped through the pages of her work. "What's wrong with it?" she whispered.

Alice was surprised. "I thought you'd know this wasn't up to your usual standard – I thought something might be wrong at home, in your personal life...?"

Dawn shook her head mutely, feeling sick.

The analysis was too blunt, Alice explained – there was no subtlety, no allowance made for individual decision-making. In places, it verged on conspiracy theory. It referred throughout to "the government" as a single entity, bent on destructive policies. A massive, flawed assumption underlay the whole essay: that the government controlled how people thought.

Dawn left the room utterly dejected. Geoff was waiting outside. Without speaking, she showed him the paper and its grade and he grimaced sympathetically. While he flipped through it, her phone beeped with a text message from Ray.

"Gone to see President. Back tomorrow. Hugs."

"Cheer up," said Geoff, slipping his arm around her waist and hugging her to him. "Let's go to my place and put a VEC on. We'll go somewhere pretty – take your mind off things."

Dawn shrugged. It would mean delaying the rewrite and probably another kissing-and-fondling session, but so what. Maybe if she joined in a bit more she'd fall in love with him, as she so wished she could. After all, he was interesting, fun, good-looking, intelligent and kind. What more did she want? Maybe this *was* love and she was just too stupid and naïve to know it.

Ray stood at formal military rest; spine erect, hands clasped behind his back Thomas stood at his side. Vice President

Warren Christian was on the sofa, one leg crossed over the other, his hands clasped behind his head. In marked contrast, another of the room's occupants – an attractive mid-forties woman – sat upright with her ankles neatly crossed. The President, however, was wearing a groove in his carpet with a dignified tread, back and forth.

"So you don't remember a single moment of the experience?" he asked, stopping and looking at Ray again.

"No, sir."

"And the on-board equipment didn't record any data?"

"Yes, sir," said Thomas, "like nothing even happened. Even the onboard clocks didn't move."

"Well, gentlemen," broke in Warren, from his casual position, "this puts us in a very awkward position. The president's polling numbers are in the toilet, energy costs are driving us into a depression, the population's addiction to VECs are further damaging the economy and the one thing…" He swung himself forward abruptly, his appearance of good humor vanishing. "The *one* positive thing that could have maybe changed the downward spiral of this presidency comes back as if nothing even happened! How in the hell is the President going to address the public with the results of Mission Last Frontier as a big, fat zero?" His glowering eyes fixed on Ray, who returned his gaze with a steady anger of his own.

"I have an idea." Thomas broke the uneasy silence.

"This better be good." Warren flung himself back into the sofa, staring up aggressively.

"Well, sir…" Thomas swallowed. "Albert Einstein believed that at the speed of light, time didn't exist…"

"Do *not* even go there!" yelled Warren.

Thomas jumped. "But sir – can't we say that the lack of data and Ray's lack of memory validate Einstein's theory? It's called negative data, sir and it is a result – it could even be viewed as a breakthrough…"

Warren leapt to his feet and paced slowly across the

room, until his face was a few inches from Thomas's. He ground his words out slowly.

"Do you really want the President of the United States to tell the American public that we have proven time doesn't exist at the speed of light?" Thomas felt instinctively that "yes" would be the wrong answer and kept quiet. "Do you think," continued Warren, his rage rising like a controlled eruption, "that this is something the American public can comprehend?"

The correct answer here was obviously "No" and Thomas responded accordingly.

"We talk to the country in simple *three word phrases*." Warren's voice was nearing a shout. "And that's about all they can handle! Proving time doesn't exist at the speed of light would be like teaching calculus to a kindergarten class! We do not tell them things they cannot possibly understand! *Do you understand me?*"

"Yes, sir," said Thomas promptly.

The awful man at last moved his face back and spoke to the room in general. "I'm going to tell you two how this going to go down." He shook his finger in Ray's face. "*You* are going to go on every talk show from New York to LA, enthusiastically bragging about how successful this mission was." He shifted his finger to Thomas. "And *you* are going to do a press conference, figure out what fucking spin to put on that 'did what' shit and brief the press on what a successful mission this was."

"How am I going to do that, sir?" The man was scary, but Thomas was determined to stand his ground. "If I can't play the negative data card and I don't have a single piece of positive data…"

"You're the fucking rocket scientist," snapped Warren, "you figure it out."

As evening shifted towards night, everyone rested from the strains of the day. Thomas caught a cab back from the airport and let himself quietly into the house, not wanting to wake Cathy. He tiptoed upstairs. She lay outstretched on her side, her face solemn in sleep. He stroked her hair gently.

"Mmm…"

"Shh…" he whispered. "It's me, I'm home. I'm just going to have some supper, okay?"

"Mmm." He tucked the duvet around her shoulders and under her feet, so they wouldn't escape into the cold again. "I wanna hear about it," she murmured.

"Sleep – you need to sleep." He wanted to be alone, to think about the day.

Downstairs, his supper stood on the kitchen table with a note on heating instructions. He ate it in the den, flipping through his programs, looking for something to take away the sour feel of the mission and the Vice President's angry injunctions. He lifted *Tumble in the Hay* and grinned. The fresh-faced cowgirl, all wholesome goodness and ribboned blonde plaits, reminded him of Cathy when they'd first met. An hour or two of her sweet, sincere attentions and he'd feel more himself.

Marianne knelt in front of her altar. A statue of the Buddha was flanked by two white pillar candles, in front of which lay a censer; the dust of burnt incense sticks sprinkled around it. At the center was Ray's birth-candle: red and brown for Capricorn. Four white candles surrounded it, then four red, for protection, purity and strength. All had burned down to stubs and now flickered and died. She didn't use candle rituals so often these days, but she'd known Ray wouldn't accept a crystal or an amulet. Her spiritual practices were eclectic and drew from a wide variety of sources. She pitied those who scorned the pick-n-mix approach to spirituality. "Be open to new light, wherever you find it," said the Quakers. Spirituality, she believed, was a force, not a rule book or set of dictates, and she'd argued the case strongly in

Open to Light.

Her vigil of protection complete, Marianne stood and stretched her stiffened legs. She browsed her collection of VEC programs, looking for something light and distracting, but not too energetic. Her fingers hesitated, shuffling back and forth, and settled on *Sensibilities*. PURE had a new line called "Classics from the Great Authors," and a brief immersion into Jane Austen's world would be just the thing. She slipped her headset on and sank into the happy frivolities of a flirtation with Willoughby. Delicious…

President Robert Priest settled himself on his knees by his bed, to pray. He felt it symbolically important to kneel: that even he, the most powerful man in the world, should humble himself before the Almighty. He took pride in never missing his prayers. Properly composed, he began to beseech the Lord for help with the trials that troubled him: a successful outcome from the apparently abortive NASA mission; an end to the oil embargo imposed by the unbelievers; an upward swing in the economy; a positive turn in his own polls; and a solution to the VEC problem.

On the VEC subject, he grew very passionate, calling on God to have mercy on those weak-willed and indulgent people. He prayed for those who wallowed unrepentantly in their sins of the flesh and their selfishness; to the destruction of their own country. Having made exhaustive reference to everything God should know about, he finished off by assuring God that His will would be done. President Priest then climbed into bed next to his sleeping wife, confident that it would be.

Dawn wandered around the house, leaving lights on in her wake. Her eco-consciousness pricked at her, but her fears won out. She hated being alone in the house at night. The windows seemed so huge and black. Drawn curtains were worse, hiding who-knew-what in their folds... When Ray called to say he was about to board a plane for New York, she'd almost asked Geoff if she could stay at his place, but then she faltered. She was still too ambivalent, and Geoff too eager, to risk it. At last, she curled up in her big brother's bed, amidst the safety of his things, and dozed off with the lamp shining.

Also in lamplight, Les sat up in bed against a pile of pillows. In his hands, he held a copy of *La Verité en Peinture* – "the truth of painting" – by Jacques Derrida. He was determined to understand the beauty of things and his own wild emotional responses to art. On the first page, he read "Someone, not me, comes and says the words: 'I am interested in the idiom of painting.'" His heart leapt – they were his own words to the librarian. Could it be that Derrida had somehow heard his question, some forty-plus years before? Excitement pounded as he began to scribble ideas and equations in the margin. Unlike most scientific types, Les dismissed nothing as impossible – how else could he have found a way for speed-of-light travel?

At the end of an hour, all the margins and the inner leaves were full of scribbles and he laid the book on his bedside table with a sigh – another library book he'd have to replace. They were starting to get annoyed with him.

Ray was also scribbling, although he used the letterhead of the Hilton Garden Inn. Between the folds of striped curtains, he could see a sliver of the night sky, to which his eyes returned intermittently. Just this morning, he had been up there, with those stars; all the petty concerns of this planet blended and dimmed by distance. Now, the atmospheric pollutions impeded once again, cutting him off from fully experiencing the magnificent starscape. He looked again at his notes, scratched out what he'd just written and stood to make himself another coffee. The car would come for him at four in the morning; carrying him to the first of his interviews. He scanned the press office's briefing again while he tore open the little packets of sugar and powdered creamer. The pile of coffee-detritus piling on the tray made him smile and think of Dawn – the wastefulness of packaging like that always made her rant. Holding his cup, he sat down again to work. Whatever he said, whatever the Vice President's instructions, he could not bring himself to directly lie. Lying to other people was the beginning of lying to himself – and that is the pathway to madness. *The truth but not the whole truth*, he thought grimly, *so help me ethics.*

5

Ray sat on the sofa, in a relaxed pose, as instructed. His face itched with the pasty studio make-up they'd insisted on applying. Matt Lauer, with the full dignity of his 63 years, was leaning earnestly towards him. From so close, Ray could see the fine coating of powder that kept his thinning pate from catching the light. The falsity of everything here – from the cosmetics to the faux "living room area" to the well-managed audience – grated him.

"So, what was it like to travel at the speed of light?" Matt asked, his eyes clasped on Ray with the utter sincerity and seriousness of a media statesman.

"You know," said Ray with a forced smile, "it's hard to say – the time just flew by."

Matt's eyes barely flickered. "That's funny..." – a quick tweak of his mouth suggested wry humor – "time is supposed to slow down, or not even exist at the speed of light."

"I know, but I got the opposite sensation – the mission was over just like *that.*" Ray snapped his fingers in the air and cracked another grin. He'd decided jocular idiocy was the order of the day. As long as he could seem to answer the questions, the host would have experience enough to supply any actual content the interview needed.

Dawn was watching at home through the slits between her fingers, hands over her face. Whatever fine things her brother was, TV personality of the year he was *not.* He was photogenic – his blue eyes shone like gemstones and with his neatly-cut black hair and strong, narrow jaw, he was practically a poster boy for NASA – but his replies were stilted and uninformative. It was almost enough to make her feel sorry for Matt Lauer. She winced through the rest of the interview. *The Daily Show* was, if possible, even worse. She liked Jon Stewart, with his easy humor and crazy hair.

"So you didn't come face to face with the big guy at the speed of light, like some were predicting?" The resolute terseness of the handsome astronaut was forcing the poor man to lead the witness.

"Oh no." Ray shook his head. "Didn't meet the big guy, unfortunately."

"*Say something!*" yelled Dawn at the screen. "Stop saying yes and no, give them an answer! Tell them what it was *like*!"

"Are you sure?" Jon raised an expertly quizzical eyebrow. "You don't sound too sure to me…" His side glance at the audience raised the appropriate titter of approval.

"Oh yes," said Ray. "I'm pretty sure something like that wouldn't have slipped my mind, unless I'd had some kind of *brain freeze* or something!" He burst into a strained laugh and Jon was obliged to join in.

"So," Jon resumed, his laughter dying quickly, "let's talk about those newly famous words – 'did what?' Not quite what the public was expecting."

"Well – you know…" Ray frantically tried to remember what the press people had told him to say about that. A sleepless night and a caffeine-fueled day were making his neurons fire sporadically in every direction at once. "You know how it is…"

"As a matter of fact, we don't, and we'd *love* you to tell us," cut in Jon jovially.

"It's…" Oh, thank goodness, that was it. "It's not what I do – I'm part of a much bigger system. I might be the man in the ship, but my contribution is just a small part of a vast machine; the engineers – who are the technical pioneers – our fine ground team…"

"But you *were* the one to actually travel at the speed of light." Jon picked up the conversation as Ray's words petered out. "So how was that experience?"

"Incredible," replied Ray, nodding sagely, thinking how easily most people forgot what their words actually meant. "Just – unbelievable. That's the only way I can describe it."

Deciding he was going to get nothing more articulate, Jon wrapped up the interview. He raised applause from the audience, got in a dig about the "strong and silent" type and finished with a flourish and a promise to be right back. To his relief, Ray saw an assistant nod to him – he was off-camera.

"TV off," said Dawn, as the advertisements began to roll.

"So where would you like to argue today?" said Marianne happily, sliding into the passenger seat. She was wearing her favorite outfit – a white silk dress that tied together with thin straps over her shoulders and then fell in simple folds around her breasts and her hips. While dressing, she'd experienced euphoria rising like champagne bubbles through her: he was safe, he wanted to see her again, and they could talk about his trip... For the first time in at least a year, she got ready to go out without any anxiety or throwing garment after garment in an increasing pile on the bed. At her neck, she wore a quartz crystal tied with leather.

"It's a surprise," said Ray, glancing appreciatively at her. She was always lovelier in person than he remembered while they were apart. "But I think you'll like it..."

The delight in her face was all the proof he needed, as they drew up outside the Mango Tree restaurant. The white stone doorway, surrounded by shaped topiary and clinging foliage, invited them down a path of wonders. Her hand in his, he followed her pace as she dawdled and marveled over orchids, swans, hanging baskets, and lush greenery. Her childlike happiness made him chuckle. She closed her eyes, her head tilted back.

"Listen…" she whispered. "'Smell that…"

Self-consciously, he followed her example. She murmured a litany of pleasures, guiding his senses. "The bird song. The water splashing against the rocks. The sound of wings slapping into place after flight. Smell the flowers and the leaves in the heat. Take in the sweetness in the air, and the smell of shaded water…"

With her low voice directing his nose and ears, he fell into a reverie. When at last he opened his eyes to the visual splendor again, he felt deep calm. He lifted her hand in his and gently kissed the back of her wrist.

"You have a way with words."

"You have good taste in restaurants," she said, laughing softly. Silently, he sent a prayer of thanks to Dawn.

"Come," he said, walking onwards. "Our table's on the patio – you can see the garden from there."

The South Pacific atmosphere continued on the patio, with pillars of soft pink, a sky-blue ceiling and huge panes of glass exposing the jungle beyond. They sat in comfortable silence, Marianne sipping white wine and Ray orange juice.

"You can hear the water," he said, turning his head to the direction of the light rippling sound.

She looked at his profile. His face balanced on the fine line between beautiful and handsome, and was now touched with the vulnerability of a much younger man – almost a boy, really. Black smudges under his eyes betrayed a profound exhaustion. She'd been longing to take him to task over those interviews – such obfuscating, clumsy answers – and suddenly remembered how tiring it must have been for him. She made a quiet decision within herself not to raise the subject, or anything contentious that night. He deserved a break.

Instead, they talked of everything else. They'd both found their paths into their chosen careers by striving and working double-time, spending their evenings on getting closer to that shining goal instead of at the cinema, or in bars.

They compared notes on holding onto a dream and the reactions of people who tried to make them more "realistic" about their ambitions. They realized they hadn't looked at the menu, briefly scanned the dishes and were lured back into conversation before they could make a choice. In the end, they went with the waiter's recommendations and interrupted bites of tender artichoke hearts and crumbling blue cheese with more talk. Each believed in reaching for the stars, demanded perfection from themselves and held honesty to be the highest of virtues.

"That's one of the things I don't like about religion," said Ray, over the salmon entrée. "I think most people are just dishonest with themselves about it. Just because you don't *like* the idea of a universe without a great-big teddy-bear of a god to look after you, doesn't mean you can go around inventing whatever gods make you feel warm and snug and better than anyone else. Wishing doesn't make it so."

Marianne nodded thoughtfully, chewing while she thought about what to say. She did believe in a benevolent force, but not in the terms he expressed. She was also determined not to argue on this night.

"Freud and Jung both talk about that," she said cautiously. "I told you my major was psychology..." He nodded. "Well, both of them talked about the human predisposition to believe in God. Freud said that, compared to animals, humans have a very long period of dependency on their parents – which creates a psychological expectation that there will always be this towering figure to say yes or no, right or wrong, to punish or forgive. That the dependency takes away some of our ability to make those judgments for ourselves, because we're used to them coming from somewhere else. He doesn't say that God doesn't exist, but just explains where the picture of this paternalistic father-figure God comes from. I mean – big beard in the sky? That's such a three-year-old perspective!"

They both laughed.

"Big beard stinking of booze," said Ray absently.

"And then Jung's take was similar, but within his own framework." She went on to give a nutshell version of Jung's theories of the archetypes, the picture-images consistent across cultures and ages: the mother, the shadow, the wizard, the crone... "And of course, the God-concept." That, she explained, was from a hierarchical view, where society was a pyramid, from God, to the king, and down to the peasants.

"So childhood, or society, makes people believe in God?" asked Ray. The waiter cleared away their plates and Marianne watched with surprise as Ray signaled him to bring her more wine.

"In *that* kind of God, yes," she agreed.

"But that's not the kind of God you believe in?"

She shook her head, smiling. "Uh-uh. You're not going to get me into an argument tonight – this is all too pretty and I'm having too lovely a time..." She waved her hand around, gesturing at the candles that now glowed on each table and the soft spotlights illuminating the garden. "Okay – here's one. Did you hear about the dyslexic atheist?"

Ray had, but waited for the punchline with glee.

"He didn't believe in Dog." Marianne groaned as Ray laughed. "I can't believe I told you that, it's the oldest one in the book..."

"You heard about the dyslexic devil-worshipper?" countered Ray. "He sold his soul to Santa."

The rest of the evening was spent exchanging all the lame jokes they knew and laughing inanely.

On the drive back home, Marianne's resolve finally broke.

"So what happened up there?" she asked casually.

He stiffened, but replied lightly. "Haven't you been watching TV? I've told every talk show host on the networks what happened."

"Oh, I watched you say nothing at all and brush them off

at every turn. I was just hoping you might tell me the truth."
She fiddled with the crystal at her neck.

"Are you saying I lied?" Quiet anger underlay his voice.

"No – of course not, Ray. I know that much about you.
But unfortunately I've dated enough men to know
instinctively when one is being… ambiguous."

He gripped the steering wheel tighter. He didn't like the
direction of this conversation. He didn't want to get back
onto the subject of spirituality, which they'd managed to
circle around so neatly all evening. He didn't want to give
her the same pointless ripostes he'd given on TV. He didn't
want to risk telling the very sensitive truth to someone who
was – however much he liked her – in the media frontline.
Attack was the best form of defense, he concluded.

"And why would I mislead you and the whole country
about my experience? What would be my motive?"

She shrugged listlessly, hating herself for not keeping
her big fat mouth shut, but unwilling to back down and say
she believed all the drivel he'd fed the media. "I don't
know," she murmured. "Look – I don't lie, you don't lie.
I'm not saying you lied. But I can't lie and say I think you
gave them the whole story. So maybe I should've copied
your example and just evaded the whole subject. I tried to
and then I just – caved. I'm sorry."

Ray drove a few more miles in silence, until he found a
spot to pull over. They sat in the car, looking out at the
Atlantic. The moon was just past new and cast barely a
flicker of illumination across its surface.

"Can I trust you?" he said, at last.

"Of course." Her face showed puzzled surprise.

"I mean – really trust you. If I tell you this, it goes no
further. No mention of it, no allusion to it, no *nothing*." He
remained in silent hesitation for a minute or two. "I mean –
this is probably a state secret. It's just – I haven't expressly
signed anything saying I'll keep it secret – although the Vice
President… Look, I don't believe in deceiving people, so I

don't even think keeping it secret is honorable. And I didn't give my word, so I'm not breaking it."

Marianne remained motionless, her nerves on tenterhooks. This had to be huge. She wouldn't breathe a word of it to another soul – but she hoped so much to hear that he'd had the breakthrough experience she expected, touched the face of the god-force... He *was* gentler, this evening, than any of their previous dates.

"On your word of honor, this goes no further?" he said.

"On my word and on my soul,'" she replied, vowing by what they each believed in.

"Okay. This is it. Nothing happened."

"*What?*" She yelped.

"Nothing. On the ground, the ship vanished and reappeared two minutes later. For me – and for my ship's mind – nothing happened, no time passed. I pressed a button and then they started saying 'come in, come in, you did it.'"

Marianne shook her head in disbelief, her stomach heavy with disappointment. She thought back over his interviews. "So that's why you said 'did what'."

Ray nodded. "They're seriously pissed about that, by the way."

"What were you supposed to say?" Despite the more pressing question of his non-experience, her curiosity was piqued.

He snorted. "You want to hear?" He cleared his throat and with proper solemnity recited, "We have broken the final barrier. It's time to explore the universe."

Marianne chuckled. Very portentous. I think I prefer 'did what.'" Then, tentatively, she asked, "You don't think it's possible that you did have a – timeless – experience – and just couldn't translate the memory into a time-filled world?"

Ray slammed his head on the steering wheel in despair. "Don't start!"

"But it's possible..."

"For god's sake, Marianne! If it looks like nothing, feels

like nothing, smells like nothing, why can't it just *be* nothing? *No – time – passed!"*

"But two minutes and ten seconds…"

"Oh, so *now* you believe in objective time?" he snapped. "Listen, Little Miss Einstein, nothing happened. Accept it. I have no reason to lie to you."

"But you have *every* reason to suppress the memory!" she countered angrily. "You're a textbook case of repression!"

They were quiet again, the bitter words echoing in their ears. "We're doing it again," she said wearily. "I really, really like you, Ray. But maybe…"

He started the car and swung back onto the road, the headlights sailing across the sea, over the expanse of beach and onto the tar.

"Maybe it doesn't matter," he said, his eyes fixed on some point ahead.

She bit her lip, fighting back tears. Another sweet possibility crumbled to dust before her eyes. At least this one had been nipped in the bud, before her heart got really involved… The twisting pain inside, however, said otherwise.

"Maybe it's okay to disagree," he continued. "I don't believe there are different truths for each person – I still think the truth is the truth – but we argue and we don't hate each other because of it? Do we?"

"No," she whispered, her voice tight and filmy with emotion.

"And I still like being with you, even when we're quarrelling about – stuff. So…there's this post-mission party coming up to celebrate the big fat zero results of the mission in style." Her lack of reaction was making his belly writhe with nerves. After the way he'd snapped at her, she probably didn't want to ever see him again, but if he didn't ask, he wouldn't know. "It's on Friday, and I'm wondering if you'd like to come with me."

She stared at him in astonishment. "You're kidding me."

He let out a slow sigh. "Fair enough. I guess I've been a bit of a prick..."

"No – no!" She shook her head vehemently. "I thought you... I mean... Yes, I'd love to come! And I'm the one who's been a prick. Or a..." She sought the corresponding word, and recoiled. "Okay, *prickly*."

Their smiles slowly returned as they drove onwards until he drew the car to a halt outside her apartment.

"Thanks for a lovely evening," she said shyly, her hand on the door handle.

"Not yet you don't." He leaned over and cupped her face in his hand, bringing her lips to his for a long kiss. "Now you can thank me," he said breathlessly as they broke apart.

"Okay." She slid her fingers through his hair and brushed her parted lips against his. Their tongues flickered tentatively, barely grazing each other in cautious passes. Through the silk of her dress, his rising palm confirmed that she wasn't wearing a bra. His moan of pleasure echoed in her own throat. When they pulled apart, they were both shaking and the car windows were fogged.

"Okay," she said resolutely. "I'm going in now. Thanks again." She giggled. "Bye." They gave each other a quick peck, which digressed into another languorous kiss. It took several more false starts before she extricated herself from the steamy car and waved him out of sight.

When Ray got in from his jog, Dawn had a fresh pot of coffee on, and the table set for breakfast.

"No class?" he called, on his way to the shower. Usually she was already on her way to university by this time.

"Not today," she yelled back. "We're mostly on study leave for finals."

When he came back, she slid eggs on toast in front of

80

them both and sat opposite him. "Eggs are brain-food," she said. "I figured maybe you'd need some, too."

"Sister of the Year Award coming right up," he said after savoring a mouthful of egg. "So what's the occasion?"

"Oh, you know… glad you're still alive and everything…" she said casually. He grinned. "And I've missed you the last month, you know." He raised his orange juice in mock salute.

They ate in comfortable silence while Dawn occasionally topped off their coffees. "So… what actually happened?" she asked, leaning forward on her elbows.

"Oh, Christ, not you too." Ray said, scowling. "Marianne was giving me enough of a hard time last night about those interviews; I don't need my sister starting in as well."

"Well then she has you pegged more than I do. *I* just thought the interviews were your atrocious TV personality. Actually…" Her fingertip traced the wood grain on the table. "I was talking about your face when you came off the spaceship. And your missed line."

"Yeah, the whole world's talking about *that* one," said Ray wryly. "I don't dare switch the radio on; every DJ on the air's going to be making wisecracks."

"So…?"

"Dawn." He set his coffee-cup down and crossed his own arms over the table, meeting her eyes. "I don't know what I'm allowed to say."

Her forehead creased in alarm. "Was there – something up there? Are there aliens? Did you make contact? Are they trying to hush it up?"

He burst out laughing. "No aliens, baby-girl." He put his fingers on his head like little antennae and made beeping sounds. "Earth to Dawn – Earth to Dawn," he said in a mechanical voice.

"So what aren't you allowed to say?"

He blinked at her. "Replay that question in your head,

whiz-kid, and you tell *me* what to answer."

"Oh. Okay. So you can't even tell me?"

He picked up his coffee again and drained it. Was it fair to tell Marianne and not his kid sister? He'd only confessed the truth to Marianne because he wanted to repair the mood between them. A small part of him admitted that he also wanted her to understand him.

"Okay," he said relented and spoke to her the truth of his experience.

"So there *is* a cover-up?" she concluded.

"Yes – and no. Ground-control considers the mission successful. They just don't want it broadcast that we don't have any positive data... I mean, the country needs some good news at the moment." He stood up to leave for work. "Hey – I almost forgot. There's a party on Friday, to revel in our so-called success. I got you a ticket – you can bring whatsisname – what is his name, anyway?"

"Geoff. But we broke up, so I'll come on my own."

Ray sat back down again abruptly, taking her hand. "You okay?"

"Fine," she grinned. "He wasn't really my type."

Ray frowned. "You didn't – sleep with him, did you? I mean, if it's serious, that's one thing, but if it was just a casual relationship..."

"Raymond Sky, that is so *none* of your business!" Dawn leapt up and began stacking the dishes briskly. "My sex-life is nothing to do with you!"

"You did, didn't you?" His light-hearted mood had vanished, replaced once more with the stern brother-father figure she knew all too well.

"No, for your information, I didn't," she said defiantly. "Actually..." her mouth quirked a little. "I didn't – you know – find him physically – umm... I mean, we got along great, and he fit the criteria on my list, you know? But up close – eww. Anyway, have you slept with Marianne?"

"No," he admitted, also starting to smile. "'But I sure

82

wouldn't mind."

"Dirty old man."

As Ray set off for work, Dawn finished clearing the kitchen and gave the house a quick vacuuming before she got her laptop out and settled down to study. For a while, though, she just stared at the lawn outside, thinking. The "list" she'd referred to had been drawn up when she was sixteen. She and her girlfriends thought they were so sophisticated to be picky and aware of everything they wanted in a boyfriend. The actual contents of the list had changed and resided only in her head these days, not on her laptop. Nevertheless, Geoff had met all the requirements, so why wasn't he what she wanted? Was it as simple as pheromones – that his skin smelled wrong to her? If good looks, intelligence, mutual interests, kindness and friendship didn't make love happen, what did?

It was no good appealing to Ray – as far as she knew, he'd never been in love. Once again, she felt a sharp pang of resentment that she had no mother to ask these questions. She pushed the thoughts to one side and turned to her work. Her finals were close, and it was time to show Ray that he didn't have all the brains in the family.

Ray was filling out endless post-mission reports when Amelia Jacobson knocked on his door and then came sailing in, wearing her brightest PR smile.

"Hello, Mr. Sky!" she exclaimed enthusiastically. "Our hero of the hour! Man of the moment!"

Ray gestured towards a chair. "You might be able to lay it on thicker if you use a trowel," he said curtly.

Momentarily disconcerted, she sat quickly, her folder on her lap. She recovered just as quickly. "Well, I do get a little carried away with my enthusiasm at times… So, Friday is celebration-night, right?"

Ray nodded without glancing up, still ticking off boxes and filling in data. He didn't see why this charade needed to be carried on inside the KSC as well as outside.

"So…" She cleared her throat. "I know you're a busy man…"

"Yes, I am," said Ray pointedly.

She went on nervously. "Well, we thought if you didn't have anyone special to bring, we could maybe help out a bit, you know? We drew up a quick list…" She produced a sheet of paper from her clipboard and handed it to him. He glanced at the photos of young women, their names and accompanying descriptions before sliding it back across the desk toward her. Amelia caught it as it sailed off the edge.

"I'm not in the habit of using escorts for dates," he said coldly, looking at her at last.

"Oh n-no Mr. Sky, these are *not* escorts!" she said, hastily. "They're all very respectable young women – all well-known figures; starlets, socialites…"

"Thanks, but no thanks." He returned to his paperwork. "I have a date of my own, thanks."

"Do you mind my enquiring as to whom…?"

He couldn't resist it. "Marianne Summers," he said curtly.

Amelia's transformation was instant – he could have showered her with diamonds and not made her happier. "Oh, Mr. Sky! Oh, that's – Mr. Sky! That's *fabulous* news! Oh, my!"

"So if that's all?" he cut into her annoying raptures.

"Okay! Of course, yes. I'll leave you in peace." She sailed out, gleefully clutching her glad tidings. Ray watched her suspiciously, and then shrugged. Another avid fan, he supposed; Marianne seemed to have an army of followers. But really, the audacity of it – assuming he couldn't arrange a date of his own! Of course, he forgot that at every previous office party. he'd arrived in the company of his sister.

When Ray and Marianne pulled up outside the Kennedy Space Center headquarters that Friday night, he understood Amelia's reaction to who his date would be. The entrance was roped off, Hollywood style, and surrounded with photographers. Ray groaned.

"I am so sorry – I had no idea…"

"Good thing I dressed up," said Marianne. "Come on – it won't be so bad. Just smile, say nothing and walk past."

Inside, however, a few select photographers were mingling – while blinding people with camera flashes every few minutes. Ray made a few quick greetings then tracked down Amelia.

"What is this about?' he demanded. "This is an internal office party!"

"Mr. Goodman's instructions." She shrugged gaily. What Thomas ordered, the astronaut couldn't countermand. "What are you worried about? You and your date look great – quite the glamorous couple."

"This is a circus."

"It's publicity," retorted Amelia sharply. "Anyway, they're only here for the first hour – the speeches and so on – and then we'll send them packing and let our hair down. Okay?"

He was grateful for Marianne's company, as photographers interrupted their conversations or dragged them over to join new groups for a better photo-op. She seemed to understand the protocol better than he did, smiling with poise at the camera and resuming the small talk gracefully. It was easier to keep his cheerful expression after a smiling glance from her. Even so, he only began to relax when the photographers and their cameras were politely escorted away; then he could chat to his coworkers without anyone trying to capture the moment.

"Hey," said a familiar voice behind him.

"Dawn!" he spun around. "Where have you been?"

"I saw the photographers outside, so I laid low till they

left. Didn't want to spoil your reputation." She said, grinning.

"You mean you didn't want Ray And Dawn Enjoying A Laugh in the society pages again? You know everyone already, yes?'

"Of course, Thomas – Cathy, hi, Lovely to see you. Harry. Marianne, you look great. I'm sorry, I don't…"

"This is Les," said her brother quickly, "the genius engineer, remember?"

"Oh of course." Dawn smiled at him. "My apologies. You're the one who engineered this whole thing, aren't you?"

"Yup," said Les. He recovered from his disappointment that Ray's pretty young sister had forgotten him now that her bright eyes were resting on his. "From the science it's based on to the engine… Oh – sorry, please excuse me!" He dashed off.

Dawn meandered around the room, joining and leaving groups of conversation, wondering why she'd bothered to come. Usually at these things, she and her brother had their own little sub-current of giggles going, but he was taken up with Marianne. Out of boredom, Dawn emptied and refilled her glass, hoping Ray wouldn't notice. She leaned against the wall, watching the folks on the dance floor.

The funny-looking engineer was dancing with a striking, shapely older woman. Her long black hair was pinned high on her head, kohl outlined her huge dark eyes and her full lips were painted crimson. Her classically-cut gown swirled around her feet as the two spun in symmetry across the floor. While dancing, Les was transformed. His usual posture was awkward, always hunched and bobbing back and forth. At that moment, his back was straight, his arms elegantly raised, and his feet weaving dexterously. The pair outshone the other dancers, who were mostly doing the traditional office-bop: a muddle of rock "n roll and salsa.

The occasional house-moves were thrown in here and there from the ones who were old enough to remember then, yet too old to realize how uncool they were. She raised her glass to her lips, found it empty, and wandered back to the bar to refill it.

The music switched to a slower number, Mariah Carey's *Without You* and Cathy put her hand lightly on Thomas's arm. "Remember this?" she said, too quietly for Harry to hear.

"Excuse us – blast from the past..." muttered Thomas.

With their arms around each other, they began to dance. They couldn't light up the floor with ballroom moves like Les and his mysterious partner, but after thirty years of marriage, they knew each other's steps and swung in easy synchrony. Thomas was reminded briefly of one his favorite VECs – a dance that quickly led to the more horizontal kind – and then realized that he liked the VEC so much because of certain dirty memories he had of Cathy. He chuckled aloud at the irony.

"What's so funny?"

"You remember why we chose this song..." he murmured in her ear. Before it was their wedding song, its teary passion had led them under the table, into the privacy of a tablecloth-tent, at a friend's thirtieth. "You were *filthy*.

She giggled. "Still am. Pity there's no floor-length tablecloths around..."

He pulled her tighter, happiness singing in his veins. Time might pass, but Cathy was still his sweet Cathy.

"Hi there, Dawn. Would you like to dance?" Les appeared at Dawn's side as the wine flowed from the waiter's bottle into her glass.

"I can't do that fancy stuff you were just doing," she said hesitantly.

"Don't worry, I'll lead."

She abandoned her glass and let him lead her onto the dance floor. He lifted her right hand in the air and put his own right hand firmly under her shoulder blade.

"Now rest your other hand on my bicep – if you can find it." She giggled. "Okay. Now just relax and follow me."

He led Dawn masterfully, the gentle pressure at her back guiding her to and fro easily. At first he whispered instructions – "Change feet... turn under my arm... and back..." alongside a steady flow of encouragement. She quickly got the hang of it, quieting her mind and just listening to the flow of Les' body giving her directions. She began to feel giddy, and little bubbles of laughter escaped as he began to spin her more glamorously. She hadn't realized ballroom dance was quite so sexy. As the song ended, they paused while he listened for the beat of the next number.

"Ooh, rumba," he said appreciatively. "They say the tango is sex, but rumba is *lurve*..."

They rocked back and forth through the steps. He held his body differently now, not gliding up and down like waves but keeping his torso at one level while his hips took the switch of weight with lazy Latin undulations. She began to copy his posture.

"You're a natural!" he exclaimed happily.

Dancing with him was easy and erotic, without being in the least threatening. She had the feeling she could just relax and have fun, without worrying that he'd read too much into her responses or try anything. When the next dance was just a boring four-beat, they sat down at the table, to rest and chat. She saw the lovely woman he'd been dancing with before twirling with Harry.

"Is your date okay?" she said. She'd never much liked Harry and wouldn't have wanted to be trapped with him.

Les brayed with laughter. "She's cool. She's my mom, and can totally handle herself," he added. "Who're you here with?"

"Technically, I'm here with my brother. But he has his

own date.

"So we're losers together."

"Guess so." They sat for a while, until the silence began to make Dawn uncomfortable. "So you orchestrated this whole speed-of-light thing?" she asked. It was the only thing she knew about him. He nodded proudly. "But Jack Firestone – he did his trip ten years ago, didn't he? So that would've made you…"

"Nineteen," he said. "But I was sixteen when I got the idea."

Dawn whistled, thinking about what she'd been doing at sixteen – making lists of ideal men and thinking she was grown-up if she went to the mall for a coffee with her girlfriends.

"So how does it work?"

Les looked at her in astonishment. "You really want to know? I mean – it's kind of complex…"

Dawn shrugged. "Sure. Try me."

His face lit up with enthusiasm as he began to explain. She recognized in his glow a real passion for physics, for the impossible, for his beautiful idea. He started by running through the basics, to check what she understood. Some of this she already knew from Marianne's book – that there were three dimensions of space and one of time, but actually there were four dimensions of space-time. Les picked up a napkin and showed her how the weight of her cell phone changed its shape. "So imagine the napkin is space-time," he said. "And the cell phone distorts it? Now, put something little – one of your hairclips – on the napkin." It rolled down to nestle against the cell phone, while the liberated strand of hair fell over her cheek. Les glanced at it and swallowed. In his experience, beautiful girls didn't take an avid interest in his scientific theories. "That's gravity; things rolling around in space-time. Now…' he crunched the napkin into a tight ball. "Imagine this ball is tiny-tiny-tiny. That's a black hole. All the time and space crunched together. Nothing gets out."

"Okay. Now, where does the speed of light fit in?"

"It's what defines a black hole. Nothing can get out because nothing can move faster than light. Well – never say never – but even I haven't managed to get that one right yet."

"So gravity's more powerful than light?"

"Bingo!" He regarded her with respect. "That was my starting point. And that led me to thinking about negative mass. You know the equation, $E=mc^2$?"

"Doesn't everyone?"

"Like they know the Lord's Prayer, yeah, they just rattle it off. But you know what it stands for?"

"Energy is equal to mass times the speed of light squared," recited Dawn, thinking wryly that she only really knew that because her brother's date had explained it in *Godspeed*.

"Okay, so that was our speed-limit – when we raised the energy, we raised the mass, so when we had enough energy to reach the speed of light, supposedly, the mass was just insane. But that wasn't taking negative mass fully into account. Of course, I was lucky," he added modestly. "There was that breakthrough in 2012 with dark matter – you remember…"

"I was eleven in 2012," she said wryly. "I remember playing with my dolls."

"Right." He was disconcerted. "What did you play?"

She blushed. "They were survivors from world destruction. I rescued them. I used to color wounds on, and then bandage them up."

"Weird.' From the way he said it, she knew it was a compliment. This wasn't a man who balked at weird.

"So – dark matter?" She led him back the subject.

"Yeah – well, once we had more of a grip on that, we could manipulate mass more effectively – you see, positive and negative mass don't cancel each other out, like plus and minus – they do, in terms of Einstein's equation, but in reality it works out – you effectively reduce the mass and the resulting energy raises the vibration to the speed of light. In other words instead of trying to add energy, you take away mass."

"Clever."

"My professor thought I was crazy, so I wrote to NASA and they offered me a position."

"Hold on a sec – at *how* old?"

"Seventeen. Yeah, I know…I was young, but I *have* got…" He was about to append his usual boast, the highest IQ ever recorded, but bit it back abruptly. His mother told him not to tell girls this if he liked them. "I… I had a good idea," he stumbled out instead.

"Are we interrupting a science lesson?" Ray and Marianne pulled up chairs at the table and Ray lifted the crumbled ball of napkin between thumb and forefinger. "I was just wondering if my sister fancied a spin with her geriatric brother."

Dawn leapt to her feet happily. Dancing with Ray was always fun. He'd taught her to rock "n roll in the living room when she was a kid, and he'd always been strong enough to send her flying through the air. It was the adult version of him swinging her round and round by her arms in the park.

When they rejoined the table, Marianne and Les were engaged in a passionate conversation, so they took their seats quietly. Marianne was explaining a notion she had about thought and time. In sleep, she reasoned, incredibly elaborate film-length dreams could spin out in the space of a few seconds. Deprived of sensory input, our thoughts speed up dramatically. In a way, thought is inversely proportional to time: the less time, the more thought.

Ray listened with growing impatience and Dawn recoiled inside. She knew from personal experience not to make unfounded pseudo-scientific claims in the presence of her brother. Give data, quote sources – substantiated statements were what he respected.

"Thoughts are neurons firing in your brain," he said

abruptly. "They'll always need a certain amount of time to fire. What's the highest speed neurons can communicate?"

"120 meters per second," put in Les.

Dawn kicked Ray's foot in warning, but he ignored it.

"*That's* the limit of how fast we can think," he went on, "Not how much time there is around."

"Neurons are only the physical manifestation of thought," retorted Marianne swiftly. "I'm talking about pure thought; free of all our physical limitations. If we think so much better without the senses, imagine how well we can without the body…"

"So what exactly is doing the thinking, huh?"

Les and Dawn exchanged looks. The other two had forgotten them, and were fired up with eyes ablaze.

"Without your body, there's sweet FA," snapped Ray.

"There's the soul–"

"That's spiritualist bull–"

"That's materialist prejudice–"

"What proof do you have–"

"Oh, so suddenly we know everything about the universe, do we? That whatever we don't have physical proof of doesn't exist? So until we made an instrument to measure radio waves they didn't exist either? Electrons didn't exist until we found them, is that what you're saying?"

Dawn had to hand it to her – the woman knew how to argue with her brother. Rather than being bulldozed by his crushing skepticism, she blew up in his face and talked over his arguments as fast and loud as he did over hers. In fact, in terms of speed and volume, she was winning.

"That's argument by analogy."

"So? You're arguing *ad ignorantiam*. Analogy doesn't make it wrong!"

"It's not proof, either!" Ray was adamant.

"I am *talking* about *not* having proof for everything – that there's a whole world of stuff out there that we can't yet prove!"

"So we can just make up what we like in the meantime?"

"No! I..." She stopped abruptly and looked around the table, embarrassed. Dawn was watching the argument open-mouthed. Les was scribbling on a napkin, his pen bleeding equations and tearing the thin paper. "Oops. I'm sorry, you guys."

"Don't apologize," said Dawn, in awe over Marianne's debating prowess. "It was edifying. I'm going to come to you for training, so I can learn to hold my own against this one." She cocked her head towards Ray.

"We have a slight clash of intellectual ideologies," said Marianne smiling, taking Ray's hand. He returned her gentle squeeze with a rueful grin.

"Actually," said Les absent-mindedly, "I'm inclined to think Marianne's right on the time-thought thing..." His eyes caught Ray's astonished expression. "Sorry, Ray," he shrugged. "In the realm of new ideas, you don't start with proof. You start with cool conjectures. And this one's seriously cool."

6

Douglas Barrymore wrapped up his presentation and hit the power button on the data projector, restoring the bright screen on the wall to blankness. Around the polished table in the Cabinet Room were the President, the Vice-President and the Chief of Staff. Helen finished making notes of her questions and reached for the jug of water at the center.

"So you want to use these VEC simulators to train the military?" summarized the President.

"Yes, Mr. President," said Douglas, closing his laptop. "We can use the brain activity of our bravest and best-trained soldiers and show simulations to our troops. This will serve to teach them how to conduct themselves during combat and, over time, get them acclimated to being in battle."

The President shook his head slowly, picking up the VEC2020 that sat in the center of the table. It was no bigger than a CD case, and boasted a matching headset. "You know I don't like these things, don't you?" he said, examining it. "I believe it is the work of the devil."

"Yes, sir, I do know," answered Douglas cautiously. "However, I wouldn't have approached you unless I was convinced that the VEC would be instrumental in developing our young servicemen and women into better soldiers, sir."

Helen set down her glass of water and signaled with her hand for the President's attention.

"I'm hearing rumblings over at the Pentagon, Mr. President," she said. "The generals aren't too thrilled about using the VECs in training. They believe that imposing such intense and realistic experiences, without consequences, may numb the less disciplined soldiers towards violence. It might make them into mindless killing machines instead of mindful soldiers." On her notepad, she had several pages of queries and propositions, but the effect of training without consequences was her major concern. Before this meeting, she'd contacted a few friends to get some information about the on-the-ground reaction.

An old college pal was on the Staff of Generals, and had confirmed that their attitude was much the same as hers. Too many of the soldiers were already indifferent about the sanctity of human life. This was the kind of attitude that inspired hate-messages on bombs, the careless victimization of innocent civilians and horrific treatment toward prisoners of war. These atrocities were already too prevalent as it was. Deadening the consciousness of the soldiers any further to the impact of their actions would create even more mayhem on the field of battle. She was relieved to see the President nodding at her words.

"Helen makes a good point," he said to the Secretary of Defense. "We don't want mindless soldiers out there."

"The fuck she does," cut in Warren brusquely. "Being a soldier isn't about being mindless or mindful. All a good soldier needs to learn is two simple qualities; how to follow orders and how to kill, in that order. Now if the VEC can help instill these two qualities into our soldiers, what the fuck do we need 'mindful' soldiers for?" He spat the word out with contempt.

"We need them to cut down on collateral damage." countered Helen. The Vice-President's aggressive, dismissive attitude always got under her skin, but she did her best to conceal it. "So as to eliminate the slaughter of innocent people when our soldiers misinterpret their killing rampage as a stroll in the park! They need to know their actions have *consequences*…"

"Screw collateral damage!" said Warren. "If the war on terror has taught us anything, it's that most so-called innocent people in that part of the world aren't actually all that innocent." He swung around to the President. "And your job is to protect the citizens of this country. If better-trained soldiers make us safer, then with all due respect, Mr. President, it's your duty to make it so."

Helen could see the shift in the President's eyes as he began to lean with Warren's argument – as usual. She flipped through her pages in frustration, gathering her thoughts. These were not decisions to be made in a gung-ho cowboy style. Unanswered questions remained and more information was required…

"Mr. President, why not at least consider a trial period with a select battalion of soldiers?" she offered. "See what the results are on a small group before we introduce it to the entire armed forces. We can conduct psychological evaluations…"

"Oh, great," sneered Warren. "So while we restrict our best possible training option to a tiny number of soldiers, your precious 'innocents' carry on bombing the hell out of our troops? Secretary Barrymore." He turned on the Secretary of Defense. "Is it your informed opinion over countless years in military service to your country that we use the VECs for training our soldiers?"

"It is," replied Douglas.

"Then I'd go with the expert." Warren shrugged, turned his back to Helen and faced the President.

President Priest considered a moment while captured in Warren's steely gaze. "You have my consent, then," said the President solemnly. "Sorry, Helen." He held up a hand as she opened her mouth in protest. "This really isn't your field."

The meeting ended, and Warren pulled the Secretary of Defense aside. "I want to see you in my office…now."

"Yes sir," Secretary Barrymore replied, eyeing Helen ruefully.

After closing the door behind them, Warren rubbed his hands together and eyed the Secretary of Defense. "How is our little project coming along?"

"Very well, sir, we've isolated the components that work well under the guise of dark matter and are currently testing its effects."

"Where?" Warren's eyes narrowed. The last thing they needed was a story to leak out.

"Sir, with all due respect, it's best that the areas coordinates are kept a secret from even you. In this regard, the less you know, the less you can be implicated if something were to become exposed."

"Is there any chance of that?"

"None, sir. But we like to take extreme precautions in cases like this."

Satisfied, Warren slapped the Secretary on the back. "Good...good. Once this weapon is perfected, we have an opportunity to rid this world of the constant threat of these so-called 'rogue' societies once and for all. We've tried the 'hearts and minds' approach for far too long, and it simply doesn't work. No, Douglas...if you want to kill a snake, you've got to cut off its head. I want this weapon armed and ready on my notice."

"Yes, sir."

Professor Alice Jennings moved around the large table, handing back the last pre-finals assignments to her class.

"Much better," she murmured, as she slid Dawn's A-graded paper in front of her. Dawn's heart sank with bitter disillusionment. She had really thought this was the one class where she didn't have to do the dance-monkey-dance routine to get grades. She'd learned over the course of her college career how to play the game; giving them what they wanted to hear in the way they wanted it said. She'd aced so many exams with a sense of disgust, knowing she'd earned herself top marks just by following orders and keeping her own thoughts and opinions to herself.

She'd also learned that if she wanted to do something differently, or to argue an idea that didn't embrace the popular opinion, her work had to be three times the quality to receive the same grade. Sloppy arguments towards an accepted conclusion got good grades; if she disagreed with the accepted point of view, her every logical step had to be watertight.

She'd chosen Media Politics as her major, because it was the one course in which she'd been able to offer up her own ideas and not got penalized for them. She believed that Alice would instantly recognize – and scorn – any formulaic conformist essay. But Dawn now stared at proof that just the opposite was true; her paper graded high only because it matched Alice's opinions. Her swallowed hard; disillusionment a jagged little pill.

"So in our last lesson," said Alice, while the students glanced through their essays or shoved them in their bags, "we're going to do one last discussion of the baselines you've observed. As you know, I believe firmly in the principles of team-work, even if the university system requires that you be tested individually. So please be aware that everything you contribute in this class will be considered public-domain material for your exams. And don't hold back your best ideas on that account – I'll be looking for how you build on that team effort in your exams. So, let's hear them…"

Various students began to offer their opinions. None of them were new or especially useful to Dawn – she'd observed much of what they talked about, but felt their points lacked any new perspectives. They were reaching for the same, tired ideologies that everybody knew – not one topic contained a spark of fresh outlook. She continued to tap notes swiftly into her laptop, knowing she'd have to regurgitate some of this onto the exam paper in order to meet Alice's ideas of teamwork. When it was Dawn's turn to contribute, she flipped through various documents to find her own research notes. She selected an idea she'd kept out of her last essay, in fear that it would result in another low grade. She believed it important, but knew that maintaining a high GPA was imperative. It was safer to test it out in class first.

"So Dawn, what do you have for us?" Alice was

beaming at her star student. Dawn's heart no longer leapt in response, however – she'd quickly lost intellectual respect for Alice.

"We don't feel guilty," said Dawn. No one reacted. "As Americans, we don't feel guilty," she repeated.

"In what sense?" asked Alice, puzzled.

"Just about every other nation that has committed major atrocities have spent decades living with remorse. Post-Holocaust Germany, for instance, has passed its inherited guilt down to each new generation. White South Africans suffer immense remorse, even those who weren't born until after Apartheid ended. The Japanese, to this day, experience repercussions from their war crimes during World War II…"

"So what are *we* supposed to be flagellating ourselves for?" scoffed Geoff. Their usual supportive pair-work in class hadn't survived the break-up.

Dawn stared at him in disbelief. "Hiroshima? Nagasaki?" she said. "Ring any bells? These events should've had some effect on public consciousness. Instead, we congratulated ourselves for ending the war – the suffering of all those people caught in the fallout never made it home to our souls. That's the biggie, obviously, but then what about other atrocities we've committed that we haven't acknowledged for what they are?"

"Such as?" Geoff nearly spat the words at her. His eyes held none of their usual warmth.

Pausing a millisecond in shock before regaining her composure, Dawn continued, "Slavery?" Geoff's non-verbal response of rolling his eyes caused Dawn even greater unease, yet she persisted, "I mean, yes, we may have made some reparations in the case of slavery, but even these meager measures have been under constant scrutiny, threat and dissolution depending on who yells the loudest. What is even more appalling to me is that there are still whole sectors of American society who actually assert the merits of slavery and continue to victimize African Americans.

"The Native Americans are another prime example. We invaded their country, murdered entire communities, stole their land, and placed the remaining survivors on reservations where the quality of life for their descendants, to this day, is scanty at best."

Geoff scoffed, "I see, so the fact that they own practically every gambling establishment and gaming organization outside of Las Vegas does nothing to compensate them?"

Dawn gaped at him. One can never really know another until something goes awry. "I'm speaking of how the U.S. doesn't feel remorse, or even acknowledge that they've done something wrong. Take the Japanese-American internments, for example. Right after the Japanese bombed Pearl Harbor, Japanese-Americans were rounded up, allowed to keep only the possessions that they could carry on their backs, and placed in shoddy internment camps. 62% of those interned were American citizens. The property and belongings they were forced to leave behind were up for grabs. It became a free-for-all as people closed in and seized what they could. After the war ended and the surviving Japanese-Americans were released, they had no homes to return to. Their lives were in ruins and they had to begin rebuilding from scratch. It took over four decades for the U.S. Government to formally apologize and offer compensation to the survivors and their descendants…compensation that was minimal at best."

"The government decided that they posed a threat to national security. What else were we supposed to do? It was the first time any attacks had ever been committed on U. S. soil since the American Revolution. The country was in a state of panic—"

"Hold on," said Alice, "you're veering away from the issue here. Let's go back to this idea about guilt…"

"Okay," said Dawn, swallowing back her impatience. "Our nuclear atrocities in the Second World War should have resulted in a massive burden of collective guilt – other countries who've done similarly suffer enormous culpability. Conservative estimates put the number of casualties from our bombings of Japan at 240,000 people, but where's our burden of guilt?"

"Are you saying Americans don't feel guilty about the bombings?" asked Alice, stunned.

"I'm saying that we don't live, every day, with the knowledge that *we did that* – not in the way that Germans or South Africans live with the knowledge of what they did, or what their ancestors did."

Every face around the classroom was frowning in puzzlement or disagreement. Dawn felt the resistance to her idea as an almost physical force, repelling her away from them. Alice persisted with her questions, trying to work out what Dawn was trying to say.

"Do you think that kind of guilt is helpful, or even healthy?" she asked. "Taking on responsibility for events you were never involved in or responsible for…?"

"Personally, yes," said Dawn. She believed passionately in collective accountability, in taking responsibility for things done in one's name, or by one's country, whether or not the individual had any personal influence over them. Every system was made of individuals, Alice had always told them. Likewise, Dawn believed that every individual had to acknowledge what systems they were part of, and to be prepared to fight for the principles of that system.

She knew her ideas wouldn't go down very well, however, so she stuck to more certain ground. "I think it greatly reduces the chance of something similar being committed again. The Germans are still wary of right-wing régimes. The South Africans are very conscious of any kind of racial discrimination. Whereas we just carry on bombing people and invading their countries. Look at how we created a war out of declaring Iraq to be a rogue country who participated in the September 11 attacks on America. There was absolutely no evidence that they had participated in any way, but the media was employed to spin it to U.S. citizens that they had. We illegally invaded a sovereign country, destroyed their existing government and reduced their infrastructure to ruins, costing thousands of American and Iraqi lives, and yet ..." Dawn stopped herself, knowing she was on contentious territory again. "But that's not really the issue – whether it's helpful or healthy to feel bad," she continued. "It's just that, comparatively, it's interesting. Where other countries feel responsibility toward their actions, the American baseline is unapologetic – we don't feel guilty."

Alice nodded thoughtfully. "I see," she said at last. "Of course, that kind of helpless guilt is very unhealthy. I suppose – being leftist – we always assume baselines are wrong, just because they tend to be right-wing. But there's no reason why a baseline can't be a good thing – it's still a baseline. Good work, Dawn," she concluded.

And good work, Alice, thought Dawn bitterly. The professor had taken an idea that threatened her own assumptions and skillfully reintegrated it to shore up her own beliefs. At least Dawn now knew what angle to take in the exam. When she wrote her final paper, she would have to leave out her own opinion: that without the guilt, nothing was stopping us from doing the same thing again.

Ray was clearing away his papers and shutting down his computer when a confident knock rattled his door. He was taking advantage of the post-mission lull to work more reasonable hours so he could see more of his sister – and Marianne. They'd made a date to watch the full moon rise over the sea; Florida's eastern coast alternative to watching the sun set. He suspected it held a more spiritual significance for her, but didn't mind much. If she saw Heaven and the Moon-Goddess, he saw his beloved stars and a pretty damn

Goddess-like face by moonlight. It managed to suit them both very well.

Jack Firestone's face in the doorway followed the knock. "Got a moment?"

"Sure, Jack, come on in. Have a seat." Ray dumped his bag back down on the desk and shook Jack's hand before sitting back down. "So, what can I do for you?"

Jack smiled. "Ray, come on, you know why I'm here."

"I guess I do." His voice was flat.

"So spill it. Tell me what happened up there." Jack leaned forward, his eyes shining with expectation.

Ray turned his face away to look out the window, sighing heavily. "Senator, absolutely nothing happened."

"Come on, Ray," said Jack, ignoring the formality of the 'senator' remark. "Something must have happened?"

"On my word of honor, nothing happened up there. Absolutely nothing."

"Oh." Jack slumped back in the seat, his eyes shifting to the nylon carpeting. "Right." He pursed his lips in disappointment. "I was so positive something was going to happen."

"I know. I'm sorry." Ray felt like he was coming back from the North Pole with the news that Santa didn't exist. He knew, from past experience, that the way to handle Jack was to be totally honest with him, but the man's heart had been so set on Ray coming back with the key to enlightenment; some kind of salvation for the world.

"What are we going to do now?" asked Jack.

"What do you mean?"

"Well, I thought – this would be it. We'd have access to God and he'd show us the way; enlighten us with the Divine Plan. Show us how to create Heaven on Earth. Dammit, Ray, I don't know, something to change the course the human race is currently on."

"Maybe these are problems that we're supposed to solve ourselves," said Ray stiffly. That was another thing he hated about religion – people placed all responsibility onto the shoulders of their deity, instead of cleaning up their own messes.

"Looks that way, doesn't it," said Jack heavily, rising to his feet again. Dejected, he suddenly looked like a much older man and Ray felt a flash of pity.

"Senator – Jack – are you feeling alright?"

The older man paused, his hand already on the door handle. "Every spiritual belief I held that God existed at the speed of light was just flushed down the toilet," he said bitterly. "How do you think I feel?"

Marianne and Ray sat on the beach, their bare toes digging into the cooling sand, their hands clasped. They weren't arguing – perhaps, because they busy just taking in the scene. In the dying light, the sea was already dark blue fringed with the pale, bluish-white of soft breakers and creased with ripples. The huge moon, lingering just above the horizon, lit its stippled path across the water in warm gold that would gradually pale to ice-white. A thin mist in the air gave it a blurred halo while all the colors of the world slowly retreated into shades of blue.

Ray breathed in the cooling salty air and sighed with contentment. Bringing Marianne's hand to his mouth, he kissed her knuckles lightly, and then pressed his lips to her bare shoulder. Her perfect profile softened into a smile tinged with sadness. She wondered if she were a fool to have brought him here; exposed her secret ritual to someone so opposed to spirituality. She liked him more than she was prepared to admit, yet wondered if she were a fool to even keep seeing him. It couldn't end well; the law of statistics and her own experience said that much, even without their opposite views making it worse.

He was so sincere, though – so genuine and warm, despite the cold amour of intellect he drew around him.

Being gorgeous just made him even harder to resist. It seemed blindly optimistic to trust to her feelings and start another relationship, however. Every moment of happiness they shared now was just building up a vault of heartache for the future, with interest. He put a warm, muscular arm around her back and despite herself, she nestled against it.

"I want to ask you something," he said hesitantly. His lips moved lightly over her temple and long hair as he spoke. "It might seem a bit – forward – but it's better than awkward doorstep negotiations. At least I think so. Anyway, I just wondered if you'd like to stay over at my place tonight."

"Easy tiger," she laughed, backing off a little. "You're too cute to go around making suggestions like that."

He turned his face back to the sea, embarrassed.

"What's wrong with someone – cute," he stumbled over the word, "asking you to stay over?"

"Oh, I get far too attached," she said lightly. "It's a dreadful failing. Very old-fashioned and usually uncalled-for." Intending her words to be humorous, she didn't notice the edge of bitterness in them. Ray was too inexperienced with women, and much too confident a believer in honesty to leave the matter there. A wiser man would have let the words fall without argument, placing trust instead in passionate kisses to state his case.

"So what's wrong with getting attached?"

She stumbled through her explanation, the principles that had formed in her bruised heart over the course of several failed relationships. Her bitter philosophies were long in the making and deeply held, but now that she tried to articulate them in words, they were somewhat less convincing.

"You're obviously been badly burnt," he concluded, with the pure wisdom of inexperience. "Tell me what happened"

"There have been too many stories to tell you all of them," she said sadly, "so maybe just one example will do."

There was a man with whom she'd been intimate.

They'd worked closely on a very spiritual project; their ideas in sympathy at every step. They witnessed the light of enthusiasm in each other's eyes, the breathlessness of awe on each other's lips, and they fell in love. They also fell, as is the way of these things, into bed.

This man had had a wife, she explained. They were separated – there were complications about getting a divorce, and she couldn't go into them. Marianne didn't play the mistress; waiting by the phone for someone to deceive their wife and sneak into the study. She wasn't living with the hope that "one day he'll leave her…"

"Except, as it turned out, I actually was." Her laugh dripped acid. "All that connection we shared, all the love we felt – and if that wasn't real, I'm a damned fool – and it turns out that he was lying the whole time."

Unexpectedly, she started crying. A man might find a few tears that trickled gracefully down a lovely cheek to be touching; endearing, even. Marianne's were ugly, racking sobs that shook her body and contorted her face. Ray drew her against him and she curled up in his strength, weeping a storm into his chest. "I thought I was over this," she wailed thickly, "I thought I was older than this, stronger, wiser. But at the end of the day, I'm still a fucking teenager – I don't cry like this, I don't do this!" she protested against her own pain, and then cried harder. "It hurts, Ray," she whimpered. "It hurts so much and I don't know what to do anymore, because I can't seem to bring myself to trust anyone."

He rocked her gently. "You can't stop trusting people," he said, only because it was the token wisdom of the age and he didn't know what else to say.

"Au contraire," she said, pulling away and wiping her eyes. "It's just scientific method. I've tested my hypothesis pretty thoroughly and I don't have the strength for another experiment." She stood up, sniffing and sheltering her puffy features behind curtains of hair. "Sorry to get all emotional and spoil the evening, Ray."

"You haven't spoiled the evening." He rose to his feet and put his arms around her again, sheltering her in the circle of his muscles. "But we'll take it slow, okay?" He nuzzled his face next to hers, forcing her to lift her face a little and meet his eyes, and his lips. "It's hard to trust anyone when people you love have let you down," he said. From the timbre of his voice, she recognized that he was speaking from experience. "But I swear I am trustworthy. And we don't need to rush anything…" He was kissing her moist eyes as he spoke.

She nodded.

"Just so you know, I could die for wanting you." He laughed. "But more than that, I want you to feel safe with me – with us."

7

Marianne and Dawn sipped their coffee in the living room, while the clatter of pots and plates echoed from the kitchen.

"Is he always this domestic, or is it a special show just for me?" Joked Marianne.

"It's a deal we have between us," said Dawn. "One cooks, one cleans up. But he gets the better half of it – I do all the cooking."

For this particular meal, Dawn pulled out all the stops, left her books to one side and spent the whole day cooking. She knew without Ray telling her that Marianne was vegetarian except for fish; her fanzine said so. Between eagerness to help her brother get the girl, and awe that her heroine was going to eat at their house, she'd been a ball of nerves over every detail. By the time Ray arrived home that afternoon, there was nothing left to do; the house sparkled, the fish soup starter was simmering, the moussaka was baking, chocolate mousse was setting in the fridge, the table was laid and a huge bowl of pale apricot roses tinged with pink was arranged at the center of the dining table. With all this anxious preparation, they were on the main course before Dawn could properly relax and enjoy Marianne's company. Now, over coffee, her nervousness was forgotten.

"Ray tells me you're in school?"

Dawn nodded. "Media Politics – I'm almost done, we're doing exams at the moment."

"Interesting choice. Why that? Forgive me for asking, but you just don't seem like the hardened media-type…believe me, I've met a few of *those*."

"I guess – it sounds stupid, but I kind of want to do something worthwhile – to make the world a better place. It's childish, I know." Dawn felt embarrassed about confessing her grandiose ideas to Marianne, but the older woman shook her head and smiled.

"It's not childish at all," she said. "Or if it is, I'm childish too. I studied psychology for the same reason – I wanted to help people. And then, I gradually decided I could make more of a difference through promoting spirituality."

Dawn glanced anxiously towards the kitchen and Marianne laughed.

"Oh, don't worry about him – he knows where I stand. Seriously, though, I think more people would do well to hold onto their dreams of changing the world. Most of us get it drummed out of us at an early age. We're taught to 'get with the system'; told that, 'this is the way the world works', and, 'who said *you* could be the one to make a difference?' People say, 'you're just one person, what difference could you possibly make?' all the while forgetting that the whole world is made up of 'just one person.'"

Enrapt with Marianne's words, Dawn forgot her manners and tucked her feet under her on the armchair. "Yes! Exactly! That's what I think! And we spend all this time in class studying what people think, what everyone thinks, and we forget that these thoughts have to come from *somewhere,* and people have to agree with them in order for them to take hold. We forget that the world *does* change and new ideas have to come from somewhere, don't they?"

"Of course." The girl's infectious enthusiasm reminded Marianne of herself at a younger age – much younger than Dawn was now. It was clear to her that Dawn had led a sheltered life. She played housekeeper for her brother in a perfectly adult way and clearly managed those responsibilities well, but at her core was a pure, untouched youthfulness. Life hadn't bruised Dawn. Marianne found herself hoping that it never would. She believed, in theory, that pain was a crucial stepping-stone on the path to personal growth. She felt strongly that what it stole of youth's freshness, it returned in valuable maturity; however, looking at the girl's glowing face, Marianne began to feel differently.

"So, do you have any idea what you're going to do after

you finish school?"

Dawn made a wry face. "Not really, to be honest. I'd like to…"

"More coffee, anyone?" Ray appeared in the doorway with a fresh pot, and both women held out their cups for a refill.

When her cup was half-finished, Dawn made an excuse about studying for exams and left for her room with her coffee. After all, there was no point in making a special meal to help things along, and then sitting there all evening like a spare wheel. She sat in her room, browsing webpages instead of studying. Soon she heard the familiar sounds of bickering and grinned to herself. She slipped her headphones over her ears and activated her loudest playlist. Dawn had a theory about Ray and Marianne's constant arguments. With all the sexual tension humming around them; and her brother already as uptight as he was – well, the energy had to go somewhere, didn't it?

"I just don't get how someone so intelligent can be so illogical about it! Okay, I'm willing to admit there's no proof either way – but that's not proof *for* any more than it is proof *against*."

Marianne and Ray were now sprawled together on the sofa, in a posture that entirely belied their heated disagreement. Her head lay on his lap, cradled in his arms. She reached up to run her hand lovingly over his roughened chin.

"If there's no proof either way - don't you think your insistence that *nothing* happened is a kind of evidence? If there were nothing to deny, would you be so intense about it?"

"Wow! Psychologists and the clergy are masters at spin!" He kissed her forehead in exasperation. "If a person agrees, then they agree. If they disagree, then they're in denial, which means that they secretly agree. It's a total catch twenty-two! So tell me, oh wise one, what would I say if I really didn't agree?"

"It's not *what* you'd say; it's *how* you'd say it. Case in point: You'd be less adamant if you had less invested in repressing the memory…"

"Well, I definitely have an acceptable mental health rating invested, I'll grant you that!" he retorted. "How long do you think an astronaut would last in NASA if he systematically repressed all memories of his missions?"

"Bingo!" exclaimed Marianne triumphantly. "You're afraid of being considered a flake."

"Am not."

"Are too."

"Am not, times a trillion."

"Are too, times infinity. I win!" She beamed up at him.

"You can't multiply by infinity. Anyway, *you* make me crazy all the time, but here I am holding you in my arms. Case closed."

They kissed for a long time until Marianne pulled away, trembling.

"Now who's the scaredy-cat?" he whispered tenderly.

"Never said I wasn't," she laughed. "But at least I confront my fears," and she pressed her lips to his again.

The paperback release of *Godspeed* required another tour of book signings and publicity appearances. Ray missed Marianne more than he anticipated. Dawn was devoted to her studies and he found himself in the position of once again wondering what other people did with their spare time. The hours he typically spent holding – and arguing with – Marianne were a vacuum in her absence. Try as he might, he couldn't spend the entire day training and studying. Eventually, his body and brain just refused to continue their efforts. When Dawn mentioned that Marianne was appearing on Oprah's Spirit Channel, he barked at the TV to activate. He couldn't wait to see her again, if only on screen. He even longed to hear her talk about her oddball theories that played such havoc with science and logic. He was startled; however, to see a large photo of himself at Marianne's side projected onto the background.

The show's set was tastefully coordinated in pastel tones that had a soothing, Zen-like minimalist appeal. Strategic soft lighting and flattering angles gave off a serene, almost meditative energy. Oprah Winfrey, the show's host, was as tastefully dressed as her set, and the two women perched comfortably on matching white plush chairs. Marianne, adorned in a flowing blue dress that had a touch of the Druidic about its style, radiated a ravishing contrast to Oprah's serene simplicity.

"So," Oprah was saying, "There's talk on the streets that cupid has come calling…"

Marianne gave a controlled smile. "I prefer not to discuss my private life in public," she said, "however yes. I did accompany the astronaut Raymond Sky to a post-launch party hosted by NASA in honor of his mission."

"And that must have a special significance for you," said Oprah, "considering what you've written about speed-of-light travel in your book, *Godspeed*, which has just been released in paperback."

They began to discuss the book. The show was clearly aimed at an audience of fans, because they didn't spend much time outlining or explaining the basic theory behind speed-of-light travel, and no time at all on its supposed scientific foundations. Rather, the questions were centered on the spiritual significance that speed of light travel could have for humankind if the effects of this experience could be extended around the globe.

"At the moment, the technology is prohibitively expensive for any but a few hand-selected people to have this extraordinary experience," said Marianne. "But history teaches us that all technology will eventually filter outwards. Cars, air-travel, computers, space-tourism, VECs – all have demonstrated that technology tends to gradually spread from the financially élite to the majority of people. I believe that when this happens, the world will become steadily transformed.

"In what way?" Oprah inquired, clearly intrigued by the subject matter. She believed that everything had a spiritual/social impact, and often steered her guests toward topics that supported the attainment of higher understanding for her viewers.

"Vibrating at the speed-of-light is an intense spiritual experience." Marianne's voice was calm and pleasing. "In that state, long-held suffering, which is rooted in the mistaken notion of separation of the self from the Universe, begins to be healed. We live in an extremely self-ish society, in the broadest possible sense of the word. Even when one turns to spiritual study, it is usually for what it can bring to one's *self*, not to the world at large. We consistently deny that we are an undifferentiated part of the Universe, and the pain of that denial only reinforces our attempts to protect ourselves. Few people have the courage to find their way to such a holistic experience on their own – and I don't blame them."

She gave a gentle smile. "In my therapeutic work, I see people handling terrible pain and fear in the way they know best, which is often not the healthiest choice. The healing process is very slow – it takes a long time for people to even accept that their deep wounds can be healed. And until those wounds are at least partially mended…well, most people just aren't brave enough to let go of their sense of self like that."

As she spoke, meditative music began to play and her face was juxtaposed with a montage of touching images. Some were the usual inspirational variety: oceans, sunsets, galaxies, flowers unfolding, and so on. Some picked up on themes from Marianne's words – the spaceship taking off, abject poverty and despair interspersed with people embracing and helping each other.

"The speed-of-light experience changes us that completely. By traveling at the speed of light, the soul is carried *instantaneously* into the highest vibration. The result is an experience of pure love. I can't emphasize enough the transformative power of this love. It flows through us, you see – it heals the wounds that hold us back and flows outwards from us to other people. Let me give you an example.

"Imagine a man was brought up in great poverty. He hates that poverty and wants to become rich to escape it. He works hard; drives himself to extremes, has a few lucky breaks and gets to the top of the corporate ladder with masses of money. Now, logically, you'd expect him to look around and think, 'hey, I can help some other people who are poor!' But he doesn't do this – he clings to his money, always afraid of not having enough, so afraid that he never even asks himself how much is actually enough.

"The great philanthropists – the Gateses, Branstons and Shuttleworths of this world – are usually not people who grew up in such poverty. They don't attach their fear to a lack of money, so they are able to be incredibly generous. Now, if our self-made millionaire could let go of his *fear*, he might be able to help other people.

"That's a very materialist example, obviously, but the principle works through all things. Our own wounds hold us back from showing love to other people. That, in turn, wounds *them* and consequently *they're* held back from showing love to others."

"And the speed-of-light experience breaks this vicious cycle?" asked Oprah.

"Exactly. It transforms them. And if everyone were able to have this experience – can you imagine how it would change our minds about everything? War – our economic interests – environmentalism – poverty and lack of education... We would feel a deeper compassion for ourselves and others than we feel now."

"And have you noticed this change in Raymond Sky?" Oprah queried.

"Oh, yes. He's much gentler and open-minded – it's softened him. It's a beautiful thing to witness."

"Mr. Sky didn't say anything about a transformative experience in his interviews," said Oprah. "Why do you think that is?"

Marianne's mouth twisted. "Well – I don't think it's fair for us to speculate on that," she said. "He might not know exactly what happened to him, but it's certainly had an effect. In time, I hope to have the privilege of telling his story."

"TV – off." Ray's voice was hard, his face white with fury.

Ray and Dawn were both in the living room, immersed in their laptops, when the doorbell rang. Dawn sat cross-legged at the coffee table, her earphones plugged in.

"You going to get that?" said Ray from the sofa, not taking his eyes from the screen. Since he'd seen Marianne's interview a week ago, he'd buried himself in his work. He still didn't fully understand how Les's theory worked. Les said not to worry about it, that most people wouldn't, but Ray was determined to come to grips with it.

Dawn slid her headphones aside. "What?"

"The door."

"You're closer."

"Yes I am, but I pay the bills and you live here free."

Dawn pulled off her headphones and stretched to her feet. "You know, you can't use that to win every argument," she said.

"And if it's for me, I'm not here," continued Ray, ignoring her words.

Dawn swung the door open – Marianne was standing at the doorstep, beautifully made-up and looking stunning in jeans and a thin light blue sweater. She gave Dawn an anxious smile.

"Marianne! Hi! Come in." She stepped aside, a beam of welcome on her face. "Ray's in the…" but Marianne was looking beyond her to where Ray was disappearing down the hallway. "…in the kitchen and headed for the garden, I think," finished Dawn, puzzled.

Marianne found Ray in the garden, his back to the door and his arms folded across his chest.

"Ray?" The word was more like a plea.

"You've got a lot of nerve," he said, turning around. His face was stone.

"What did I do? Why won't you take my calls or see me?" She felt tears beginning to rise, threatening to spoil the beautiful face she'd spent so long perfecting before she came. She dabbed lightly at her moist eyes, which only made him scowl.

"You don't know?" he said incredulously. "You betray my trust and you don't even notice?"

"No – how – what have I *done*" she wailed.

"'He might not know exactly what happened to him, but it's certainly had an effect. In time, I hope to have the privilege of telling his story, '" he spat. The words had seared themselves into his mind over repeated playbacks. "You gave me your word, but it's all grist for the mill with you, isn't it? All of your fine spiritual-babble, but in the end it just boils down to the next best-seller and the next publicity stunt, doesn't it? Well, you can do whatever the fuck you like, but I won't be a part of it."

She stared at him, stunned. "The interview…" she murmured. "That's why you won't speak to me. Were you ever going to even *tell* me what happened? Weren't you going to give me a chance to defend myself? If I hadn't come over today, would you have just kept refusing my calls? Letting me continue to try and hope and wonder what the hell was going on?" Her voice was rising to near hysteria.

"I don't see how you can possibly expect to defend yourself." His arms still crossed his chest like a barrier, blocking her out. A few yards away on the lawn, and he may as well have been standing on the moon. "I told you, in *absolute secrecy*, that I didn't know what happened – and you blurted it out to the whole world. Not to mention that bullshit about me being oh-so-nice all of a sudden."

"Well, I can see I was wrong about that!" Tears fell from her eyes now, carrying trails of mascara with them. "Are you going to even give me a chance?" Her mouth quivered as she slowly lost her resolve. Suddenly, looking lovely didn't matter anymore. "I said what I believed…"

"No!" he snapped. "You said what you *knew* and you only *knew* it because I told you!"

"That's not what I meant, Ray – I meant that you might not grasp the spiritual significance – I meant…"

"You can put whatever spin on it you like, Marianne, but don't expect it to change anything."

Marianne plopped down hard on one of the garden chairs and hid her face in her hands.

"And don't expect your crocodile-tears to make a difference either," said Ray, contempt ringing through his words.

"You won't even listen," she whimpered. She'd known he was obstinate and nearly incapable of seeing another point of view, but she'd assumed it was just about other things – spirituality, science, belief – not this. Not about the woman he said he loved.

"I listened to those words about twenty times," Ray growled, "and that was all I needed to hear. It's been nice knowing you, Marianne, but you won't be telling this astronaut's story, so you can go now." He knew his words were cruel and her parade of misery tore at his heart – but she'd duped him. It wasn't about *him*, it was about furthering her own greedy ambitions. When the choice came between loyalty to him and her own publicity, she'd already demonstrated where her true priorities lie.

"You said you loved me," she said, lifting her tear-stained face to stare up at him. "You said I could trust you. You had me thinking I was the fearful one, and it turns out that you're too much of a fucking coward to even *tell* me – do you *know* what sort of week I've had wondering and waiting to hear from you?"

"Well, I'm telling you now." Ray shifted uncomfortably.

"I *trusted* you!" she howled, flinging her bag at him. It bounced off his chest and fell on the ground, scattering its contents. "I opened my heart, you *bastard*, and now you stand there too goddamned self-righteous and uptight to admit that there's even a remote possibility you're wrong!"

"Unlike our other arguments, this time there's concrete proof," he replied icily.

She scrambed in the grass, shoving her things back into her bag, eyes blinded with tears. He stepped backwards, away from her.

"Trust me, trust me, you can trust me," she sobbed. "That's what you said." She kneeled on the grass, too shaken to collect her things. "Well, this is what happens when I trust men, Ray! They kick me in the teeth and betray me."

"I think when you look back on this rationally, you'll find that *you* betrayed *me*," he said. "What – did you expect me to just carry on with you, knowing every word I said to you could end up on international television whenever it served your career? And for God's sake, get up – have some self-respect." The sight of her kneeling, weeping, and using her weakness to manipulate him made him see red.

Marianne leapt to her feet and dealt his face a stinging slap with her open palm. "How's *that* for self-respect?" she spat. She swung her hand again, but he caught it in an iron grip before it could land. She looked into his hard, ice-cold eyes and found no mercy there. Her arm slackened and he dropped it.

"Pick up your stuff," he said, turning back towards the house. "Excuse me if I don't see you out."

"So that's it?" she cried. "That's it – it's over? You won't even talk to me?"

He stopped and glanced over his shoulder at her. Even in the mess she was in now, she was beautiful – as beautiful as Sampson's Delilah.

"Yep," he said. "It's over."

Oh God...I'm back here again, thought Marianne dully. She'd cried herself out for now and sat curled on her sofa, lights low, the sound system playing her "pathetic" playlist. An open bottle of wine stood on the table, from which she repeatedly topped off her glass. She knew she was "self-medicating," a behavior she gently discouraged in her own clients. It made no difference, though: nothing did. Whether she played it super-careful or flung caution to the winds; it didn't matter. She still got hurt. Whether she stayed sober or got drunk; the pain remained. Happy music made her cry for the happy times; sad music made her cry for the now. Wallowing in self-pity brought on despair, and keeping up a brave face brought on a lingering deadness in her soul.

She didn't have the energy to follow any of the advice she gave her clients. They had her warmth and sympathy to help them along, to motivate them, and encourage them. She had a handful of dust and yet another heartbreak to add to her repertoire. She could see her own therapist, but the woman had gone on some blasted yoga retreat in Egypt. Maybe she should've slept with Ray – she would have at least gotten some fun out of it while it lasted.

She thought she was keeping her heart safe by not having sex with him, but his gentle acceptance of her fears had only made her trust him more, so in the end the pain was the same. Whatever she chose, it always came back to this – crying on the sofa with a bottle of wine, berating herself for reacting so uselessly to her own misery, all the while expecting much more of others. Layers of guilt on top of heartache. Well, she could do something about one of those, at least.

She loaded up one of her meditation VECs, slipped onto the floor and sat in the lotus position while the music played out gently into her ears. The scene was a waterfall, streaming over the bushes that had sprung up between the rocks; the columns of water like white swaying trunks. Bluish spray softened the outlines, and the steady roar of the waterfall filled her ears. The mist touched her face, light and cool. She sat cross-legged in a shallow hollow in a rock, overlooking the scene.

The guiding voice advised her to look into her surroundings and observe the emotions she felt. Soon, she was crying with the same force as the waterfall. The breathing exercises calmed her eventually, but didn't ease the deep well of misery she felt inside. She tried to open herself to the Source, to feel its love and light surrounding her, but all she felt was alone. At the end of the meditation, she opened her eyes feeling none of the sense of calm she usually felt.

Perhaps I'm in the wrong frame of mind, she thought, *but then, what is the right frame of mind? If meditation only works when one doesn't desperately need it – if the Source will only surround people who aren't unhappy – what the hell kind of system is that?*

Ray got one thing wrong in his dismissal of spirituality: as consolation in moments of weakness, it was useless. Maybe it only worked in therapy because of the therapist's presence. Maybe there *was* no loving Source, just the comfort of having someone else around, even if they were paid to be there. Nothing made a difference – "working through" pain didn't ease it – but some kinds of distraction worked better than others.

"Load VEC titles – Category, Romantic. Sub-category, Naughty," she said. PURE's programming stopped short of the truly salacious, but had a very nice line of beautiful, compliant men; the kind who didn't blow you off for giving an interview or suddenly turn around and say "Oops, forgot to mention it, but I'm married." The Pure men didn't stand you up, argue, cheat, get freaked-out by the L-word... The list of VEC-men virtues was endless. She scrolled through the list.

"Cleopatra – play," she said. Instantaneously, she was reclining on a long divan, with young men in short, Egyptian skirts feeding her grapes and fanning her with palm leaves. She could see Antony standing by the window. She'd get to him, but for now she'd just lie back and enjoy being fawned over.

Dawn and Ray sat in silence over breakfast. She glanced at him occasionally, but he resolutely avoided her eyes, staring down at his food and chewing. After a while of deafening silence, she dropped her fork on the plate with a clatter.

"So what on earth *happened* between you and Marianne?" she said.

"I told you, I'm not discussing it," said Ray. He pushed his plate away and swiped at his mouth with a napkin. "How's your studying going?"

"Fine – I'm on top of things. I've been working hard throughout, so..." She shrugged and a little smile crept onto her face. "I think I'm in line for that A. I've got the system pegged and I know my stuff."

"Excellent." He smiled with more warmth than he had for days. "And once you get the coveted A? What's the plan? Media internship?"

"Actually," said Dawn carefully, "I thought I might take a year off – go traveling in Europe."

Ray frowned. "How will you afford that?"

"I'll work my way through it – picking fruit, bartending, whatever. It won't cost much if I stay in youth hostels and things. And I can use some of my trust fund for the ticket."

Ray shook his head in disapproval. He knew what most kids did with their gap-years in Europe; got drunk, took recreational drugs and generally lived in a dissipated, escapist fantasy world.

"That fund is for your *future*," he said. "To help you get a good start in life – not to fund a great big holiday and live like a hippy for a year."

He stacked the plates and started clearing the table. Dawn followed him and sat on the island at the center while he cleaned up.

"Oh, come on Ray! Don't be so down on everything. It'll be an incredible experience – different cultures, different languages – I want to *see* stuff. I'm not going to lie around on beaches smoking marijuana, if that's what you're afraid of. I want to see all these places for real, places I've only seen in VECs – like France, Italy – see the *real* sights…"

She cut off quickly as Ray dropped the pot he was holding in the sink and spun around. "What VECs?" he said dangerously.

"Sightseeing ones…" She shifted nervously on the counter top.

"Where did you get them? Where did you get a VEC?"

"Geoff's house – I watched some with him…" Her brother's eyes darkened with anger. She knew he didn't think much of VECs, and that he wouldn't buy her one, but she hadn't expected him to react this badly.

"I have tried to keep you safe from those things," he said, his voice shaking with fury.

"Jeez, Ray, it's just a bit of fun…"

"It's not *real*."

"I *know*. That's what 'simulation' means. Not real. What's the big deal about a little escapism?"

Ray smashed his hand down on the counter and the chopping-board jumped. "Escapism killed our parents!" he yelled. "The reason we're *orphans* is because of escapism! I had to bring you up because *they* couldn't face reality! You know the stats about children of alcoholics – they're way more likely to go the same way…"

"Mom wasn't an alcoholic," said Dawn, feeling scared. Ray rarely spoke about their parents and she only had muddled memories herself.

"No she wasn't; she was a drug-addict," snapped Ray. "She couldn't face life any more than Dad could, so it was down to the drugstore she went; loading up on Valium or whatever the fuck they would give her, so she could float around in her little druggy dream-world pretending everything was fine, while our dad drank himself to death. Jesus Christ, Dawn! You do not escape from reality!"

Tears started to prickle in Dawn's eyes. "You're yelling at me like it's my fault," she said. "It's not my fault…"

"I'm yelling at you because you're talking like *them*. Where's the harm, it's just a bit of fun, what's the big deal – you're the daughter of *two* addicts and you think escapism is okay? Well, it's fucking not! And I forbid you to ever use a VEC again."

Dawn leapt up, outraged. "You are not my father!" she shrieked. "I'm twenty-four and I have the *right* to decide some stuff about my own life! You can't keep telling me what to do forever!"

"Fine!" yelled Ray. "You're right; I'm not your father, I'm your brother and you're a grown-up, so I don't know what the hell I'm doing supporting you and looking after you! You can move out and live your own life tomorrow if you'd like!"

He slammed the door behind him and she heard the roar

of the engine in the drive. Left behind, Dawn began to weep. In her bedroom, she shoved clothes into a duffel bag.

Ray drove halfway to work on pure rage before he had to pull over. He was shaking too much to drive. What had possessed him to fly off the handle at Dawn like that? It wasn't her fault that she didn't understand. She hadn't lived with their parent's addictions the way he had. Trying to manage a drunken father is heavy work for a boy of fifteen. He remembered dragging his dad in from the yard so that the neighbors wouldn't see him passed out on the lawn, the man's weight straining his young muscles. When Dad got really clumsy, staggering around, Ray tried to keep the baby safe and out of sight, in case he hugged her too hard or dropped her. Every time he tried to enlist his mom's help, she'd be spaced-out on her pills, saying it didn't matter, or she'd just start crying helplessly and then reach for the pills. Ray had these memories, but Dawn didn't – how could he expect her to understand the dangers she faced?

He'd practically threatened to throw her out. It stung so badly when she said he wasn't her father – after he'd been so much of a father to her. He tried so hard to be adult enough for the responsibility; baby-sitting and helping with homework. While his college buddies played sports and got on with their lives, Ray desperately strove to keep his baby sister safe.

But it wasn't just what Dawn said that bothered him. It was the ache in his chest where his love for Marianne used to be, and maybe still was, despite everything. It was his gnawing anxiety about the mission and whether something had happened that he'd simply blocked out.

He pulled out his cell phone and punched the speed-dial for home. The answering machine came on. He tried Dawn's cell, but it went straight to voice-mail. "Dawn – it's Ray. I'm so sorry I got mad, baby. It's not your fault. Ring me at work, okay? Love you."

At the same time, Dawn was knocking on Marianne's door, awash with tears, holding a bag of clothes and her laptop.

8

In Marianne's soothing living room, Dawn set about converting a box of tissues into a pile of crumbled white rags. Her jumbled words flowed as rapidly as her tears. Once she started talking, she found she couldn't stop. Marianne sat quietly, radiating gentle concern, occasionally offering a word or reformulating a feeling, mostly just listening.

It wasn't just the fight with Ray that upset Dawn – it was everything that suddenly rose up and swamped her like a freak flood. She was uncertain about her future, longing to make a difference in the world but without the first idea of what to do or even what kind of job to apply for. Disillusionment with her course of study still ate at her – it wasn't the forum for finding the truth that she'd hoped it would be. All the old confusion about Geoff came out, why she couldn't fall in love with someone so obviously suitable, all this with the attendant longing for a mother who could advise her on these things.

She found herself saying, "I want my mommy," and hating Ray for calling that beloved absence a drug-addict, while simultaneously loving him so much and needing the security of his love so badly. He was all she had – if he got angry and threw her out, it would be just her against the world. She wasn't ready for that; she didn't know what she wanted to do with her life yet. Her laments went round in circles.

Marianne listened as she would to a client coming to her for therapy, keeping her own thoughts to herself. Much of what was hurting Dawn so badly was the natural growing-pains of her age and situation; she was getting ready to leave the nest. That was always a scary process, fraught with tension for both the baby bird and the baby bird's parents. In Dawn's case, it was obviously complicated by the fact that her "parent" was also her brother. From the trauma of her

126

childhood loss, she clung to him too tightly to allow space for rebellion or flight. Young women with mothers didn't find the process much easier – but in the absence of a real mother, Dawn idealized the wisdom and understanding that would flow forth from such an influence. In reality, all that would've likely flown forth at this stage would be quarrels.

"How old were you when your mother died?" she asked gently.

"Six," sniffed Dawn.

Marianne nodded. That also explained a lot. To a six-year-old, a mother is still a holy saint of unspeakable beauty; an angel of light whose presence transforms the house – no matter what the mother was actually like.

Marianne knew that telling Dawn any of this wouldn't be much use. She had to find her own way to understanding. A few words of reassurance and a guided meditation would help more than all the psycho-babble in the world.

"Dawn, regardless of what happened between your brother and me, I know this much: he is a good person and he loves you very much." Dawn nodded tearfully. "It sounds like he got angry because he's worried about you and perhaps a bit hurt that you want to do your own thing – that's normal." What a host of ills those magic words eased – "it's normal." "I am certain that he doesn't really want you to move out. So this is what we're going to do. I'm going to take you through a meditation, to help you center yourself and find your inner peace." She chuckled at Dawn's face. "I know, right now it feels like you don't have any inner peace, but trust me – there's a place of absolute tranquility inside you and you can draw strength from that. And then you need to go home and talk to your brother. You don't have to resolve the issue of traveling or VECs today – just reassure each other you're still there and still love each other. Okay?"

"Okay," said Dawn.

"And if at any time you want to chat, you just give me a

call. Deal?"

Dawn smiled a little. "Deal."

The meditation did for Dawn what it didn't do for Marianne – or perhaps, it was the promise of love and support in Marianne's presence that made the difference. Regardless, when Dawn left, she was calmer and happier. Marianne's smile faded as she closed the door. The siblings would make it up easily enough. She had no such hope for herself.

"I love you, Ray…" she whispered to the empty room. The two VEC headsets still lay on the table from the guided meditation. She should be working on her current book project, *The Inner Light*, but how could she write about spirituality when all she felt was raw pain? She lay down on the sofa and pulled the headset into place.

"Load VEC titles – Category, Romantic. Sub-category, Naughty." A little light liaison with a perfect man and no consequences would lift her spirits.

The quarrel with Dawn had given Ray a lot to think about. Somehow, when he'd lashed out at her, he'd gained some insight into his own feelings. He thought he'd just written Marianne off as a bad investment and that was that. In reality, he was hurting deeply and had taken it out on his kid sister. Marianne's insistence that he *had* experienced something nagged at him. What if there was something he'd repressed and he managed to unblock it? What would he find – monsters, aliens, God? Marianne had some insight – she'd touched a nerve when she said he was afraid of madness. He knew it to be true and she'd seen it. Maybe the routes she took were nonsense, but her intuition and conclusion were valid – that had happened often enough in the course of physics. If there were some way of experiencing his mission again… He thought of the argument with Dawn and an idea started to form.

Early the next morning, Ray strolled into Harry's office. The doctor was leaning back in his swivel chair, eyes closed, wearing a VEC headset. Lost in whatever fantasy he was currently simulating, he didn't hear Ray's footsteps or see his approach. Ray reached down and flipped the off switch, causing Harry to jump, his eyes springing open.

"Jesus Christ, Ray!" he yelped. "You scared the shit out of me!"

"Don't tell me you use your VEC at *work*?" said Ray, disgusted.

Harry looked pointedly at his watch. "What are you, the labor police? We officially start at 8 a.m. and it's only 7:45, so chill out."

Ray shrugged. He knew what kind of programs Harry liked and didn't think they were *ever* okay to use at work, regardless of what time it was. Harry pulled the headset off and flung it on the desk.

"Don't you want to hear what I was simulating?'

"Um – no," said Ray. The man had no shame.

"You sure?" Harry was leering, and Ray cringed.

"Yes."

Harry pulled a mirror out of his drawer and started to rearrange his hair – all three of them had been ruffled by the headset. As he examined his reflection, he spoke. "At least I don't simulate with my *mother*, like some of our colleagues I could mention."

Ray's mouth twitched in a little smile. "You didn't seem to think too badly of Les's mother when you danced with her at the party," he pointed out.

Harry dropped the mirror. "*That's* Les's mom?" he yelped. "Jesus Christ, no wonder he has an Oedipus complex the size of the Empire State Building!" He stared at Ray, then grabbed the mirror again, trying to regain his composure. "Okay, Ray," he said gruffly, "since you deemed it important enough to interrupt my morning ritual with Madame Raven, what important issue would you like to discuss?"

"Do you still have the brain activity recording from the mission?" asked Ray.

"Of course I do. Why?"

"Can I have a copy?"

"Sure. You interrupted Madame Raven for *that*? She'll be even more punishing next time…" A devilish smile crossed Harry's face. "Thank you," he beamed.

Ray rolled his eyes and handed him a data-stick. Harry hit a few keys on his computer, transferring the relevant files across.

"Don't know what you'll make of it that I can't," he said, watching the file transfer, "but hell – it's your brain."

Les was also reclining on his chair, a VEC headset in place, when Ray opened his door. His body twitched slightly from side to side. Ray tapped his hand gently and Les's eyes opened.

"Hey, Les, am I interrupting?"

Les gave him a friendly grin, sliding the headset off. "No – come in, I'm just finishing up."

"Does everyone in this building sit with their VECs on till eight? I just came from Harry's office…"

"I don't usually," Les said quickly, not wanting to be grouped with Harry. He didn't get along with the doctor and disliked all that dirty talk. "I've got a big ballroom dance contest tonight, so I'm just practicing. Pull up a chair."

Ray slid a chair opposite the desk and sat down. "You use the simulator to practice?" he asked curiously.

"Of course. I use simulation to train my brain and learn the steps and then that helps with the actual dancing. You can't just learn from the sim – but it does help."

Ray nodded approvingly. "That's a very healthy

attitude, Les. You don't get carried away with the illusion, like everyone else does."

"Like I always say – if you can't apply the simulation to real life, why do it at all?" said Les.

"If more people thought like you," said Ray with a sigh, "maybe I wouldn't think those things are so damned evil."

Les squawked in laughter. "Technology's not *evil*, Ray! It's what people do with it that is."

Maybe people shouldn't be allowed to do some things, thought Ray, but he held his peace.

"So, what can I do for you this fine morning?" Ray handed him the data-stick and Les slid it into his computer. "What's this?"

"It's the recording of my brain activity from the mission. I got it from Harry."

"Okay – what do you want me to do with it?"

"This is going to sound hypocritical…" Ray said sheepishly. " But I was wondering if there was any way you could transform it into a VEC program. If there was any way I could try to experience whatever – happened – during the black out. That dark spot Harry was going on about, remember?"

Les whistled. "You know, when they make the VEC programs of exact experiences, they have all the sensors attached to the model, in order to separate the strands of senses – they don't just work from raw brain data, like this."

"Actually – I don't know that much about how they make them," Ray said, embarrassed. "It was just an idea – if it's impossible…"

No word captured Les's interest as much as those four sweet syllables: *impossible*.

"Nothing's impossible. Difficult, yes. Ray, I came up with speed-of-light theory, I built you a spaceship to take you there – I can probably unravel your brain scan for a VEC." He grinned. "I take it you want the moment you came back – when your brain still registered whatever it experienced during the trip."

"If there was anything, yes. Is that possible?"

"Your brain doesn't work at the speed of light, so yeah. Even after allowing for the extra lag of data traveling through the atmosphere, it's still faster than your brain. So we received the data before your brain had a chance to catch up." His hands were moving restlessly over the keyboard as he spoke. "You know, this suggests something did happen – you say no time passed, the ship said no time passed, but look at these two scans."

Ray sat on the desk while Les turned the screen around. He'd brought up the two images of the superior parietal lobe that Harry had shown them – one the instant before he'd vanished, the other the instant he arrived back.

"Your brain doesn't work this fast!' Ray felt slightly insulted, but Les was bubbling with enthusiasm. "I can't believe I didn't think of this before!"

"Les – I don't get what you're so excited about."

"Okay – sorry. You think when your neurons fire, yeah? And they take time to travel. So a thought takes *time*. The speed of light is much faster – radio waves travel pretty much at the speed of light. Well, they do, unless you take into account atmospheric..."

Ray held up a hand to halt Les's detour. "Back to my brain. please?" he suggested.

"Yeah. So when you got back, we received an image of your brain before you had a chance to think – because the image traveled faster than your thoughts. *And*, we got an image of the last *nanosecond* before you left. Now – the ship says no time passed between the two events, right?"

Ray nodded. "And that's what it felt like to me."

Les twitched his head, as if Ray's feelings were immaterial compared to the ship's data.

"But your brain changed. You arrived back home with a different pattern. So something had time – somehow – to happen. Ray, this is awesome! This is big! I can't *believe*

Harry didn't see this!" Les was bouncing up and down on his chair, making its wheels squeak against the floor.

"And you can put this into a VEC program for me?"

"If I can't do it, no one can," said Les proudly.

"One thing." Ray met Les's eyes, holding them while he spoke. "I'd rather no one else knew about this, for now. Whatever I was thinking, this is *my* brain. I want to know what happened before anyone else gets access, or knows any kind of access is possible. If there's any kind of… irregularity…"

"You don't want the good doctor knowing you're a fruitcake?" said Les innocently.

Ray sighed. "Something like that. Just keep it under your hat, okay? I owe you, big time." He swung off the desk and moved towards the door, then stopped, turning back. "If you manage this, it could change so much for me. I don't know how to ever repay you."

Les scratched his neck and looked at the floor. "I know how," he mumbled. "You could give me your sister's phone number…"

"You *gave* it to him?' said Dawn, in disbelief.

"I needed a big favor from him…"

"So you pimped your sister?" She laughed and Ray joined in.

The reunited siblings were sharing their usual Saturday post-jog breakfast. All tension from their blow up had resolved itself, and they were back to business as usual. They'd developed a habit, over the past few years, of always lingering over this meal with a second pot of coffee. During the week, Ray's work and Dawn's drive to college made breakfast a brisk affair or a piece of fruit grabbed en route; in the evenings, Dawn was usually studying or glued to the day's media coverage, laptop at the ready to leap on any telltale slips that showed bias. On Saturdays, they could catch up with each other's' lives a little.

"I didn't think you'd mind – you got along with him at

the party, didn't you?"

"Getting along with and dating are different," retorted Dawn, but without malice. "Hey – I'll get a coffee or something with him if it helps further your glowing career..." She stood up, draining her coffee, and gave him a mock bow. "I'll catch you later, okay?"

"Where are you going? Don't you have to study?"

She was already putting her cap on and slinging her bag over her shoulder. "Geez, Ray...even God rested one day a week. If I watch another news bulletin, I'll throw up. Oil talks, economy, the government posturing... Yeurgh. I need a break."

"So where are you going?" Ray wanted to go shopping for a VEC, for when Les had the program ready and dreaded the thought of Dawn catching him red-handed. He couldn't admit what he was going to do – not, at least, until he knew what the program showed him.

"Just to a friend's house." She hoped he wouldn't push it. A few more visits to Marianne had made the older woman feel more like a friend and less like a therapist, but she didn't want to spring their friendship on Ray quite yet.

White pillar candles glowed on carved teakwood stands. Their soft light turned the walls to muted peach, gentle against the dark wooden lines of the two massage tables and the elongated masks on the walls. Dawn and Marianne lay on a table each, both naked except for a thin white sheet. Another low table at their heads had been painstakingly whittled to create a wild jungle scene in low relief, like another world floating beneath the pane of glass. This supported a bowl of chocolate-dipped strawberries and two brimming champagne flutes.

Despite the Thai scene, their masseurs were two powerfully-built blonde men, whose hands dug rhythmically into their shoulders.

"Oh my god…" groaned Dawn, while the tight muscles around her neck succumbed to the program's ministrations. "This is like a dream come true…"

"Oh yeah," sighed Marianne. "PURE programs are the only place where dreams do come true."

"Is this actually going to relieve my real tension? In my real body, I mean?" Dawn was in knots from hours spent hunched over her laptop and exam tables.

"Mmm…" affirmed Marianne. "The relaxation filters through… Maybe not as much as a real massage, but this has certain advantages over a real massage." She popped another strawberry in her mouth as her masseur moved down to work on her feet. "Like no calories," she giggled.

Dawn took a swig of her champagne. "And no hangover." They stretched their arms out to clink glasses and Dawn settled back to enjoy it. The dreamy sensations spilled over her body as one by one her muscles surrendered beneath the kneading hands. The masseur began to move towards her buttocks.

"Hey, Hans," she muttered, "where are you going with those extremely yummy hands of yours…?"

"You can't blame Hans," giggled Marianne. "The Artificial Intelligence chip is reading your body chemistry, and it believes that's exactly what you want Hans to do."

"Who am I to argue with an AI chip?" the girl murmured. "But first…"

The masseur leaned forward and held a strawberry to her lips.

"Oh my…" she said through a mouthful of dark chocolate and sweet red flesh. "That chip does know my everything, doesn't it? Hey…" She half sat up a moment. "He won't – you know – I mean…"

"It's PURE, Dawn – not RUSH. He won't take advantage of you." Marianne smirked and Dawn blushed.

She closed her eyes, a content smile on her face, as Hans resumed her massage.

Les and Dawn sat at an outside table at Rusty's Café, that
overlooked the ships docking in the harbor. The scent of the
wooden deck sweltering in the sun mixed with salty, fishy
sea smells and the garlicky aroma of plates carried past them.
Les took a nervous sip of his Margarita. This wasn't how he
expected a date to be. He'd dressed nicely, and then his
mother had told him to change and put his on his casual
clothes. Dawn chose where to go and didn't want to be
picked up, suggesting they meet there. She'd originally
suggested coffee, but then ordered a cocktail, so he had one
too.

He'd asked his mom what to talk about on a date, and
she clucked her tongue and heaved a deep sigh; the way she
always did when she felt he was being dim.

"You've met this girl already, yes? And talked to her?"
He admitted he had. "So if she's agreed to go on a date with
you, maybe she liked the way you were then; the *authentic*
you. So just be you."

He thought about this advice and decided to ask about
the coffee. Dawn laughed and blushed.

"Sorry about that. My brother's really anti-drinking, like
even the tiniest sip, so I always just say coffee. It's my code-
word for cocktails."

Les liked the little giggle she gave and the way she
leaned over the table when she spoke, as if they were
conspirators. When she introduced a topic of conversation,
they were on their way, chatting quite normally. He hated
feeling inept in social situations. Everyone always said "Just
be yourself," then when he followed this advice and talked
about things he really found fascinating, he got the brush off.
Dawn, however, seemed sincerely interested.

They were talking about VECs – something else her
brother despised. Les opened his mouth, and then shut it
again, remembering he'd promised Ray not to let anyone else
know about their project.

"You know, I've heard they started using them for

military training. I don't get why NASA doesn't use them. I mean – surely they're cutting-edge simulations?" asked Dawn.

Les nodded and thought about it. "People die in the military," he said, "and we try not to kill people. That's the biggest difference. Using sensory simulation – the SMS – we try to recreate the experience, not just simulate it. This produces an actual physical experience, not just a mental simulation."

"But that's exactly what the VEC creates – a physical simulation." She was eating the salt off her margarita, pinching it off with her fingers then licking the tips.

"We think so… but we don't know for sure. Take zero-g, for example. People feel *sick* in a zero-g situation."

Dawn nodded. She remembered her brother's colorful stories of just how much he'd thrown up in his suit when he first started using it. He'd told her all about the "vomit comet" and the "sickie sphere".

"But a really experienced astronaut, like Ray, doesn't feel so sick anymore. Or does he? I mean – he's learned to cope with it, by doing mental exercises and breathing techniques to suppress it. So if a rookie astronaut uses a VEC program that we based on Ray's current experiences, would he actually get the full-blown nausea that he'd have in a zero-g environment himself?"

"Can't you perform tests to find out that sort of thing?"

"We are. You see, we can find out some answers, but we don't yet know all the right questions, you see. Everyone thinks we know so much about how the brain works, that VEC technology has peeled back the last frontier, but that's not necessarily true. The links between physical sensations and thoughts aren't fully understood yet. The VEC companies *say* it's just simulated physical sensation, because telling us they simulated other people's thoughts would just freak us out, but they don't know for sure exactly *what* they're simulating."

"But they *must* know! I mean, they built it!" Dawn felt bewildered. As a date, this was not her most romantic experience ever, but Les intrigued her. She signaled to the waiter for more drinks, wondering whether he'd seem more romantic if she had another cocktail. She chuckled at the thought. She sure wasn't going to drink him pretty, that was certain.

"Not really – the AI chip does the processing and we don't know how it reasons, exactly."

"But surely someone programmed it?"

"No, not quite. You don't program AI, you see – you train it. Okay, here's a classic example. They wanted to use AI to recognize tanks, right? So they showed the chip lots of photos with and without tanks in them. It was kind of like saying 'This is a tank, this isn't, this is, and so what's this?' Know what I mean?'

"Uh-huh." Dawn began demolishing the salt crystals around the rim of her second margarita. Around them, the deck had emptied a little; the late-lunch crowd departed and the dinner rush not yet started. Only a few other tables, like them, lingered over their drinks under the setting sun.

"So the AI learned to recognize tanks, then they showed it more and more pictures where the tanks were partly hidden – behind a tree, with just a bit sticking out, or cresting a hill, and so on. *Then* they showed it a picture where the tank was completely hidden behind the hill and the AI said 'tank.' He looked at her triumphantly, waiting for her to reach the conclusion.

"So it could see where a tank would be even if there wasn't one there?" hazarded Dawn.

Les shook his head. "All the photos with tanks in them had been taken in the morning, when the tanks were out for practice. All the photos without tanks were taken in the afternoon, when the practice area was empty. The AI was looking at the angle of the shadows, not at the tanks at all."

"So it's stupid?"

Les frowned at her and Dawn realized she was the one being stupid. "I get it. It doesn't know the word 'tank.' It's just like saying x, or not-x – it didn't know what you wanted."

Les's grin told her she'd got it right. Hanging out with him was going to be slightly more demanding than Geoff's company.

"So we'd trained it badly," Les went on. "But the point is – we don't know how it's working stuff out. We add checks and things, but we can't get it to answer questions we haven't asked. What if no one had realized it was looking at shadows in the tank pictures? That's what I'm saying about the VECs. We think it's just duplicating the senses, but we don't know what the AI knows about how the brain works."

Dawn put her hands to her temples. "I think my brain has stopped working…" she laughed. "Overload – overload – imminent collapse…" She used Ray's mechanical-alien voice and was rewarded with Les's laughter.

He was weird, she thought – in a good way, but maybe not exactly a romantic candidate. Visually, he couldn't hold a candle to the extremely tasty men she and Marianne had been conjuring up in the VEC. She'd enjoy seeing more of him, but she didn't really want to be seen *with* him, and hated herself for being so shallow.

A week later, Ray sat at his desk, the headset in place, his hand trembling over the play button. He glanced at the clock – would he know time had passed? He wrote the time down on a piece of paper. A new, awful thought struck him: would he even retain enough self-awareness to know he was inside a VEC? Would they find him on Monday morning, badly dehydrated, locked in a world of which he might – again – have no memory? *Be sensible,* he chastised himself. *People in VECs must know they're in VECs, or no one would ever get out. It's only manipulating your senses; it's not shaping your thoughts. It's purely sensory.* He took a deep breath, as nervous as he'd ever been for a launch, and pressed play.

9

"Using VEC simulations will provide us with the most effective form of interrogation, which we believe will help us meet the challenges to security that terrorism poses." Steven Black, Director of the Central Intelligence Agency, was an intimidating man in both body and voice. Even while sitting, he towered over the others who sat around the conference table, his words booming out in an authoritative tone. Even though he wore civilian clothing, his military background was evident in his bearing, his officious grooming and short-cropped hair.

"What is the legal position on this idea?" asked Helen Cross. The Chief of Staff had the usual barrage of detailed notes in front of her. "I believe the UN has made addendums or rulings on all simulations. What is their position on this one?"

"Obviously, we've taken legal advice from our experts and they find in favor of this option," declared Mr. Black. He turned away from Helen and toward the President.

"In what way would your agents use these VECs?" asked the President.

Helen's eyes flickered, but she remained expressionless. Sometimes she wondered if the President just slept through every presentation that was ever delivered to him. The man insisted on covering every main point in a Q&A session afterwards, as if the contents of the meeting itself were irrelevant.

"Basically, Mr. President, we'd disengage the pain control feature from the unit and then have the subject simulate activities that would range from mild humiliation to quite painful." Tactfully, he didn't skip back to the part of his presentation that had already explained this.

"Give me a few examples of what would take place during an ordinary interrogation."

"We've obtained a few preliminary simulations," said Mr. Black. "They seem a little unorthodox, but we've selected options that are both psychologically and physically effective."

"Such as?"

"The subject may be forced to run with the bulls on the streets of Spain with their pants around their ankles, or swim naked in a piranha tank during feeding time – those are just two examples, naturally. We believe the wide variety of activities will contribute to their efficacy." Helen stared at her papers, hiding her revulsion. She breathed deeply, took a gulp of water, and then turned toward the CIA Director.

"Mr. Black, it appears that your experts have overlooked the legal constraints around obtaining that type of VEC data. What you're suggesting crosses the line between interrogation and torture. You'd never get the programs."

"With all due respect, Ms. Cross, we already have them."

The President scowled, to Helen's relief. "Where exactly did you get that kind of brain activity?"

Director Black's eyes darted toward Vice President Warren, who returned a barely perceptible nod. Helen's eyes narrowed as she caught the exchange. She never agreed with the President's decision to hand the responsibility of overseeing the CIA to Warren – that act wasn't power-sharing, it was sheer folly. If he hadn't allowed the Vice President so much power, would the CIA Director have deliberately withheld information from the President?

"Not all countries share our policies on human rights, nor do they recognize the Geneva Convention," Black said diplomatically. "In some of these countries, such simulations are easily available."

Helen coughed into her fist, signaling the end of the meeting to the President, who responded with, "Thank you, Steven. I'll need some time to consider this information. Let's revisit this in a couple days."

"Thank you, Mr. President." Black responded, turning on his heel and glancing at Warren as he headed toward the door. Warren responded with a quick nod. The door had barely closed behind him when Helen spun toward her Commander in Chief.

"Mr. President," she began, "I'm very concerned about this idea. It smacks of torture. We cannot afford another Guantanamo Bay or a Gulfstream Five incident – the rest of the world simply wouldn't stand ..."

"Hold on a second," Warren held his hand toward her face, turned his back on her and stepped in front of Helen, blocking her off from directly addressing President Priest. "Mr. President, this is an entirely different scenario than the Gulfstream 5 flights."

"That is *absolute…*" began Helen, but Warren raised his voice to talk over her.

"Desperate situations call for desperate measures, Mr. President, but we are stopping short of truly desperate measures. We will not be engaged in physical torture, on American soil or elsewhere – simulated torture is not technically torture, because it is a simulation."

"How did you come up with that brilliant rationalization?" flared Helen, still on her feet.

Warren stood too, but slowly, using his fists on the table to haul up his weight. *Trying to scare me with his cave-man postures*, thought Helen disdainfully.

"I came to that *conclusion*," he said in his measured don't-make-me-angry voice, "when I came to the *conclusion* that any information received using this technique could save thousands of American citizens. *That* is how; by recognizing my patriotic duty."

"Patriotism is important," mused the President.

"You are talking about a return to torturing human beings!"

"Simulated torture," Warren interjected.

"If any other country was using the VEC for this purpose we would denounce their actions publicly and impose trade sanctions on them, demanding they stop. However, when we decide to use the exact same despicable methods, you claim we're saving lives and that it's our patriotic duty. Mr. President," Helen shouldered her way past Warren to again face President Priest head-on. "We cannot wrap ourselves in the flag every time we want to do something terrible, and then justify our actions by claiming it as a means of winning the war on terror. We must maintain our moral high ground. This kind of behavior places us on a slippery slope towards becoming exactly what we are fighting against."

Warren waited a beat before asking coldly, "Are you done?"

"Yes," she said, turning to face Warren with her chin jutted out.

Warren smirked at her before turning again to Priest. "Mr. President." His voice was calm and measured. "Intent is everything. If action is taken with the intention of saving American lives and to win the war on terror, it is considered by the majority of Americans to be good. When action is taken with the intention of punishing people for no other reason than for the amusement of some crazed dictator somewhere, it is considered a bad thing. Using the VEC to smoke out information on potential terrorist activities, therefore saving countless American lives, it is a good thing."

"So basically, you're saying that if 'good people' torture, it's good. And if 'bad people' torture, it's bad?" Helen cut in.

"Exactly!"

"So based on that logic, since we insist that this administration's intentions are good, any actions taken by order of this office are automatically good ones?"

"Yes!"

Helen and Warren stared at each other from their opposing positions, both attempting to stare down the other.

"It is my duty to protect the interests of the American people," said the President after a long silence. "It is my duty to preserve the safety of this country's citizens. I have to agree with Warren. Since our intentions are good, we must use all tools available to us to save American lives. This will not be torture – this will be a simulation; a valuable interrogation technique."

Helen lowered herself slowly into a nearby chair, disbelieving what she was hearing. She wanted to shake the President until his teeth rattled in his head and some sense returned. Her contempt for Warren inspired an image of him enduring a "simulated" torture session… *No*, she stopped herself. *Don't start thinking like them.*

Helen often wondered what kind of bizarre hold Warren had over the President, since every foul policy decision he initiated got pushed through with barely a minimum of discussion. This particular decision; however, was diabolical.

Ray floated in an ocean of burning golden light, its particles interweaving seamlessly with his, rising and falling gently with the waves. Once, when Dawn was a teenager, he found a pack of meditation cards she'd bought and pulled one out to read. "Imagine you are a drop of water in a boundless ocean," it read. "Now – where are your boundaries?" At the time, he'd howled with laughter. Dawn, flushed with embarrassment, locked the pack in her bottom drawer.

This current experience; however, was not illusory. He felt the flaming excitement of falling in love – the lurch and warmth that came with a glimpse of the new beloved. Except here, the anxiety that usually clung to that feeling like burrs was absent. A warm, heady sense of security existed in its place, like lying in post-coital adoration while gazing into a lover's eyes. He felt limitless. He could expand to fill the world – but there was no rush of power with this sensation; just a deep feeling of gratitude. He seared through existence like electricity through water. Was he extending to fill the ocean or melding into it?

Dawn stood at the center of the dance floor, the lights spiraling through the steam of sashaying bodies around her. Her foot began to move to the quick, syncopated Latin beat and the motion traveled up into her hips. A tight red dress, gathered at the sides, clung to the shape of her body, slit high and cut low. She glanced at Marianne who stood, hips aslant. Her sequined little black dress started very late and finished very early, emphasizing every curve in between. A man was stalking towards her like a cat, intent in every lean angle of his body. His mouth twitched knowingly as he swung his arms to grab hers into position for the tango. As Marianne's body twisted, Dawn saw the back of her dress was cut away to the base of her spine.

Dawn looked away, straight into the dark eyes of her dance partner. His face was triangular and feline, his dark hair slicked back into a ponytail. He raised one eyebrow seductively, his mobile mouth curving into a smile, and held out his hands to embrace her.

As their feet began to dart back and forth, their hips whipping from side to side with the beat, Marianne called over to her.

"I gave you Rico – you like?"

Dawn stared at Rico, feeling the heat of his body rising so close to hers, and a tremor ran down the length of her.

"Oh yes," she said. "I like…"

They moved swiftly, Rico changing style with every new song that played, Dawn following his lead effortlessly.

Tango, rumba, salsa, mambo – he knew them all and guided her by his smoldering eyes, taut arms and deft feet. Amazingly enough, Dawn knew them as well. The dances were sending storms of electric charge through her. It was the ultimate erotic experience, following the form of the dance with precision, knowing every movement of their bodies was communicating something wordless and forbidden; because after all, it was just the dance, wasn't it? And the spell of the dance would not be broken, so desire, like her partner, was held at arm's length.

Dimly, like a sleeper who knows he is dreaming, but clings to the story unfolding in this more marvelous interior world, Ray knew he was also sitting at his desk and wearing a VEC headset. He knew, vaguely, that some smaller and less magnificent version of his self would call that the true reality and this the dream, but within the dream, he knew better. This was the numinous experience that the entire world sought. Its importance filled his heart like red-hot coals: *this* was the truth of the matter, not that little body in its defensive shield of skin! *This* was the level at which he truly existed and could be real – the petty priorities and self-important little thoughts of that other self were laughable in comparison. A deep, gentle laugh filled him – he was amused, not scornful. The feeling was joyful, really…and ripples of his laughter ran through this ocean.

He became conscious then of something he'd surely been aware of all along: the intelligent center of this place. It, too, was bubbling with mirth, like a parent listening to a toddler's earnest explanation of how clouds stayed up. Pure love flowed from this center, infusing the ocean in which he drifted, encouraging him to flow freely and without barriers through the Universe.

Understanding, long dormant as the seed of a desert flower, blossomed within and without him. When he could feel that unconditional love, he was seeing the light, experiencing God, falling in love, going to heaven – all these aspirations were one and the same. The small self that still sat at the desk was lost in a deep gloom, trapped in a darkness which simply could not exist at this level of vibration.

Why don't you just get rid of the darkness?

Even as he asked, he knew it was the wrong question, and a sense of gentle resistance confirmed that.

This is not a parent-god to give and take away and set rules. He felt how, despite his proclaimed atheism, he too had always looked to a deity to take responsibility for people, just like a parent. *We are Source. We are, always. Air is, always and we breathe it. Water is; we drink it. This is – we are – meet it.*

He fell away – tumbling down a spiral, spinning down a whirlpool, the collective gold of thoughts, passion, lives, all around him, all striving to reach this, meet this, some touching it for an instant, then falling back as he was now doing…

He lifted the headset off and set it on the desk with shaking hands.

If dancing with Les had been sexy, Dawn thought, this was pure lust. Several times, its frissons nearly muddied her steps, but she kept her concentration and pace though her pulse was pounding. The Argentinean tango was a lot more intimate than the others. When their thighs scissored between each other's, Dawn thought she might faint, but they followed the steps – pulled away – came so close again that she could feel his breath on her lips – and then she was sent off, to parade around him while he knelt. Just when she began to feel a sense of power over him, he twirled upwards again. Pinned against him, still following the inexorable laws of the dance, she looked up and saw him smiling down at her like a snake.

The dance ended, but Rico still held her trapped close against him. He lowered his head, never breaking his gaze, and she shuddered with fear and elation. She could do as she pleased, she realized, and the freedom almost scary. There was no other person to consider; to worry about their wishes, their responses, how they might feel about it, what they might assume it to mean or expect... All the passion, without the awkward negotiations around two people, trying to work out if their desires coincided. The AI chip ensured that whatever she wanted, Rico hungered to offer – from taunting her lust to the feel of his lips, now, on hers.

She succumbed to the kiss. Her lips parted, allowing his tongue to swirl deep inside her mouth until she responded with equal fervor. Her head spinning and her breath short, she pulled away at last and looked around self-consciously for Marianne.

The other woman was clasped in her partner's arms and smiled wickedly at Dawn.

"Is this heaven?" gasped Dawn.

"Yes – this would be heaven..."

Ray stared at the headset, his throat tight. Two contrasting forms of knowledge were at war in his head. On the one hand, he knew, with the empirical certainty that underpinned his whole life, that whatever he had just experienced was an artificial simulation. At the core of his soul; however, he knew its absolute reality, no matter how much he wanted to deny it. It was the same part of him that called out to Marianne like a magnet, despite his logical objections, despite her obvious unsuitability to be the romantic partner of a physicist, despite the knowing that she'd betrayed him. The golden kernel at the center of his being had turned to face her – and no matter which way he turned, it would still spin like a compass to point due-Marianne. In the same way, he knew, against everything he stood for, that the dreamlike experience he'd just had was in fact reality.

Was *this* what had happened during the mission black-out? But whatever *that* had been, this was just a simulation, an echo, a playback. He had to keep his head about him and *observe*, not just wallow in bliss. He straightened up in his chair and engaged in some of the steadying breathing exercises he used in zero-g and before launches. Then he pulled the headset back on and hit play.

He again floated in an ocean of burning golden light, its particles interweaving seamlessly with his, rising and falling gently with the waves. He strained to keep his conscious mind about him, the objective and discriminatory sense of self that would let him observe this experience. The resulting misery at what he was doing tore at his soul. He felt the sentient center's rush of compassion and grief for his efforts. Like listening to an agonized song during a time of great pain, his feelings were recognized, understood and mourned.

This is a simulation, he cried out desperately. He was holding the light at bay, but felt it run gently over and around him, wrapping him in a net to keep him safe.

Love cannot be simulated. It did not speak this in words. It planted certainties in his mind.

It's a chip, it's an AI chip. He clung to certainties that felt like trivia. *I know this!*

Know? There is knowing and there is Knowing. What do you Know?

He knew he was wearing a VEC headset equipped with an AI chip and a program that Les had formulated from his brain scan. He knew trying to hold on to his sense of self here made him suffer and cut him off from something beautiful, but that even so he wasn't actually cut off. He knew opening himself fully to this experience was what he truly wanted; more intensely than he had ever wanted any ambition, woman, or sense of security. He let himself soften and felt the love-light rush in to heal the wounds he'd inflicted upon himself. It didn't forgive – would water forgive him for not drinking it earlier when at last he gulped it down? This sentience was of a higher order and not separate. It was a part of him as much as he was a part of it, as one they rolled through the bliss of being perfectly understood and perfectly joined.

Unconditional love, he understood. *No check-lists, no balance sheets, no terms and conditions, never withheld and never portioned-out according to virtue, never waiting for a response to give more, never little-by-little to judge how it's used – this is unconditional love.*

The wine was crisp and cool. Gradually, it calmed Dawn's fluttering nerves. She and Marianne were sitting out on the balcony with one candle burning on the table, its golden glow a warm contrast to the silvery twinkle of the stars.

"It felt so *real*," laughed Dawn, exhilarated. "The music was hot, the dancing was hot and the men..." She bit her hand. "The men were *extremely* hot!" As Marianne had promised, PURE's programming didn't take things too far, but Dawn still felt bashful about just how well the AI chip had recognized her responses. And while there was a limit to how much the programming would allow, the chip had no control over what it could make Dawn want.

"Oh, when it comes to the Latin Dance Club programming, there are no two better than Rico and Enrique!" said Marianne.

Dawn raised her glass to Marianne. "To new friends," she said.

"To new friends and fantasies to experience."

Their glasses met with a soft, full chink and they each took a deep sip.

"And to the programmers at PURE," Dawn went on,

"who must have been women to create men like Rico and Enrique."

"Oh yes." Marianne leaned back with a sigh, holding her glass up to the night sky. "To the programmers at PURE who did what God wouldn't…"

"What's that?"

"Create men that won't drive you crazy! Or at least, not in a bad way…" She gave a low chuckle and Dawn began to giggle too. Marianne didn't seem to think any worse of her for having kissed Rico like that – and after all, what could be more normal than a kiss? Especially when it was so uncomplicated – the perfect setting, the purely physical delight without a messy tangle of confused feelings or fussing over whether or not you were "in love."

When Ray removed his headset for the second time and began locking up his office, he found his face wet with tears. That much was real, then. He chuckled, though, to discover it and then laughed harder, aware of the innate joy of everything. Looking out his office window at the palm trees in the floodlight and the distant sea in moonlight, nothing had ever seemed so perfectly picturesque. His blood sang in his veins. His future sparkled. A thought came to him and he grinned, pulling out his cell phone. He scrolled down to Marianne's name and was about to press call when he hesitated. Right now, he felt so cheerful and gleeful that it seemed nothing could go wrong – but he didn't know where she was, how she was feeling.

He wanted to tell her she was right, about – oh, probably everything – and that he loved her, but second thoughts gave him pause. In the VEC, he had been convinced it was true, but outside he remembered again that it was a simulation. *Love can't be simulated*, the VEC had said – but there was no reason a simulation couldn't say that. Logic returned to him, slightly eroding his optimism. Right now, he was still under the influence of the VEC experience. He hadn't yet decided how real that experience was. If he phoned Marianne and told her about it, then changed his mind later, it would bruise her even worse than he already had.

He walked down the corridor, deep in thought. Marianne was right: he had experienced something during his speed-of-light mission which, for whatever reason, hadn't made it through to his conscious mind. She'd accused him of repressing it. It wasn't the so-called "betrayal of trust" that had made him so angry about the interview; he realized that now. It was her speaking to the world about knowledge he couldn't face himself: that something extraordinary *had* happened. The specter of madness, of a mind out of control, haunted him. For that, he lashed out at her, using his pig-headed "principles" to defend himself.

Outside, Ray leaned against the car, looking up at the galaxies' endless swirl across the sky. What had he done to her? Promised her love, and then snatched it away. Offered support for her past heartache, and then broken her heart. Asked her to trust him then ruptured her trust. Before he could even consider asking her to risk her heart with him again, he needed to be absolutely certain about this transcendental experience, or simulation, or whatever it was. He would not risk hurting her again.

The week before her last exam, Dawn was once again glued to the TV screen from morning till night, the rapid tapping of her fingers on the keyboard like the clatter of mice in the floorboards. The last paper was an extended essay, at Professor Jennings' discretion, written under exam conditions, and might ask anything about contemporary media. Dawn had already decided to choose the politics option. She watched every national news channel she could, then went online to watch the BBC news – the British usually covered American politics, because their own Prime Minister invariably ended up backing American international policies. Their angles, however, were refreshingly different and gave her more insight into the American perspective. She wished, not for the first time, that she understood Arabic, so she could see how the oil embargo was represented in Middle Eastern media. Now *that* would surely readjust her perceptions!

Four days before the exam, a news bulletin aired that made her throw out half of her research. Alice simply couldn't ask about anything else – this had to be the single most important media event of the year, maybe the decade.

"A White House spokesperson has just informed ABC news…" began the anchorman in the heavy tones reserved for dramatic bulletins. Dawn was idly noting down that egocentric phrase, as if ABC news had been contacted exclusively, before anyone else, when his next words froze her hands on the keyboard. "…that diplomatic talks with the Arab nations about dismantling their nuclear arms program and dropping the oil embargo have been cancelled until further notice. The tension between the United States and the Arab nations has not been this great since the Iraqi war began almost two decades ago."

The bulletin cut to the Secretary of State as he addressed the nation. "It is with great regret that we find ourselves unable to continue reasonable negotiations with the Arab nations," he said. "Their insistence on continuing with this embargo amounts to a form of global terrorism, and the United States will no longer be held for ransom."

"Oh, Jesus…" whispered Dawn, her eyes huge with horror. If the all-purpose boogieman of terrorism was being invoked, that meant the government would now stop at nothing; UN resolutions and the Geneva Convention be damned.

"We are a powerful country," continued the Secretary of State, "and it is time that we remembered that. We have made every possible effort to resolve this issue diplomatically, but now the time has come to say: enough is enough."

Dawn knew that the stern and sorrowful rhetoric, with all its vague expressions and strong phrases, amounted to a declaration of war. Feeling sick, she thought of how the army's training had been notched up a few levels with the VECs. They'd been preparing for this. While the negotiations were still supposedly going on, the military had, in reality, been preparing for war.

The anchorman was back on screen. "With diplomacy off the table, pundits are speculating that military action may be a more viable solution to resolve our Middle East crisis."

Dawn was too stunned to take any notes, though she automatically registered the word "crisis" – another nice vagary – and its automatic situation elsewhere. *It's never our fault*, she thought. *It's never the American crisis – it's never the American régime – we don't bomb places, we have 'air strikes', we've never fucked up, we've 'worked with available intelligence' – oh shit...* Too upset to think clearly, her angry thoughts ran down their familiar lines. She'd have to watch the news bulletin several more times before she could say anything sensible about it. She'd have to watch everything from now on.

The next few days were a blur to Dawn; reading the papers, watching bulletins, trying to keep her intellectual clarity despite the immense outrage she felt towards the government. How could representative democracy be a good idea, she wondered, when it enabled the supposed representatives to do things like this, in the name of people who would surely never support slaughter for oil? If someone shot a gas station attendant rather than pay for their gas, that person went to prison. If the U.S. bombed a country for its oil, they were heroes. That was the problem – the electorate didn't seem to notice or care.

She jogged through the streets, dazed by the ordinariness of the lives continuing around her. Bit by bit, the bitter pill was being swallowed with great big mouthfuls of sweet rhetoric to wash it down. People were being groomed to accept a no-holds-barred war. She sat in coffee shops with her laptop and heard them quoting the media sound bites as if these were their own opinions and conclusions. Believing they were having political discussions, they espoused everything the government was leading them towards. Even scarier, perhaps, were the people who sat chattering about inconsequential things, oblivious to what was unfolding. How could a nation so huge and powerful never stop to think what it was doing to the rest of the world? She felt like the only person awake in a great procession that was sleep-walking its way to hell, and was being carried along in their wake.

The night before her exam, she spoke to Ray about it. He'd been spending a lot of time at work lately, though it must have been going well. There was a spring in his step she hadn't seen since he and Marianne had split up.

"What can we do about it?" he said.

Dawn was incensed. "We live in a *democracy*," she shrieked. "Our government is going to kill innocent people, they've basically announced it, and everyone just nods and agrees and you say what can we *do*? What the hell is democracy for? What the fuck is the point of having free speech if no one in the government listens to a word you say?"

Instead of flaring up in return, he sat calmly listening to her words, nodding. Then he spoke. "I didn't mean it in a rhetorical sense," he said. "I'm serious. I believe you and I agree with you and I want to do something. So, what can we do?"

Dawn sat down, too surprised to speak for a moment.

"But – you never support my causes," she said at last, her passion dampened momentarily by shock. "I'd even started to agree with you – that they never make a difference; these protests and all."

"I guess I was wrong," said Ray. "People have to try. Even if we don't see a difference immediately, or get what we hope out of it, surely we have to try."

"Are you serious?"

"What's the alternative?" he said, dead serious. "Silence implies consent. I don't want to consent to this and neither do you. So…you know more about this kind of thing than I do. What can we do?"

Dawn considered. "I'll check the main activist websites," she said, "see if there are any protests organized and if there aren't, suggest one – usually the protests start too late, of course. By the time we hear anything about it, the government's already declared war, its troops are already mobilized, and the decision's been made. I'll also look up petitions, and either join or start one. We can write to the papers; national and local and write to our congressmen. All the usual stuff."

Ray was impressed. "This is the usual stuff? This is what you do with all these causes?"

Dawn nodded. "It's not all about getting bailed out by my big brother," she said wryly. "Most of it's a lot of less glamorous, admin stuff; posting letters and standing around holding signs. But Ray – are you serious? You're kind of famous these days. If you endorsed the cause, there'd be a lot more publicity. Are you even allowed to?"

He hadn't considered that. "I guess I'll have to ask," he said reluctantly.

Dawn slept better that night than she had since the day she heard the news. If even Ray agreed with her, perhaps there was hope. Perhaps people wouldn't stand by and let this happen, or sweep it under the carpet as something that's happening "over there," in a place far removed from their lives. Every right-minded person had to recognize how important this was. Her newfound faith in humanity was violently jolted the very next day, when she opened her exam paper and scanned down to the question on politics.

"Discuss how the U.S. government's stance on new technology, such as speed-of-light travel and VECs, is represented in the media, with reference to baseline assumptions and recent broadcasts."

Alice Jennings considered the government's attitude towards gadgets to be more pertinent than its attitude towards war. Dawn considered writing, "This question sums up your own baseline assumptions more disgracefully than I ever could," and then with a weary sigh picked up her pen. Grades mattered to her too much to sabotage them. All her research was wrong, but she had a retentive memory. She could dredge up the information from articles on the required topic that she'd previously glanced at and rejected; at least enough to make a convincing essay. For several minutes she just sat, pen poised above the paper, wondering how to begin and steadily realizing that she couldn't.

10

When Les didn't answer the door, Ray stuck his head inside to see the young engineer wearing his VEC headset, eyes shut, hips twitching from side to side. He grinned and tapped his hand.

"Ray! Good to see you!" Les pulled the headset off.

"Another dance contest?" said Ray. Les nodded. "I never asked how the last one went, by the way."

"Oh, I did fine, but unfortunately my partner let me down'" Les replied regretfully. "It's a shame; we had a really good routine."

"How'd she let you down?"

"My mother's sciatic nerve flared up and we couldn't finish our tango. But she got a cortisone shot and says she's good as new for the cha-cha contest tonight."

Ray laughed spontaneously and tried to cover it up by saying, "That's great! It sounds like your mom is really game."

"She's amazing," said Les seriously. "So – what can I do for you? You're getting on all right with that VEC program I made you?"

Ray sat down on the edge of his chair, with a sigh. "That's kind of what I came to see you about… It's working fine," he added hastily, seeing Les's concern. "It's just – look, I know how the VEC works."

Les grinned at him. "Then you know more than most people."

"I know it only simulates a physical experience – but what if it's simulating something that's not a physical experience, then is the experience real?" Unwilling to describe his encounter yet, Ray tried to put the question as a generality. Les looked bemused. "For example – what if it's simulating love?"

"Oh, wow." Comprehension dawned on Les's face.

"You mean – is emotion a physical experience? Is it sensory? Or can the VEC also simulate things like thought-processes, rather than purely sensory data? You know – the question of where emotions are situated is a very old one and one we haven't entirely resolved yet…"

Ray could see Les was about to fly off into neurology and philosophy. "What I can't figure out," he cut in, "is if the emotion is *real*."

"Define *real*," Les answered wryly.

Ray's answer was quick and certain. "Real as in something that has a right to exist outside the VEC and to continue to exist without a simulation. Something that has a concrete, tangible source. The way your mom is real and your simulated dance partner isn't."

"They're people," Les reasoned. "You're talking about emotions."

"Okay, the way you feel about your mom and the way you feel about your dance partner!" Ray was getting exasperated.

"If emotion is real by your definition…" began Les cautiously. The astronaut was asking a profound philosophical question, but obviously wanted a more practical answer. "Then – well, I guess the pragmatic answer is this: Real love comes from the heart or the soul or wherever, and simulated love comes from an AI chip that tells your brain you're experiencing love."

Ray's face fell.

"I assume that's not the answer you were looking for."

"No," sighed Ray, picking up a ballpoint pen lid. As he spoke, he absently bent the plastic against the desk. "Although, that's what I thought, too. You're only confirming what I believed to be the case." He finished destroying the lid and began to dismember the ballpoint pen itself. He clearly wanted to say more, but couldn't bring himself to do it. Les tactfully moved his favorite fountain pen out of Ray's reach, replacing it with another ballpoint.

Personally, he didn't think people knew enough about emotions to make distinctions between "real" and "artificial." *Try telling someone with a panic attack that the feelings aren't real,* he mused. Ray clearly considered the distinction important, though.

"Why does it being only a simulation make it a bad thing?' said Les eventually, when Ray finished dismantling the second pen.

Ray didn't look Les in the eye as he spoke, his voice halting. "Because there's something there; a sort of a 'being' in the simulation. It's…like God. No, that's – that's not the right word. The presence is even better than what we imagine God is. And it says that, when you're experiencing love, you're touching God, heaven, the Source – whatever you want to call it. We don't have proper words for it." His hands were now absently putting the pens back together. "So if the love I'm feeling during the simulation isn't real, the interaction I'm having with – it – the being – isn't real either."

He tried to straighten the pen lid again, and then dropped it, frustrated. He raised his eyes to Les's, expecting to meet derision or disbelief. What he saw was pure interest, and it urged him on. "I had some kind of out-of-body experience, Les. I'm terrified to show it to anyone in case they use it to make a case against me – I mean, all we've got is the contents of my head. There's nothing tangible to point to, no specific sensory experience, to say this or that happened. There's nothing to prove that anything happened outside my own head. It made me wonder if it was real or not…" He trailed off again.

"A simulation isn't necessarily a bad thing," said Les.

"No." Ray exhaled heavily, then rose to his feet, becoming business-like once more. "But reality's better than simulations, right?" He gave a brief, strained smile. "Thanks for that. Catch you at lunch."

"Before you go, Ray – I have a question for you…" The

engineer was blushing and Ray raised his eyebrows. "Do you know – I mean, when you ask someone out on a date, and you go on one, when is it okay to ask them out again?"

With an absolutely straight face, Ray replied, "I think a week is the normal length to leave between dates. You can usually phone again a couple of days after a date. And if the date goes very well, it's okay to phone the next day." He managed to maintain composure until he left the room. In the hallway, he let out a soft chuckle. *Oh Dawn, baby, what have I gotten you into?*

The sun soaked into Dawn's skin and bounced off the silver fabric of her neatly-fitting bikini. Marianne lay in a lounge chair beside her, her face tilted towards the rays, dark glasses hiding her eyes. In front of them, the blue water of the pool sparkled, its far edge hidden so that it seemed to blend into the vast vista of sea. Around its edges lay the lawn, speckled with broad-leafed tropical plants and shrubs. Two young men, dressed only in shorts in the heat, were grooming the bushes. The sweat of their labors glistened on tanned skin.

"So what's going on here?" asked Dawn. "Am I seeing double, or what?'

"No – that's just Kirk and Dirk," said Marianne. "They're twins; they do the yard work."

Dawn sighed in contentment, her eyes relishing the sight of their well-formed bodies. "Only yard work?" she said, regretfully.

"Oh no – much, much more." Marianne picked up her bottle of suntan lotion and raised it in the air. "Oh, Dirk…" she called. "Can you come here and rub some suntan lotion on me?"

Dirk set down his clippers and hurried towards Marianne, a huge smile on his face. Dawn glanced between them, then at the remaining twin still hard at work.

"Oh, Kirk…" she called softly.

The two women reclined while the men's firm, large hands roamed over their skin, spreading the slick lotion. Dawn sat up to let Kirk do her back, then giggled when he began to smooth the white cream over her stomach and upper chest, just skirting the lines of the bikini.

She should be doing something productive, she thought – something to avert the war she was so sure was being planned. She'd posted on the message boards, sent off the usual letters, and tried to do what she could to raise the alarm, but it all felt hollow. She'd done the same for all her causes: campaigning for free contraceptive, against political torture, against environmental destruction, for proper food labeling, for Afghanistan's freedom, for equal parenting laws… None of her efforts seemed to have any effect, so why should this? People really didn't seem to care, ever, and jolting them awake with an electric cattle prod was frowned upon, so why even bother?

Kirk's hands dug into her shoulders, his fingers occasionally skimming down across the slope of her breasts, and she shivered with pleasure. She'd done what she could, for now, so why not just relax and enjoy? He moved onto her legs and she glanced at Marianne. She was sitting forward while Dirk's hands ran over her upper back and shoulders, over the front past her collarbone, then back to her shoulders again. A little smile was playing about her lips. She pushed her sunglasses up and raised an eyebrow at Dawn.

"What do you think? Time for a dip?"

"Oh, that sounds like a plan…"

"Boys," said Marianne flirtatiously. "Time for a little swim."

As one, the twins walked over to the horizon pool, dropped their trunks and dived in naked, the bare skin of their bottoms flashing through the air before disappearing into the water's splash.

Dawn stared, entranced. "Now how did they know I wanted them to do that?" she wondered aloud.

"I'm telling you," said Marianne, "The AI chip knows everything." She rose to her feet, stretched and sauntered over to the pool.

Yes, it does, thought Dawn, *A little more than I'd like, sometimes.* She looked at the guys swimming lazily back and forth, their hair plastered to their heads, their handsome features shining with water drops. The thought of them being naked beneath the shimmering surface of the pool made her throat tighten and alarmed her. Having a fantasy flicker through one's head wasn't the same as confronting it. She joined Marianne at the pool edge, her eyes shyly averted from even glancing underwater.

"Which one's Dirk and which one's Kirk?" she said.

Marianne laughed. "Does it matter?"

"Guess not." Dawn gave a naughty grin while her eyes flickered back and forth for a moment, then down. "We going to skinny-dip too?"

"For sure."

They slid their bikinis off and stood at the edge, their shapely bodies like golden cutouts against the blue sky, before diving in.

Jack Firestone sat in Ray's chair, the VEC headset over his immaculate silver hair, while Ray paced restlessly up and down the office. After five minutes, he considered touching Jack on the hand or the shoulder – but no, he shouldn't interrupt. He returned to wearing a groove in the carpet, and then abruptly left to get himself a cup of coffee. He was standing by the machine, hand poised over the button, when he remembered Dawn's complaints about "disposable" goods.

"What's 'disposable?'" she'd rant. "They're not saying degradable – they're just giving you permission to chuck it away, and add it to a landfill!" He began the longer walk to the cafeteria, where coffee was served in mugs rather than plastic cups.

He'd wrestled over and over with the question of the VEC simulation and what it implied. If he accepted it as truth, he would have to rethink his atheism, his principles and all of his opinions. If it weren't true, it was still a product of his own mind, so he'd have to conclude he was mentally unstable and fantasized the existence of a Divine force. He didn't dare ask Marianne. He knew what she'd think and couldn't approach her with half-offers and a divided mind, not after what he'd done last time. Finally, he'd thought of Jack – the only other person in the world to have shared his experience.

When he returned with two mugs of coffee, Jack was holding the headset in his hands and staring at it in a daze. He looked up at Ray.

"I'm talking to God here?" he said.

Ray put the mugs down. He hadn't conceived of it as "God," exactly; he didn't like the term. "Close enough," he said.

"And this is only a simulation of what you experienced?"

"Yes. Only a simulation."

Jack put down the headset and straightened his hair. "It felt so real," he said wistfully. "I felt the same inner peace – that sense of wholeness, an overwhelming experience of love – like I did on the mission, but so much stronger."

"I know." Ray sat down in the chair opposite and lifted his mug. "But it's the computer simulation that you're experiencing, not the real thing. At least, that's what I think and what Les confirmed."

"Les has seen this?" Jack was surprised.

"No, he made it – from the brain activity – but I don't think he's actually experienced it."

"And you don't remember any of this from the actual

mission?"

"Not even a moment. But it is similar to what you felt? I know it's made from my brain scan, but even so, I thought maybe I was just..."

"Making it up?" said Jack sympathetically. Ray assented. "I'd begun to wonder about that myself, about my own mission. I try to tell people about something so amazing, so precious, I feel like it could change the whole world and they all just nod and smile like I'm a nutcase, until I begin to doubt myself."

For the first time, Ray realized what courage Jack must have had to go public with his experience. Hell, Ray didn't even have the courage to tell his own sister!

"I still believe what I said to you – before your mission," said Jack slowly. "The world's going to hell in a hand-basket. I thought that when I told everyone what happened in a book, they'd believe me. I was a scientist, a national hero, not some fruitcake. And then I thought if people believed me, maybe they'd change. Instead, I just got shunted over to the fruitcake section." He sighed. "Then I thought to myself, 'I don't know what to do with this experience, but surely God does. And access to the real God would be just what this planet needs right now. Before we all blow each other to smithereens.'"

"Maybe that would be the best possible thing for the planet," said Ray dryly. "Maybe *that's* the divine plan."

"You really believe that?" said Jack, stunned. "After experiencing *that*?" He gestured towards the VEC.

Ray shook his head. "So what do we do now?"

Jack stood and crossed to the window, leaning on the sill and absorbing the view while he thought. For a few minutes, the two men sat in silence, and then Jack spoke decisively.

"We have journey at the speed of light again and talk to God for real," he said.

Ray stared at him. "How are we going to do that? As far as NASA and this administration are concerned, my first mission was a complete failure."

"That's before they knew you'd talked with God."

"Come on, Jack, I can't go to Thomas, or the President, and say – oh, I remember what happened on my mission now, I chatted with God. It must have slipped my mind."

"I'm sorry," said Jack firmly, "but that is exactly what you have to do."

"But I won't remember anything!" cried Ray. "I mean – why should this time be different?"

"We'll both go," said Jack. "I remembered my experience. And you might remember yours, this time – now that you've already sort of relived it."

Ray slumped in his chair. It was a crazy, astronomically expensive, career-suicide idea and it just might be a good one. "How do we know it's not just an illusion?" he said. "That maybe speed-of-light does some funny neurological thing so we think we're being enlightened but it's actually all bull, just illusion, like a dream?"

"You felt that absolute love, like I did, correct?" said Jack.

"Yeah…" Ray admitted.

"So maybe that feeling is real. Maybe the human experience of hate, greed, envy and lust are the illusions, clouding our real perception."

Ray stared at him, taken aback. "Wow, Jack. That's quite – insightful. For a politician."

Jack beamed. "Well, I can't take credit for it. It's what God told me in the simulation."

Ray smacked his forehead. "'Great. Now the AI chip to simulate reality is telling us what's real. It's fruitcake section for both of us if that gets out."

For Les and Dawn's second date, he booked seats on the Sunset Eco-Cruise, an electric boat that toured the waterways of the Merritt Island wildlife refuge. He'd seen the boat carrying its cargo of happy couples so many times, with a flicker of envy. This time, he'd be on it; an intelligent and pretty girl at his side.

Dawn accepted the invitation. She didn't have much to do while she hung around waiting for her exam results and Marianne was out of town for a few days. She did want to see him – it was just embarrassing that he'd chosen something so blatantly "romantic."

"I hope I'm not leading him on," she said to Ray. "He's really interesting, but I'm not sure I'm... interested. In that way."

The two were lying out in the yard, enjoying the freshly-mown smell of the lawn and the lazy afternoon sun. Dawn was half-heartedly reading an e-book and playing with her cell phone, thinking how nice it would be take a dip in the horizon pool with Kirk or Dirk. It was such a shame her brother was so opposed to VECs. On a mellow, do-nothing Saturday like this, what could be better?

Ray shrugged, without glancing up from his Sudoku puzzle. "Isn't that what dating's for? To find out?"

"So says the master of dating," teased Dawn, kicking him lightly. She rolled on her back and looked at the time on her cell phone. "I'd better get ready, though."

"Huh? It's two hours from now!"

"Hair, shaving, make-up, nails – these things take time, Ray." Dawn stood up, collecting her rug and empty juice glass. "I've got to look good for the occasion."

"Sounds like you are interested," he replied, grinning. "Hey – I forgot to ask. How's it going with the anti-war office?"

"Oh, you know," said Dawn, with a pang of guilt. She hadn't thought about it since Kirk's suntan lotion techniques had distracted her. "I put out some feelers on websites and stuff – I don't know that there's been that much interest, really."

Ray sat up. "I asked at work – they said that I can do

stuff as a private individual, but not with any reference to my position at NASA, and they said fronting a campaign would be out of the question." He frowned. "Actually, I tried to push it a bit and they said they'd made me a national hero and if I abused that they could unmake me. It wasn't very nice."

"I'm sorry…" said Dawn, feeling bad that she hadn't done more herself. But what more was there to do? The usual avenues were the usual waste of time. She lingered, awkwardly.

"It's fine. Go on. Go pamper yourself. Dawn started to walk off and Ray called after her, "Don't make yourself too drop-dead gorgeous though. Les might not survive the experience!"

Once again, Dawn found herself enjoying Les's company more than she had expected. He wasn't what she'd call handsome, but his looks were nicer than she remembered. Maybe his face was a little pointy and the way he combed his black hair back didn't help. Regardless, his eyes were lively and when conversation animated him, he was almost attractive. He seemed to have an immense fund of knowledge about everything – VECs, physics, philosophy, art.... She soon learned that he could even be mistaken for an expert on manatees.

They saw the strange, almost-human faces break the water some distance from the boat. Along with their habits, perils and migrations, Les told her how they had been confused with mermaids at one time.

"Perhaps they were even the source of legends about mermaids," he said, "but it's a pity to think mermaids never existed."

Dawn smiled – she'd just been thinking the same thing. "I like the way you think," she said. "You're so different from my brother, that way. He's all about the facts and things being proven or disproven, when sometimes ideas are just… pretty."

"I try not to rule anything out," said Les, earnestly. "I think that would be very arrogant. Ray is very true to what he believes and I respect that, but I think there's so much we don't know that any assumption is dangerous. I don't want to assume anything – I want to find out…"

"Find out what?" Dawn enquired gently. The flaming sunset, the tranquility of the reserve, the glass of champagne and the simple pleasure of his conversation were all softening her toward him.

"Everything!" His face was alight, making hers brighten in sympathy. "There's so much to learn – and to study – I feel like I can never learn fast enough…"

"You must learn pretty fast to know as much as you seem to," said Dawn.

Les leaned on the railing, looking out towards the Atlantic, where the reflected sunset was making soft strands of purple run across the horizon. He said softly, "To myself I am only a child playing on the beach, while vast oceans of truth lie undiscovered before me…"

"Newton?"

"Uh-huh." He was glad she recognized the quotation.

The marshes stretched out in drifts of reeds and grasses, with streaks of water reflecting each one in symmetry. A heron stood poised and silhouetted in the water, its mirror image echoing it. The light was fading as they stood in silence, the wild crimson and gold threads of the sunset giving way to soft lavender and sage.

"You could believe in anything out here," whispered Dawn, as if reluctant to break the stillness. "Ghosts… mermaids… spirits…"

Les's hand found hers. She'd thought she would mind, but she didn't. His warm palm felt good against hers.

"Look," he said in a hushed voice, pointing with his other hand. The huge scaly bulk of an alligator was creeping cautiously along a stretch of beach and sank, silently and with barely a ripple, into the water. Dawn imagined it sliding imperceptibly through the water; massive, silent and powerful, and she shuddered.

"I'm glad I'm *in* the boat," she said with a nervous laugh.

He fetched them another drink each as the boat began its way back to the pier. The stars were beginning to show as darkness fell. She was glad when he leaned over and kissed her, his lips just brushing hers, light and dry. Dawn felt glad that he kissed her and that it was such a little, ordinary kiss. She still hadn't quite made her mind up about him.

"You want to do *what?*" bellowed Thomas. Neither Jack nor Ray flinched, though inwardly Ray regretted allowing Jack to present the idea. The senator was a little too confident of his power. Ray's explanation would have been drier, more factual and – he suspected – more to the tastes of the Head of NASA.

"We want to travel at the speed of light again," said Ray.

"Why? So you cannot remember a thing again? This is a space program, Ray, not the fucking tourist department!"

"No, Thomas," cut in Jack, "Ray wants to talk to God again."

Thomas turned quickly, bewildered. "Talk to God? What do you mean, talk to God? When did he talk to God the first time?"

"Last time he traveled at the speed of light – just like I did," answered Jack smoothly.

"And how would you know that? Ray doesn't remember a *thing* about that last trip! It's been all we can do to keep that under wraps…"

He tugged at his hair in frustration and Ray decided it was time to step in.

"Les managed to convert my brain scan into a VEC simulator program," he said. "I asked him to – not officially, just as a favor. I was as worried about the memory lapse as anyone else – maybe more. And when I tried it, I experienced…" He glanced at Jack. "Maybe 'God' isn't the word I'd choose and maybe 'talking' isn't quite how I'd put it either, but yeah, for lack of better words, I spoke to God."

"Oh, this is great." Thomas leaned heavily on his desk. "The guy who thinks VECs are the work of the devil and the most evil form of illusion now believes it when it tells him he chatted with God. Now I've heard everything."

"We're not saying that the simulation is real," said Jack, "We're agreed on that. We're saying it simulates what Ray really experienced, and that was a conversation with God."

Thomas stood and began to pace the room, his fingers and thumb creasing and smoothing his forehead. "You know this is nuts, don't you?" he said. "Nothing but my lifelong respect for you two is stopping me from throwing you out. And I can't go along with this craziness."

Jack grabbed Thomas by the shoulders and looked him square in the eyes. "Thomas, think about it. Going the speed of light is where science and faith meet. Don't you want to be the scientist who joins the two opposing views as one?"

Thomas extricated himself from Jack's grip. "I'm not just a scientist, Jack, I'm the fucking head of this organization – I can't do whims. This is not just some blue skies research program…" He frowned, studying the carpet. "And Ray!" he burst out. "You, of all people! You're the most level-headed, logical…" He sputtered to a halt.

"Yes," said Ray, "I am level-headed and I haven't lost it, Thomas, I promise you. And I do believe this is important – necessary – crucial, dammit. Will you agree to consider it?"

"And be the scientist who gets fired because he spent billions of dollars to repeat an illusion that won't even be remembered?" asked Thomas.

"That's why we'll both go," said Jack. "Ray might remember his experience this time, now that he had it again in the VEC, but I remembered mine last time…not that anyone believed me," he added, "but with both of us, there'll be simultaneous corroboration – or at least, it'll corroborate previous data. This project needs both of us. We both survived the previous flights – we can afford redundancy now. And you know as well as I do that I'm qualified."

"Yes," said Thomas, "you're probably over-qualified. Look, you know I have to get the blessing of the President for this one, don't you?"

Ray and Jack nodded.

"So you want me to tell President Priest that I want to send Raymond Sky and Senator Jack Firestone on a speed-of-light mission so that they can have a chat with God?"

"Yes!"

"The same Senator Jack Firestone who's rumored to be running against the President in the next election?" Thomas pointed out.

Jack hesitated. "Yes – that may be a slight problem."

"A slight problem?" spat Thomas. "Even if the President buys this bullshit about chatting to God – and I wouldn't put it past him – what candidate would send his opponent up in space to talk to God right before an election? What's your campaign slogan going to be, The Man Who Talked With God?"

Ray's eyes shot from one silver-haired man to the other; the senator and the powerful Head of NASA. He hadn't expected Thomas to agree all at once. He figured the man would take a lot of convincing about the spiritual dimension. Ray knew he'd question – like Ray – whether it were an objective reality or some fantastic illusion produced by Ray's own brain. He'd anticipated Thomas asking to try out the VEC. Ray felt squeamish about this. The idea of letting his boss simulate his own intensely personal experience was an uncomfortable prospect. However, instead of what Ray had anticipated, the two men he most respected were arguing about politics and their own careers! Faced with the prospect of speaking to a deity, all they could think about was their own petty concerns.

"Look, screw the politics!" Ray snapped at last, cutting their argument off mid-stride. "We are talking about God, here! Can we stop this idiotic banter for a moment and grasp the importance of what we are talking about?" The older men stared at him, shocked. Ray took a deep, calming breath before he continued. "How can we not go forward, not at least try this, if there's even a slight possibility that we really can – talk to God? Surely that takes precedence over anything else?"

Jack looked down as if ashamed. *And so you should be*, thought Ray angrily. *You had the same experience I did, but you don't want to put that above your own ambition? You don't think that should change everything? You want to change the world but you hesitate to change your own life?*

Thomas was nodding slowly. "Okay," he said reluctantly. "I'll set up an appointment to see him. But I'm not facing the President alone here – you guys are coming with me."

11

Ray, Thomas and Jack sat in the President's Executive Secretary's office, waiting for admission to the Oval Office. Ray knew he might have to lie – Thomas had been very explicit on that, when they prepared their strategy. Trying not to let his agitation show, he fixed his eyes on the Rose Garden visible through the glass doors. Around the expanse of lawn, the bushes and trees were in full leaf, the red and yellow roses overblown in the summer heat. Somehow, he would have to remain true to his principles, while persuading the President to let him go on the flight that would establish what his principles were. If there were a divine being, was it okay to lie in order to meet it? Thomas had expressly forbidden him to mention the VEC – "He's like you," the NASA Head had said, "he thinks it's the devil's playground – just say your memory of the mission came back to you." Jack had advised them to play up to the President's messianic ego and sell the mission as a tool for spreading the word of God to an uncivilized world.

"But what the VEC says is nothing like what he preaches!" Ray protested.

"He doesn't know that and we're not going to tell him," Jack countered.

Ray found himself thinking hackneyed thoughts about the roses – the soft, widespread petals which released their fragrance, and the curved thorns that clung to the stem – the beauty and the pain. Grasp the flower and cut your hand – was that what he would have to do? On the TV interviews, he'd managed to give half-answers and evasions, but that wouldn't wash here. He'd also been more certain, then, about what he believed: his principles, his ethics and only himself to answer to. Now there was a possibility that far overreached him: a Divine being that could perhaps help the whole world, and here Ray was, wriggling and writhing because he didn't want to lie? If soldiers broke into the house, hunting down Dawn, would he hesitate to lie for her? Of course not. His love for her took precedence. Love took precedence. Roses were romantic love; roses had thorns. How did Marianne reconcile ethics and spirituality? What would she advise?

"The President is ready to see you, now." The secretary's voice broke into his thoughts and the three men rose from their seats.

"So your memory of your first mission has come back and you believe you chatted with God?" The President turned from the window, through which he had been staring in what appeared as deep thought, though now he simply repeated their words. His hands were clasped behind his back.

"Yes, sir," said Ray. He, Jack and Thomas were sitting in a stripe across one of the plush sofas, opposite the Secretary of State, the Chief of Staff and Reed Polman, the President's political advisor. Vice President Christian sat on a separate armchair, leaning back with his legs folded and his fingers entwined.

"And you want to go the speed of light again, so you can chat with God another time?" pursued the President.

"Yes, Mr. President, I do," said Ray sincerely.

"And you want to join him?" The President turned to Jack.

"That's correct, Mr. President" he replied.

The President resumed his seat opposite Warren's. He leaned forward slightly, hands on his knees. "You know," he said gravely, "I speak to God every day through prayer. Have you tried that?" His solemn eyes were fixed on Ray's.

"Not on a regular basis," said Ray uncomfortably.

"And how about you, Senator? Do you ever get down on your knees and pray to God?"

"Not as much as I should, Mr. President." Jack displayed regret more convincingly than Ray.

"You should try it more often, you may just like it."

"Yes, sir."

The President looked at Ray expectantly, like a headmaster waiting for penitence. Quietly infuriated, Ray nodded his head obediently. *You're elected to run the country*, he thought bitterly, *not to tell us what to believe or how to relate to the Divine!*

"So tell me," the President continued, "why should I authorize that taxpayers spend billions of dollars to do something I do on my knees every morning and every evening before I go to bed? I speak to God already."

Yeah, you speak to God, but we want to listen to God speak to us, thought Ray, not trusting himself to speak. Fortunately, Thomas picked up the ball.

"Because you do it through faith, Mr. President, and this interaction with God will be done through science. By going the speed of light again, with two scientific observers, you'll have scientific proof to take to the rest of the world to show them your god is the true and only God."

"Yes," said Jack, "Like Moses climbing Mount Sinai to bring back the Ten Commandments."

The President raised his eyebrows. "Now that's an interesting comment from a man who is considering running against me in the next Presidential election, Senator."

"Some things are above politics, Mr. President," Jack replied soberly.

"And you wouldn't use personally talking to God as a political advantage over me in the next election?"

"No sir," said Jack, his voice ringing with sincerity. "In this mission, I am merely the foot soldier – you are the general – the credit must, and will, go to you."

"There's a practical aspect I'm concerned about," said Helen, the Chief of Staff. Thus far, she had sat quietly making her usual neat notes. "How can you guarantee you'll even remember the mission, or that the onboard equipment won't fail again?"

Thomas took over the explanation, offering the various safeguards they had developed. Now that they knew traveling at the speed of light was not a life-threatening endeavor, they could afford a redundancy of observers: Jack, who had memory of his previous mission, although he hadn't actually *traveled* at that speed, but merely reached it; and Ray, whose memory recovery suggested that he would indeed recall the second mission. In addition, they would have the information from both brain scans to compare and Les Hamilton was "working on" a way to make that information accessible. Tactfully, Thomas didn't mention VEC programs as the solution. As Les Hamilton's name was their strongest currency, Thomas used it again. The equipment's previous failure was because it did not have time to record anything – the tiny time-lapses in their machines were too high to do the job effectively. To record speed-of-light data, they would need speed-of-light technology, he said. Of course, he didn't mention what Les thought of his gross oversimplification, but the young man was working on the problem.

Helen's face had softened as he spoke, and she nodded her head in approval. *For once,* she thought to herself, *we're being given some proper data to base our decision on – even if they are being a bit vague about the memory-lapse episode.*

"What are your thoughts, Reed?" asked the President.

Of course, thought Helen, *there's the election to consider. Why rely on science if there's an available poll-adviser's opinion?*

"Politically speaking, I do believe having scientific proof of God's existence will be an excellent thing. It'll pull some of the secular, separation-of-church-and-state nutcases over to our side, the faith-based side, and strengthen our party."

The President nodded. "That's probably true, Reed, but I also think Jack is right – some things are above politics."

"In what way, Mr. President?" asked Reed.

The President straightened, his eyes fixed on the middle

distance. "Because doing so could allow this Presidency to bring the world a new testament of the Word of the Lord." His voice was deep and portentous, shifting into the special tones he used for big speeches. He rose from his chair, walked a little as he spoke, as if he were striding a stage. "Imagine the word of God, flowing from this Oval Office and putting the fear of God back into people's hearts. Imagine the people putting down their simulators, getting down on their knees and praying to God for His forgiveness. Imagine preaching the word of God with ten scientists at my side, verifying that my word is scientifically indisputable. Imagine the atheists finally admitting the error of their ways and falling down to worship the one true God."

"That's a wonderful vision, Mr. President," said the Secretary of State. "We can build that Christian nation we've always dreamed about."

"Neal," said Warren, "the President is talking about building a Christian *planet*."

"Our own heaven on earth," said the President, "just as intended in the divine plan."

The three men from NASA exchanged glances. Mad and pompous as he sounded, he was at least behind their plan.

"And prove to the Muslim world," said Warren, "that their beliefs are a heresy, that the only true path to God is by taking Jesus as their personal savior."

"Yes – that's a beautiful thought, Warren. Beautiful." The President's eyes were almost misting over with evangelical joy.

Helen opened her mouth and shut it again. She wanted to ask what the President would do if the astronauts came back saying oops, we were wrong, it's Allah up there – but questioning the President's faith was not worth her job. She suppressed a droll smile, imagining the President having to convert to Islam and fall on his knees for forgiveness. Or what if Buddhism was the ruling order? What if there was an entire pantheon up there? Her grin transformed into a beam of pleasure.

In the small ante-chamber between the Oval Office and the Roosevelt Room, the President's staff closed the door on his beatific smile and turned to each other.

"They're hiding something, Mr. Vice-President," said the political adviser softly. "I can just sense it."

"Of course they're hiding something," replied Warren. "I've smelled less bullshit in my last cattle drive than what they were dishing out there."

Helen lingered in the doorway, despite having a bundle of work to attend to and another meeting waiting for her.

"So what are we going to do about it?" asked Reed. Warren scowled in thought. "Follow them," he said eventually. "Tap their phones, place surveillance cameras in their homes, their work – you know, the usual."

Helen stepped forward. "I agree with you, they're hiding something," she said. "but I don't think FISA will approve the wiretap and surveillance warrants. Not for a U.S. Senator and Raymond Sky, not without evidence."

Warren turned his head to meet her eyes, scorn on his face. "Silly little girl," he sneered. "Who said anything about getting approval from FISA? This is a matter of national security, and in cases of national security, I don't need no stinkin' warrants."

In the taxi and then on the airplane, the three men from NASA barely mentioned the mission. It was too sensitive to discuss in public. Only when they settled into Jack's car, back in Florida, could Ray say what was on his mind.

"This is madness. We've sold this mission under false pretenses. Where does the lie end? How do we come back and tell him his beliefs are just so wrong? Everything in the simulation – it was just love, pure love – and he's waiting for us to bring back the news that God is gnashing His teeth at the unbelievers? That hatred – that fear – that's what brings the darkness around us, what separates us from the pure light…"

In the front seats, Thomas and Jack shared a brief skeptical glance at his ravings.

"You did the right thing, Ray," said Jack. "We needed to sell this mission to the President and to do that, we needed to tell him what he wanted to hear."

"But you know what's going to happen!" cried Ray. "Whatever information we bring back from our mission – even if we have the courage to tell it like it is, he's going to spin it to his point of view!"

"Yes, he will," agreed Jack.

"And you don't have a problem with that?" Ray was mystified. His own experience of the VEC simulation had left him in such a quandary, unsure of what to believe or how to act. Slowly, however, he was becoming convinced that the love he had felt was the most important thing in the world, and that opening himself to that bathing light was the only thing that mattered. Jack seemed relatively untouched by his experience – but then who was Ray to judge him?

"You're forgetting something, Ray," Jack answered. "The President won't be president forever." He shot a quick grin into the passenger seat, and then turned his eyes back to the road. In the rearview mirror, Ray could see big smile creases around his eyes.

"You're going to use this in your campaign?" said Thomas.

"Hell, yeah." Jack's eyes met Ray and he gave a wink. "Remind me to ask for forgiveness for this little white lie when we meet God, okay?"

I must not judge Jack, thought Ray resolutely, although his heart sank with disillusionment. *Judging is not love – the love matters – but how do you not judge? Oh fuck, I wish I could ask Marianne these questions. I don't know how to think my way through this stuff.*

He stared out the window, watching the edge of the road flicker past. He had been so wrong to judge Marianne as illogical. What was his logic but a blind obedience to rules, no different to the people who blindly obeyed their religious dictates? He saw her beautiful, pure face in his mind, that tender smile playing over her lips. She knew how to *think*, how to carve out new thoughts, not just join the dots. His heart contracted at the thought of her. If she gave him a second chance, his love would enfold her like a warm cocoon, he would keep her fragile, brave heart safe forever. Could he approach her now, while doubt still lingered in the corners of his mind? *Soon*, he promised himself. *Very soon.*

Already mentally selecting a VEC to help him unwind, Thomas unlocked his front door quietly. As usual, his dinner sat on a plate in the darkened kitchen, a note with heating instructions propped on the side. He popped a piece of cold roast potato in his mouth, but didn't really feel like eating. The interview with the President had left him stressed, and now the fading adrenalin made him queasy. An energetic and passionate romp would do more for him than food; releasing his stress and replacing it with pleasant thoughts.

"Honey, I'm home," he called softly up the stairs, not really wanting to wake her. In the living room, he poured a large whiskey, still running through his list of VECs in his mind. Nothing too sweet or coy, he thought. *Latinas* would do just right: a fiery Latin girl who sulked, bitched and scratched all the way to the bedroom. He felt himself stir just thinking about it as he walked down the stairs to the basement. The light was burning – he must have left it on...

Cathy sat on the sofa, still fully-dressed and made-up, her face hard as nails. Arrayed on the table in front of her was Thomas's extensive collection of porno-VECs. She gave him a long stare and he felt his stomach turn hot and cold with guilt.

"Oh. Shit." he exhaled.

"Have a seat," she said. "We need to talk."

You mean I need to listen, he thought. He sat in the old armchair opposite her, a hunted, wary look in his eyes. This was going to be a scene – a screaming, ranting bitch-scene – and he just didn't feel like going through it. He wished he could fast-forward to the point where everything had been said, accusations and tears over, apologies and promises made. Why, when it was all so obvious from the start, did they have to play this out?

"I know I invaded your privacy," she said stiffly, "but I thought I'd like to find out where my husband went before I gave up on this marriage completely."

"Gave up?" he said, startled.

"Don't be dense, Thomas, you know as well as I do that we're fucked. Or rather, we're *not* fucked." She laughed bitterly. "When did we last have sex – with each other? Or even speak, or have a little fun?"

"The mission party," he said, wounded. "That was fun, wasn't it?"

"Yes." She sighed and curled her legs up under her, leaning on the arm of the sofa. She looked tired and sad now, not confrontational. "That was months ago, Thomas. And it reminded me of the fun we used to have." She fingered the worn grain of the upholstery thoughtfully. Somehow, one expected the marriage to outlast the sofa, but here it was – worn but whole – while their relationship was in shreds. "So," she said, sitting up again and hardening once more. "It may interest you to learn that not everyone regards me as a useful domestic appliance, devoid of sexual interest."

"I don't!" he said, but she paid no attention.

"I didn't want to have an affair, so I was going to leave you first," she went on. "Then after the mission party, I thought it was a hopeful sign – that things might be getting back on track. And then, everything just carried on as stale and dull as ever and I thought – maybe it was the last dying flicker. But before I gave up completely, I wanted to know. Where do you go in your VEC worlds? What are the wishes and interests of this man who wanders through our house like a zombie, mechanically eats what he's given, wears the clothes that are washed for him, sleeps, returns to work, repeats it all, as if every spark in him is completely dead? I just wanted to know – if you were still alive, *where* were you alive?"

Thomas sat, dumbfounded. Cathy was planning to leave him? Cathy thought he was boring?

"So – this is what gets you off," she said, gesturing at the display of VECs. He scanned them, trying to see them through her eyes. They were neatly arranged, like little tiles, pushed together to make a square and a rectangle. Each had its voluptuous, leggy lady or ladies, occasionally in the arms of a muscular man – or over his lap, at his knees, or towering over him.

"Hey," he said, pointing to rectangular arrangement. "Those aren't mine!"

"I know," she said dryly, "they're mine. Compare and contrast."

This wasn't turning out to be the guilt-and-accusation scene he'd anticipated. She stood up.

"I'm getting myself one of those," she said, gesturing towards his whisky. "You have a look at our choices." She left the room and he moved onto the sofa.

Admittedly, her collection was smaller, but his *wife* had a *porn* stash? He knew about her PURE collection, all massages and pools and shit like that, the VEC equivalent of a trashy novel. These, however, each bore the RUSH logo. He began to study them. Christ, she had *Dracula* – he'd been thinking of getting that himself!

Cathy returned, her drink in a tumbler and the bottle in hand. She set it on the coffee table in the narrow line between the two groups of VECs.

"You've got *Tumble in the Hay*," he said flatly. "I've

got that."

"I know." Her voice even sounded amused. "There's a few that match. We could've saved a bit of money, if we'd been honest with each other."

"I got it because it reminded me of you," he said defensively.

"Really? It reminded me of that last summer – before graduation..."

"God, that was hot," he breathed. "Trying to hide from your parents all the time – all that corridor-creeping..."

"And the hay-loft," she whispered.

He met her eyes, slightly dilated at the memory. "You don't hate me for this?" he asked, still uncertain.

She smiled wryly. "That would be a bit hypocritical, wouldn't it? Thomas..." She shook her head gently. "But I thought – okay, here's the deal. See what you think. We both go through every program and tell each other why we bought it and what we like about it. Things we both like go in one pile. If you're prepared to do that... I bought this." From under the sofa she pulled a new VEC machine with two headsets. "It's kind of state-of-the-art and quite expensive, so if you're not interested we should take it back unused. But if you are interested..."

They both swallowed, their eyes locked on each other.

"Okay, I'm interested," he said quickly, breaking off. She topped up their drinks from the bottle and they bent their heads together over their collections. Giggling, shame-faced and blushing, they began to make their confessions.

Dawn and Les rolled together on the slender crescent of beach in the reserve, their feet splashing into the water and digging into the sand as they tore each other's clothes off. The whole sky was lit with the plum-colored clouds of a lowering sunset, its edges blurring softly into gold. He was kissing her neck passionately while she tore his t-shirt upwards, hungry to press her skin against his. His body was taut and thin – she could feel the strong, vulnerable lines of his ribs beneath his skin. Somehow their jeans were gone from between them and his hips were beginning to slide between her legs.

"Les," she breathed, "I'm not sure – I don't know if I want this…"

"You do want it," he said, his eyes shining into hers. "The AI chip told me."

"But…" She moaned, the surges of lust rolling up and down her body. "Yes, I do, but I'm not sure…"

There was more to consider, she knew, but she couldn't think what. She was mad for him – his narrow body, his thin smiling lips.

"The AI chip knows everything and we don't know what it knows," said Les. Her thighs were starting to part. "We must obey the AI chip."

She sat up abruptly, gasping. The lines of her bedroom were falling back into place as she looked around, half-blinded by the red light of dawn. Blinking and rubbing her eyes, she reached for her water glass and checked the time. It was six-thirty in the morning. *I guess I'll have an early start then,* she thought. *And what a start.* She giggled.

All day, the dream kept coming back to her in flashes. She was embarrassed by the intensity of the desire she'd felt – and for *Les*. She didn't believe that she thought about him like that at first, but now, with the dream playing in loops through her mind, she was in fevers at the thought of him. She didn't know how she would look him in the face that evening. She was supposed to be going to his place for dinner, with his mother. It was absurd: on their third date, he wanted to introduce her to his mother? And he was twenty-nine and still lived with her! How could she feel anything lustful towards someone like that? Nevertheless, the sexy dream kept prowling through her. His words also deeply unsettled her and she tried to make sense of their dream-logic. He'd explained to her about VECs and artificial intelligence and she had felt uneasy, in a VEC, about having the chip recognize what she wanted. These simple facts had been distorted in the grandiose world of dreams. She had seen that beach with him, on the cruise – it was where the alligator had been... She shuddered, spoiling her careful toenail-painting.

"You are *jumpy*, today," said Ray. He was lying on a deck chair, reading one of Marianne's books. Dawn hoped that was a good sign.

"Weird dream," muttered Dawn. She wiped the toenail clean and started again. As usual, her restlessness took the form of cleaning and grooming. She'd already spruced up the whole house and now had started on herself. As she polished, waxed, plucked and painted herself, she wondered if she was preparing for anything. She wiggled her toes in the breeze, waiting for them to dry.

"Ray?"

"Mmm-hmm?" He looked up from *The Spiritual Seduction*.

"How do you know if you have the hots for someone?"

He raised his eyebrows and started to grin. "Well – I suppose I'd have to tell you some time." He put his book down and leaned forward. "When a mommy and a daddy love each other very much, they get certain urges..."

"C'mon!" She batted his chin lightly with the back of her hand. "You know what I mean."

"Not really," he said honestly. "It's something you kind of – feel."

Dawn grimaced. "Yeah, okay, the feelings are there, but they're kind of flickersome. And disturbing. I mean – they come and go, you know? So sometimes I think, yum and sometimes, yuck – well, no, I don't actually think or feel 'yuck,' but I just think – weird. Like those feelings are not – part of my thoughts. Why are you looking at me like that?"

He had his chin resting on his hand, a soft look in his eyes and a small smile. He chuckled.

"Sounds like you've definitely got the hots for someone. Can I guess we're talking about Les here?"

"No!" she yelped. "I mean – yes – sort of – but I don't know how I *feel*!"

"Apart from horny?" He was grinning broadly now.

"Yuck! Stop it! I meant – if I like him…" She was writhing in her seat with embarrassment. "Fine, for whatever bizarre reason, some maladjusted part of me finds him physically attractive, on some buried level. But he's so weird. Can you see us together?"

"If you stand next to each other, yeah," Ray joked.

"Be *serious*."

"Okay, try this." He picked up his book again, flipped backwards through the pages, and began to read. "Often we ask whether someone is right for us, without clarifying what 'right' may be. We may feel guilty about our desire and want to justify it by placing it in the context of a relationship with long-term possibilities. We may be unsure about our own feelings and try to reassure ourselves with proof of compatibility: similar backgrounds, interests, jobs and so forth. We may have expectations about our own future which we want someone else to fulfill, whether that's a big house in the suburbs or a life of travel and adventure. Of course, all these other things are important to us: long-term relationships, compatibility, the lifestyle we want to create for ourselves. What is most important in a relationship, however, is the other person. Too often, we end up making love to our own dreams of the future or our own check-list. When the dreams coincide, two people can live happily together for years before waking up and realizing that the other person has been a stranger the entire time. They have projected their own desires onto their mates as if onto a screen.

A spiritual seduction is seducing someone's soul, and unless you learn what that looks like, it will be impossible. Rather than asking, 'Is this person right for me?' we should ask 'What does this person's soul look like?' Once we have answered that question, the rest becomes clear."

Ray looked up. Dawn was staring at him, lips parted. Everything was coming clear for her. The words showed Marianne's own approach to relationships: why she adored Ray, despite the constant arguments, and why it must have cut so deeply when he ended it. Equally, Marianne's words illuminated her own conflicted feelings towards Les and how her negative judgments were so shallowly based on how she, herself, wanted to be perceived. The biggest shock, however, was the change in Ray. He'd read that aloud with absolute seriousness – the same man who, a few months before, had called souls "spiritualist bull."

"Is that – um – helpful?" asked Ray uncertainly.

Dawn nodded slowly, wide-eyed. "Very."

Okay, Les, she resolved, *Let's see where this goes. I'll get to know your soul. And maybe your body, in the bargain.*

Les's house was like a warm cocoon of love. His mother was Italian – not American Italian, but had emigrated from Italy when Les was two. Their origins showed in the décor: a soothing simple muddle. In the kitchen, the units were painted green and pots, strings of garlic and a branch of bay leaves hung in easy reach of the stove. The large kitchen table was well-scrubbed wood and the ceramic crockery was chunky, plain and beautiful. Within their Florida house, Les's "Mamma" Oriana, had created the interior of an Italian villa. No TV screen adorned the fridge or hung on a wall of the living room and nobody muttered commands for lighting or music to control panels. It was like stepping back in time. With easy contentment, the two hosts lit candles, opened red wine, chose music manually, creating a homeliness that brought a lump to Dawn's throat. She thought wistfully of being part of a family like that – then remembered, it was just the two of them, like Ray and her. She wondered whether visitors to their own house felt the same sense of being included in a circle of love. She hoped so.

Dawn complimented Oriana on the food and the woman laughed heartily, telling her to flatter her instead for her mothering skills – the beautiful lasagna had been all Les's making. They splashed wine bountifully into her glass and Dawn muttered nervously that her brother didn't like her drinking much.

"Nonsense!" cried Oriana. "A meal without wine is like a day without sun, tell *that* to your brother."

They talked about the differences between Italy and the States, about how hard it was to find unprocessed food to cook with these days and about Dawn's future plans. She tentatively put forward her idea of traveling around Europe, with a flickering glance towards Les. Oriana seemed to think it was an excellent idea and that a year spent traveling was far from wasted. All the young people in Europe did this, she explained. One must see something of the world, she said, learn other cultures, or one ended up thinking that his or her little part of it was all that mattered and that his or her ways were the only right ways. Her eyes shone with joy when she spoke about places in Italy that Dawn should visit.

By the end of the evening, Dawn was swimming in her unstinting approval and roaring with laughter at her stories of Les's childhood idiosyncrasies.

"So then," said Oriana, wiping tears of mirth from her eyes, "He comes to me when he's ten and says, 'Mamma, I know what I'm going to do when I grow up. If I'm the cleverest boy in the world, it's my job to learn everything I can and find out everything I can, so people have a head start when I die!'"

Dawn choked down her wine. "The cleverest boy in the world?" she laughed.

"I didn't say," muttered Les to his mother, caught between embarrassment and pleasure. He explained hesitantly to Dawn that his IQ was the highest on record, then hastily went on to explain the statistical difficulties with recording IQ at those levels and some of the criticisms around IQ tests. Halfway through his explanation, Dawn cut him short.

"Don't worry…" she slurred, "you just convinced me."

They finished the meal with imported cheese, grapes and Vin Santo, sitting out on the porch by candlelight. Around them, wild jasmine ran riot up the pillars and onto the roof, the tiny leaves and buds making a soft veiled overhang. Their yard was laid out as a formal, ornamental garden and the late evening breeze carried the whispering scent of flowers and the warm scent of the central bay tree. When Oriana stood up and began to clear away the dishes, the other two leapt to their feet.

"No – no," she insisted. "You two sit here, let me be a proper Italian mother for once." She poured more Vin Santo into each of their glasses and disappeared into the kitchen.

Left alone, Dawn and Les continued to chat quietly, increasingly distracted by each other's eyes and the shape of their lips. After a long silence spent gazing at each other, Les said "I'd like to kiss you." The heavenly sweet wine must have given him courage, he thought, but still terror at his own words made his insides flip over.

"Okay," whispered Dawn and leaned forward.

10

After all of Ray's preparations for the last mission, he had only some brushing-up to do for this one. Physically, it seemed speed-of-light travel wasn't demanding, but he put the hours in anyway. He knew the ship itself so well by now that he thought he could reassemble it blindfolded. All the same, revision was never wasted. In addition to his previous training régime, he was privately embarking on exercises of his own. This time, he'd be prepared – mind, body and soul. Late in the evening, when most of the building was empty, he locked his office door and took out the VEC machine. The others spoke of "talking to God" in the mission, but if there was conversation involved, it was of a different order. Once more, he fastened the headset in place and pressed play.

The limits of his physical existence fell away. He sloughed them off, like a cloud of light bursting through old rags that crumbled and dwindled away. He was limitless, because he was connected. Threads of light flickered around him, and his own light merged with them. In the sea of splendorous light, he could feel a vast pulse, like millions of hearts beating in time.

We are all one. We are all connected. Simply allow…simply connect.

The small confines of his body had kept him believing that as all people were physically separate, so their minds, souls and destinies were separate. He flowed along the light like a surfer carried by the huge barreling power of a twenty-meter breaker. Triumph and awe surged through him. The wave broke, pulling him deep into the flow, tumbling and churning him. He gave himself up to being rolled and tossed about by the golden currents of Love, his soul yelling *Yes!*

Yes! in glee and laughter. The hopes and desires of every soul in the world were here, and only the joyous Love that embraced him kept him from weeping for eternity as he sensed their longings. *I'm here, I'm here…* whispered the divine force, soothingly. *I'm here, I'm here…* he crooned in turn to the tender souls of which he was a part. He felt Marianne's mantras and Dawn's anxious wishes and felt his own love-light enfold them – except it wasn't just his own, he was a part of something infinite, he was tiny and everywhere. The sweet, rippling waters of gold reached out to flow around the innocent, the seekers, and those who were newly-freed from the confines of perceived mortality. It flowed around those returning to the physical world where confusion would soon settle in, the earthbound ones who looked to the sky and yearned to see beyond, the children who prayed beneath the careful watch of nuns and grandmothers, the devoted, the unsure and the ignorant… They were all here, and the light strove to reach them all, to heal them all, and to connect them all. Love flowed unstinting to conscious believers and non-believers alike. It flowed to those who made the trade agreements, developed scientific hypothesis and bought the utilities, who recycled and reused, who protested and who obeyed, who made shrewd financial decisions, and who bought lottery tickets. To everyone, regardless of what their focus, it whispered *I'm here – I'm here – simply connect…*

We are coming to meet you, cried Ray in his soul, *to teach you how to know the Truth…*

Simply connect.

We'll come – for real – this is still a simulation… He knew the words were untrue. What he was experiencing could not be simulated. Love washed him back and forth as understanding grew deep within him. Speed-of-light travel was just a means among many to know this Truth.

Throughout the history of the world, Love had always been within reach, the underlying truth of existence. His emotional wounds and the fears he gathered like briars to protect his heart were what closed him off from what would heal him. Speed-of-light travel and the VEC served to thrust him where on his own he hadn't dared to go – but now he dared. Now, those seeping sores were washed clean and the lessons of Love burned inside him. There were no "others" to do unto – all were one.

Ray laid the headset on the desk and stood. He was about to do something he would once have dismissed as utter madness. Now it seemed the madness had been his absolute intellectual arrogance; so sure that the limits of his mind were the limits of the world. He closed his eyes and opened up. The limits of his physical existence fell away. He sloughed them off, like a cloud of light bursting through old rags that crumbled and dwindled. He was limitless, because he was connected.

He floated downstream, placid and unquestioning. Around him, the sides of the tightly-woven basket rose, quiet golden-beige like old straw. He watched the leaves of the overhanging trees float above him. In layers, they caught the light and passed it downwards, creating a full spectrum of greens and soft green shadows, and cutting the blue sky into little shapes. He laughed as the dappled sunlight ran over his face and stretched up an arm as if to catch the trailing leaves. The soft rocking of the water lulled him. His eyes began to open and close lazily, until his eyelashes fell against his cheeks and his breathing grew long and steady.

When he opened them again, the sky was dark violet with a single star burning in it. Marianne stood by him, waist-deep in water and crooning softly, her dark eyes shining with love. She gathered him to her, carrying him easily to the bank and there he lay in her lap gazing gladly upwards. His hand ran across her smooth jaw and was rewarded with a beam of pleasure. Her arm supported his head and his cheek pressed against the soft swell of her breast. She sang softly as she rocked him, her pure voice piercing the air with sweetness. The song explained that he was safe and had no cause for worry; that all was taken care of and only this remained: to feel the peace of her cradling arms.

"Heaven…" he whispered, snuggling closer into the warmth of her.

"Yes," she said tenderly. "This is your heaven."

Through the glass doors of the coffee shop, Marianne could see Dawn sitting at a table, stirring her coffee and staring off into space. She lingered on the pavement, waving with her free hand and gesturing at the cell phone clamped to her ear. Her publisher was on the line, anxious for news of how *Inner Light* was progressing.

"What I write comes from very deep and personal spiritual developments," Marianne said. "These are not the sort of things that can just be hurried along. I have to experience the wisdom of the Inner Light myself before I can pass those teachings on."

The editor chirruped in her ear, making flattering remarks about how eagerly everyone awaited her next book and more anxious remarks about printing schedules and publication slots.

"I understand you have a lot of practical concerns that are very important," soothed Marianne, "and everyone must respect the organization that you put into the whole process, to make books like this possible. I really appreciate the efforts you go to. I know that as soon as *Inner Light* is ready, you will do wonders with it."

The conversation wound up with the editor feeling gratified and Marianne not having committed to a deadline. How could she? She felt cut off from any sense of the divine force and the only thing lighting her inners was the sexy VEC boys. She had no genuine spiritual advice to give anyone and refused to make it up. Sometimes, she thought even the editor suspected that her writing was a lot of meaningful-sounding nonsense, rather than her sincerest distillations of her own experience and connection to what was higher.

She slid into the chair opposite Dawn, who signaled for the waitress.

"We could just head over to my place instead," said Marianne. "I've bought us the most divine new VEC program…" From her bag, she pulled the little case. On its cover was a breathtaking waterfall, above which stood South American cliff-divers wearing teeny-tiny little loincloths. "Yummy or what?"

"Marianne…" Dawn took a deep breath. "I think I'm going to take a little reprieve from all the VEC fantasies we've been sharing."

"Oh. Okay. Well, I guess I'll have a latte, then." She was visibly disappointed.

Uncomfortably, Dawn tried to explain. "I think maybe my brother's right about VECs, in a way – that all these fantasies are a wonderful escape, but it's also becoming an excuse not to face up to reality, a real life, a real future."

"Well, he can just add it to the list of things he disapproves of in me," said Marianne, tears springing into her eyes. Dawn winced. Her other reason was going to sound doubly harsh, given Marianne's hurt.

"I've met a guy – a real guy," she said in a small voice. "And I keep comparing him to these fantasy men with perfect jaws and hunky bodies and I don't want that, I want to learn about *him,* learn his soul, like you said in *The Spiritual Seduction.*"

The waitress brought over Marianne's latte and another coffee for Dawn. When she'd withdrawn, Marianne spoke.

"Here's *The Spiritual Seduction Part Two,*" she said

bitterly. "It goes like this: 'don't bother, it doesn't work.'"

"Marianne..." protested Dawn.

"Well, it doesn't!" She swiped a tear from her eye fumble with a napkin. "But it's so true – so wise..."

Marianne sat pondering a moment before she replied. "All my so-called wisdom is just old ideas in new wrapping paper," she said. "We have this ridiculous old-fashioned notion that we're supposed to find Mr. Right and have a happily-ever-after and that book was just one more desperate attempt to make something that doesn't exist real. I thought at the time, maybe if you try to match souls, it'll work – but for Christ's sake, what's the 'soul' anyway? 'Find out what someone's soul looks like' – honestly! It's all bull, wistful self-deception; Maybe This Time, Lady Peaceful... Trying to shore up an illusion we'd do better to abandon."

"But you can't say love's an illusion!" wailed Dawn. She had never seen Marianne so hard and bitter.

Marianne's eyes, half-slit, met hers. "Oh no," she said acridly, "It's real alright – a real collection of delusions and doomed ideals. You know, we're all brought up with this mythical wonder of falling in love. The whole fairy tale with Prince Charming riding up on his white horse and sweeping you off your feet. Romance and adventure and plenty of beautiful children. Then growing old together in each other's arms. And all the time, quite enraptured and dizzied by each other, sharing everything, passionate, yadda yadda yadda. You know, the whole fairytale dream young women are poisoned with. Look around you, Dawn." Her hand swept the coffee shop. "Guess what? It's *not true*. It's as much an illusion as anything in the VEC. We all think we're destined to be gloriously happy in love forever with one perfect man, and we're not. And if we ever, once, had the courage to look at the world honestly, we'd realize that. I don't want to see you go through what I went through; chasing rainbows, getting my heart smashed into little bits again and again, learning the hard way and ending up so hurt and bitter. If you can believe my books, why can't you believe *me*?"

"Because this time I think you're wrong," said Dawn.

"Dawn – please don't take this the wrong way, but you're young and naïve."

"Okay, I'll try not to." Dawn laughed and Marianne joined in reluctantly.

"I'm serious, though. I was young and naïve too and I love you like a kid sister. I don't want you to experience all the pain and disappointment that I went through. Your brother was my last attempt – hoping against hope – General Custer's last stand. And it blew up in my face, just like every time before."

"Ray's – changed," said Dawn hesitantly.

"Yup, he used to love me," said Marianne shortly.

"I mean… since then." With a modicum of trepidation, she began to describe the alterations she'd observed in her brother's behavior. He was taking a genuine, caring interest in her political causes that he used to laugh at. He even wanted to become involved in them. He'd become more environmentally aware, careful not to buy or use anything with wasteful packaging. He bought eco-friendly cleaning products. He listened to other people's ideas. The change was in none of these things – they were symptoms of a cause that Dawn couldn't identify, but somehow his rigidity had softened; he had warmed and gentled. "And he's reading your books – not to pick holes in them, but sincerely wanting to learn from them. He even quotes them."

Marianne gaped at her. Dawn examined the dregs of her coffee, wondering whether to make one final revelation. It could be seen as a betrayal of trust – by the old Ray. This new Ray might just understand her reasoning and that Marianne needed to know this.

A few evenings before, Ray had opened up to her about his and Marianne's break-up. He'd confessed – there was no other word for it – to being unreasonable and rigid with tears in his eyes. The pain he felt at wounding her was equal to what Marianne was suffering. At first haltingly, then all in a rush, he'd poured out his heart about why he'd been so angry, how he'd used his own fears to lash out at Marianne in the name of righteousness, how he was rethinking all his beliefs and so desperately wanted to speak to Marianne about it. Dawn asked where his sudden change of heart had come from and he'd shaken his head.

"I can't tell you – not yet – not until I'm sure about it… But that's the thing, you see, I don't dare tell anyone until I'm sure, so how can I tell Marianne? What if I change my mind again and go back to how I was before? God, I love her Dawn. I love her *so much* that I would rather never see her again than cause her pain."

What Ray didn't know, which Dawn could see at this moment in front of her, was that he was still causing Marianne pain. While he was coming around to her way of thinking, she was abandoning all her beliefs in despair, nursing her heartache with bitterness. Dawn sighed, accepting the risk. The old Ray would never have forgiven her, but who knew how the new Ray would react?

"Let's have another coffee," she said. "There's something else I want to tell you."

The high-angled shot from the hidden camera showed Ray sitting at this desk, eyes shut, a VEC headset strapped on. Only the time counter at the bottom of the screen indicated any change.

"So what?" said Warren. "Sky's using a VEC like everyone else on the planet."

"Keep watching," said the CIA Director.

The two were in the Vice-President's office, sitting on the central armchairs facing the flat screen on the wall. On the table in front of them sat a remote, next to a bowl of pale peach roses. Warren hated them. Housekeeping insisted on putting the damned things in his office every day, making it look like some mamby-pamby gracious home with all womanly touches. The only womanly touch he liked was the kind that wielded a whip.

On the screen, Ray took the headset off and stood up. His image began to flicker in and out of sight, and then vanished completely.

"What the fuck!" exclaimed Warren. "Did he tamper with the video…"

Director Black shook his head, pointing at the timer continuing in the corner. "Keep watching," he said.

"What am I watching?" snapped Warren. "It's an empty room! If this is some kind of technical fuck-up…"

Ray flickered back into visibility and Warren stared as the astronaut put the headset away, locked his drawer and left the office.

"Jesus Christ, how did he do that?" he whispered, as Steven skipped backwards to the moment of vanishing.

"We don't know – but it's not a technical failure, we know that much."

Warren let out a long stream of air through his nostrils. He stood, indicating the meeting was over. As he ushered Steven out, he said, "I want to see what Sky was looking at on that VEC. Get it discreetly."

"Understood." Steven nodded. It would be an easy enough job for one of his agents.

In Thomas's office, the Head of NASA was briefing Ray and Jack on their mission, a sheaf of papers from the White House on his desk. It would be called "Newest Testament," he said, and would be a stealth mission from the secret launch pad the military used for their Star Wars exercises. Absolute secrecy was required, which included no information being passed to family members or close friends. Their cover would be a meeting in New York City with the military, to brainstorm how light speed could be used for defense purposes. The alleged meeting would also be classified as top secret, so if anyone asked what they were doing that weekend they should reply that it was classified. Confidential footage would be taken for publicity purposes, if the mission were deemed successful.

Ray listened with half an ear, preoccupied by other things. Thomas turned the page and sighed.

"You're going to love this," he said wearily. The administration had compiled a list of questions to ask God and he passed copies to Ray and Jack. Ray glanced at them and looked away again. The list was pointless. Whatever communication could exist with the divine force, it wasn't of the question-and-answer variety.

Jack began to read the questions aloud in disgust. "When is the Second Coming of Jesus Christ? When is the rapture going to occur? How do we convince the world to take Jesus as their personal savior? What kind of bullshit questions are these? I'm not going to ask God these questions!"

"What do you expect from this president?" said Thomas. "He's a born-again Christian, for fuck's sake. Whatever you may want to ask, that's what *he* wants to know."

"We don't need to go," said Ray quietly.

The other two looked at him, surprised. He was staring out the window unseeing, lost in thought.

"What was that, Ray?" asked Jack.

"We don't need to go," repeated Ray. He turned to face them. "I think we can access God directly – we don't need to go the speed-of-light to make it happen."

"And how do we do that?" said Thomas skeptically.

Ray half-shrugged, shyly. "Just...connect," he said. "Forget the pain – just feel love – and connect. That's all."

Jack rose, concerned, and walked over to Ray. With his hand on the younger man's shoulder, he said gently, "Ray – I really appreciate your newfound spiritual enlightenment, but you learned that from an AI chip in a VEC simulating God. We're going to find the real God."

Ray was shaking his head. "I've done it without the VEC."

Jack and Thomas swapped a look that said all too clearly, *the boy's losing it, humor him.*

"That's great, Ray," said Jack gently, "but what the world really needs now is scientific proof of God's existence and that's what this mission will provide for us."

Ray shrugged again. "I'll go," he said, "but it's not necessary."

The barbecue's spray of red-gold sparks showered through the darkness like tiny meteors. From the house, music trickled out into the night. The smoky scent lingered thick in the air, clinging to Dawn's hair and making her feel nostalgic. She and Ray had just finished eating in the fading light and now sat together in the dark, roasting marshmallows. Held just above the heat and turned carefully, the outside would turn to a golden shell, full of sticky melted sweetness inside. Occasionally, one would escape its stick and slip slowly off onto the coals, where it bubbled, filling the air with burnt sugar.

"I've got to go away for the weekend, Dawn" said Ray. "Is there anyone you want to stay with? Les is going to be with me, unfortunately."

"I don't think we've reached that point yet, anyway." Dawn gave a little laugh and withdrew her marshmallow from above the embers. "Do you want this one? I'm stuffed."

Ray ate it and Dawn stared dreamily at the dying fire, thinking about kissing Les. He was so gentle and uncertain that she wondered if he'd kissed anyone before. She couldn't ask, not yet. She smiled, remembering the taste of his mouth mingled with sweet wine and the bolt of lightning that had run through both of them when their tongues touched. She speared another marshmallow and began roasting it, for the pleasure of watching it change color and to have something to give Ray.

"What do you want to do, then?" said Ray. He knew she hated being in the house alone.

"I could..." Dawn stopped. She hadn't told him about her friendship with Marianne, but perhaps now was as good a time as any. "I hope this doesn't upset you," she began cautiously, and started explaining how she and Marianne had become close, from Dawn first seeking her advice to really enjoying each other's company.

"I'm glad," said Ray softly. "Glad that she's had you as a friend – your company could cheer up anyone... So will you stay with her for the weekend?"

Dawn nodded. "I'm sure she wouldn't mind. But Ray – there's something else. And I really don't know how you're going to feel about this, but it seemed like completely the right thing to do at the time. Because she was getting into such a bad place and I just couldn't stand seeing her like that – so and hurt and hardening..."

Ray winced, his heart twisting inside him. "Go on," he said.

She told him about Marianne's struggles to write her next book and how severed she felt from her own spirituality now, to the point of repudiating everything she had written.

"I don't think she's really stopped believing," said Dawn, "but it was like she'd given up hope – that if that soul-connection she felt with you wasn't true, or could just vanish, then maybe she'd been misled about everything. Then I told her something I had no right to tell her, but I was worried that maybe if you left it any longer she'd be so bitter that she wouldn't..."

"Trust me again?" said Ray, sadly.

"Trust *anything* again." She passed him the roasted marshmallow and started on another. "I told her how much you've changed – and you *have* changed, Ray, in the nicest ways. It's like I have a brand-new brother, everything you were, only…better, somehow."

Ray smiled, though his eyes were misted at the thought of Marianne's misery. To have not only hurt her, but caused her to doubt her own pure spirituality…

"And I told her what you told me," admitted Dawn. "About still loving her – and afraid to ask her to risk her heart again. I'm sorry. I just thought she really needed to know that right then."

Ray's eyes brightened, his heart beating faster. He sat up straight. "What did she say?" he asked anxiously.

Dawn smiled. "Oh, I see how it is. I'm the go-between. She said – well, the exact words were that she couldn't get any more unhappy than she was already, so maybe it was worth a shot."

Ray covered his face with his hands and Dawn ruffled his hair with her free hand.

"Don't look so despondent, you twit, that was sad-girl-speak for yes, okay? She wants to meet up."

"I'll call her now!" said Ray, leaping up. He glanced at his watch. "Shit – it's eleven. Okay, tomorrow – oh shit, the…" He caught himself before he said "mission" and finished lamely, "'meeting." *Meeting with the divine force*, he thought wryly. "Maybe I can meet her on Monday when I get back?"

"Consider me your carrier-pigeon," laughed Dawn. She passed over the last marshmallow and leaned back, her face resting from the heat of the fire.

They sat in comfortable silence, listening to the distant music and the quiet hiss of the barbecue. The playlist was their own family compilation, made together when Dawn was thirteen and getting into making playlists. It was full of cheesy classics and long-forgotten pop one-hit wonders. Dawn sang along softly, every beat and note a familiar friend.

"Your results come out on Wednesday, don't they?" said Ray. She nodded, nerves suddenly fluttering in her stomach.

She deserved top grades, she knew, but whether she'd get them was an open question. "We'll go out for dinner, to celebrate – don't look like that, of course we'll be celebrating."

Dawn smiled.

":And then? Do you still want to go traveling?"

"Yeah…" she admitted. "Oriana – Les's mom – thought it was a really good idea, that seeing something of the world was as important as starting a career. Especially if I'm not sure what the career is, yet."

Ray leaned forward, stirring the coals to help them die, and sending another shower of sparks into the air.

"I'm warming up to the idea," he said. "I think my issue with it – at least partly, is that I just didn't want you to go." He gave a lopsided grin. "You're quite nice to have around the place."

"Thanks a bunch," said Dawn lightly.

"And I suppose I'm still trying to – look after you. But you're a big girl, so if you want to go, you should. You need any help, planning?"

Dawn's heart rose as he spoke and she smiled hugely. "I'd love some!"

Ray stood up. "We can look at it together when I get back. Time to turn in, though. I'll be leaving straight from work tomorrow. And you'll speak to Marianne for me? Promise?"

"Promise." Dawn said, beaming.

Ray and Jack were gearing up, fastening the bulky white spacesuits over the little vest and long-sleeved tees they wore beneath. Ray looked down at himself and grinned, thinking of marshmallows. Just so long as God didn't mistake them, spear them and slowly roast them over the sun, they might be okay. He chuckled. The thought of seeing Marianne again was singing in his heart. Dawn was the perfect ambassador for this situation. She knew him well enough, and loved him enough, to ring the changes without implying he'd turned into some kind of saint. Some of the thoughts that flowed through his mind concerning Marianne were far from saintly. It wouldn't be easy – he had so much trust to rebuild – but they had all the time in the world. He could *talk* to her again, and this time really listen to her ideas, in an attempt to understand and not just to disprove.

"Hey, Jack, you know Marianne Summers, don't you?" he said.

"I did," said Jack cautiously.

"You must have worked pretty closely with her when you were writing the book. What do you think of her?" Jack's opinion hardly mattered, but Ray wanted an excuse to talk about her.

"Why do you ask?" Jack asked levelly.

"Oh, we're…" He couldn't say "seeing each other," because that was still up in the air. "I like her," he said instead, grinning.

Jack gave him a sharp look and moved closer so no one else could hear him speak.

"You have to stay away from her," he said in a low voice.

"Why?"

"Okay – I'm not proud of this, but Marianne and I had a pretty passionate affair when we wrote the book together."

"Jack…" Ray's voice was calm, but tight. He had a sudden sense that he didn't want to hear this.

"Hey, it was stupid, I know, but she was young and attractive and writing about spirituality brought us very close together."

"I see," said Ray stiffly.

"Then, when the book was finished, I wanted to end the affair and go our separate ways. Marianne suddenly went psycho on me – she wanted me to leave my wife of twenty-eight years, for Christ's sake! Honestly, Ray – the screaming, the bitching, the scenes… It was not a pretty sight."

Ray breathed in and out deeply, trying to relax his jaw and loosen his suddenly tense muscles. He knew this story, though not quite as Jack represented it. He also knew, to his shame, what Marianne looked like in grief. *When you twist the knife in someone's heart*, he thought furiously, *you do not expect them to look pretty.* His arms were shaking with the desire to beat Jack to a pulp, but he may as well lay into himself. Still – to have lied… To continue to lie and misrepresent her… *Love*, he reminded himself, *Love Love Love, unconditional love – how the hell do you respond to something like that with love?*

"You okay?" said Jack.

"Yeah," said Ray gruffly and then the only thing he could think of. "She must have loved you very much."

Jack grimaced and then shrugged. "Water under the bridge," he said. "Let's go."

Warren tore off the headset and flung it on his desk, shaking. Steven Black jumped in alarm – the Vice-President had pressed play only a few seconds before. His face was now black with fury.

"Implement code 'lights-out,'" he growled. "*Now*"

Steven blinked, shocked. "Is that really necessary, sir?"

"It's a matter of national security!" barked Warren. "We need code 'lights-out' initiated *immediately* and do not question my orders!"

"Understood, sir. I'm not questioning your orders, sir – but what is on that program that's so dangerous?"

"Some of the most seditious bullshit I have ever… If this got out, if this got out to the masses, it would undermine our entire society and way of life." He leapt to his feet, pacing the length of his office. "Everything on that program goes contrary to this country's honor and national pride. It's a whole lot of fucked-up crap about loving everyone just the same, unconditionally – *unconditionally!*" He spat. "Including those fucking Arabs who're stealing our oil and every psycho little layabout…" He paused, mid-stride, trembling with rage. His eyes fell on the bowl of fresh roses, pink this time, and he kicked it across the room. The glass smashed on the opposite wall, ricocheting in a mess of shards, flying water and battered blooms.

"Lights-out," he said shortly to Steven. "And destroy that program. Make sure not a single copy gets out."

The Earth lay before them in all its marbled splendor. The sloping curve of its horizon filled their screen, a blurred arc of bluish atmosphere bordering the planet from the black reaches of space. Foreshortened countries sloped off into the distance, with swathes of green and patches of brownish grey showing vast metropolises or the ever-expanding deserts. Between them, dwarfing them, were the huge deep blue oceans, a colossal, interconnected body of water clinging to, and sustaining the planet. Swirls of cloud hovered white over everything, patchy, streaked, scattered or in huge whirling clumps. Ray thought he could see the remnants of Arctic ice, but it may just have been drifts of cloud. For once, he had no pre-flight nerves, just a sense of happy wonder.

"All systems go?" came Thomas's voice from ground control.

Ray glanced at Jack, who nodded. "All systems go," replied Ray, his fingers already moving across the control panel.

"Godspeed, men." said Thomas over the countdown.
The ship vanished in a brief burst of flame.

13

"What the *hell* was that? Ray!" screamed Thomas. "Jack! Come in! Solar, this is ground control, *report* for Christ's sake!"

He was hunched over the desk, roaring into the microphone. Around him, technicians and engineers ran helplessly from workstation to workstation or frantically keyed instructions into their computers. A few just sat, frozen, their hands halfway towards their mouths, their faces staring and immobile.

"Give me visuals, for god's sake!" yelled Thomas to the room, swinging instantly back to the microphone. "Solar – come in Solar, this is ground control – come in Solar…" he repeated, like a mantra.

Next to him, Les's fingers flew over his keyboard, his face white.

"Thomas," he said hoarsely, "I have visuals."

Calm descended on Ray. Peaceful joy subsumed him. After all the determination, struggles, wrestling with uncertainty and fearfully tentative hope, he found a sense of understanding here. He floated in an ocean of burning golden light, its particles interweaving seamlessly with his, rising and falling gently with the waves. The limits of his physical existence fell away. He sloughed them off, like a cloud of light bursting through old rags that crumbled and dwindled.

Thomas raised his head slowly from the microphone, still repeating his plea, which faded into silence as he saw what the screen revealed.

"Dear god…" he whispered. Others in the room turned to the huge central screen, their activity dying away.

Everyone stilled, speechless, just watching.

A whitish-peach cloud, huge at the center and streaking out at the edges, burned against the blackness of space. What seemed to be a cloud of blurry dust around it were fragments of the spaceship, spinning away. Destruction and debris were all that remained.

Thomas lowered his mouth to the microphone again, opened it to speak and sat down heavily. "Ray..." he whispered. "Jack..."

The Director of the CIA knocked briskly on the Vice-President's door. Unlike other visitors, he didn't enter through the secretary's antechamber, nor did he need her permission. He opened the door. Warren was standing by the window, a drink in his hand. Steven cleared his throat.

"Mr. Vice-President – code 'lights-out' has been successfully implemented. It is done."

Warren nodded, sipping his whisky without taking his eyes from the window. "It's time," he said.

"For what, sir?"

"Implement Mission Rapture."

Steven blanched. "Mr. Vice-President – with all due respect – are you sure...?"

Warren turned at last, his eyes as cold as death. Steven knew killers. He hired them, trained them and deployed them. The CIA was less about death than people imagined and more about it than they knew. He had his cadre and he saw their eyes when they reported back from a successful mission. Some were guarded and wary, some inscrutable, some determinedly honest, but all those gazes were masks. The Vice-President's eyes were stripped bare of any pretense to humanity.

"The President..." began Steven, trying not to show his desperation.

"The President is an ass, as you and I both know," said Warren. "But if he took it into his head that you were no longer fit to be Director of the CIA, I don't know that I'd be able to dissuade him. He may have put the CIA under my jurisdiction, but he still has the final say over any appointments."

The threat was clear and Steven nodded. Warren turned away again.

"It's time to purify the world of evil," he said. "We finally have a clean, decisive way to do it. Initiate Mission Rapture…now."

"Yes, sir."

Dawn and Marianne were lazing around Marianne's apartment. The mid-August weather was too hot for anything but sarongs and iced coffee. The faint breeze that floated in the open balcony doors carried sticky humidity with it. The two women preferred the open air of the outdoors as opposed to air-conditioning.

"Ice," said Dawn wistfully. "Snow. Mountain rivers. All manner of cool things…"

Marianne stretched lazily across the floor, her laptop open in front of her.

"Kin sends bucks for charity," she said. "Eight letters – fourth letter D."

Dawn looked up at the ceiling thoughtfully. "Kindness," she said after a moment.

Marianne twisted to look at her. "How'd you get that?"

"Bucks – jumps, so it's an anagram of kin sends. For charity is kindness."

Marianne whistled. "Not just a pretty face," she teased. "So that's what your genius boyfriend sees in you."

Dawn giggled. "Yeah," she said, "he explodes assumptions about space-time theory and I solve cryptic crosswords. Together we'll conquer the world!"

Marianne laughed and stood up, re-knotting her sarong around her neck. "More coffee?"

"Mmm… I keep thinking about swimming in the sea and then remembering there's no shade on the beach." She wrinkled her nose up at the thought of sandy stretches of hot sunshine.

"You could take a dip in the horizon pool," called Marianne from the kitchen.

"Nah," called back Dawn. "Not unless they've got a Les simulation in there to replace Kirk and Dirk… All those muscular tanned bodies just don't do it for me. Give me pale and scrawny every time." She flopped back onto the floor contentedly, disappearing into a happy fantasy world until Marianne came back with icy frothy coffee.

They sat on either side of the knee-high table, sipping their coffee and talking. Dawn traced the carvings with her finger. "I like this," she said. "Where'd you get it?"

"India. I went looking for spiritual enlightenment and found a table instead. Fair swap. Although they probably wouldn't have charged excess baggage for the spiritual enlightenment." She took a thoughtful sip of coffee and issued a contented sigh. "Tell me again how much Ray loves me," she said dreamily.

For the fourth time, Dawn repeated every word he'd said on the subject, finishing again with the explanation, "and he was scared to say anything in case he hurt you again."

Marianne had a blissful, far-away look in her eyes. "I know this must be the grossest thought for you ever, but I would really, *really* like to have sex with your brother…"

"Just don't confide in me with the details," said Dawn. "In principle, I'm all for the idea. But spare me the nitty-gritty."

Marianne chuckled. "So I shouldn't talk about his powerful muscular arms?" she taunted. "Or his hard-packed chest? Or his…"

Dawn swatted her over the head with a cushion. "If you tell me that, I'll tell you what his farts smell like."

Marianne squealed. "Okay! Touché. We keep our

information to ourselves. Hey, you want a tarot reading?"

With the thought of Ray's still-constant love, all Marianne's energy and light had come rushing back into her. Overnight, ideas and thoughts for her book had swarmed into her head, from whatever forgotten place they had been locked. As she guided Dawn through shuffling and laying out the cards, she felt her connection with the divine force locking into place once more. Dawn turned the cards over and Marianne leaned forward to look. Her eyes clouded with alarm.

"Isn't that Death?" asked Dawn nervously.

"It doesn't usually mean literal death," replied Marianne automatically, scanning the cards with growing anxiety. The major arcana, the all-important archetype cards that weren't found in normal playing decks, were all over the reading: Death, as Dawn had pointed out; the Tower; the Devil and the Magician both reversed; and – thank goodness – the Star. It was the only bright spot in the spread and sat in the position of Final Outcome – new hope of sweetness. Everything else was bleak. The card signifying Dawn in the future was the three of swords, anguish and misery. That echoed the central card representing Dawn: the Queen of Swords, her head bowed with sorrow, one hand clasping the upraised sword and the other stretched out, open, facing down, letting go of things once dear. Another sword card, the seven, showed her in an environment of dangerous deceit.

Marianne bit her lip sadly. One didn't cheat the cards, whether by asking and then refusing to read the answer or lying about what they said. Haltingly, she took Dawn through the distressing tale they revealed, emphasizing as much as she dared the positive outcome.

"What did you ask?" she said, after the reading was complete.

"Nothing," said Dawn, her eyes puzzled and anxious. "Should I have?" She studied the cards again miserably. "Could this be about Les?"

"I don't know," said Marianne. "But normally – for something about a love affair, I'd expect to see more cups." She swept the cards up and slid them back into the pack.

The reading cast a pall over the afternoon, which grew hotter and more humid as the tropical storm clouds gathered. After listlessly trying to finish the crossword, they agreed to watch a comedy to cheer them up.

"By the time we finish it should've rained and it'll be cool enough to go out for dinner. TV on," said Marianne, as Dawn drew the blinds.

The screen scissored into life, showing the news channel, and Marianne opened her mouth to order up the video collection before the image hit home. "Sound – up," she said tightly. Dawn turned around.

The news anchor's tie was black and his voice tense as he spoke. "We now have confirmation that both Los Angeles and the city of New York have been hit by terrorist attacks." The picture behind him zoomed in and filled the screen with a massive heap of rubble, chunks of grey concrete tumbled around twisted iron girders. Firemen moved around the edges, their uniforms covered in thick grey dust. A half-crouched woman, her hair matted with soot and dirt, was helped away from the scene. The news anchor was still speaking.

"It is now being reported that at 1:10 pm Eastern Standard Time, explosive devices were detonated in both the Hollywood section of Los Angeles and the Upper East Side of Manhattan, possibly killing hundreds of innocent Americans. At this point, as you can see, emergency personnel are frantically looking for survivors as a devastated nation looks on in agony. We do not yet have reliable information on the nature of the devices – only that they were powerful enough to decimate these massive buildings. We now have Susan Sparks reporting in Central Park. Susan."

The image switched abruptly to an attractive woman in her mid-thirties, her hair disheveled by a protective hat, standing in front of another scene of destruction.

"John, I'm being told by city officials that ground zero of the detonation was the Hancock building on the Upper East Side of Manhattan, where Adam Enterprises is headquartered. Adam Enterprise, as people may know, is the provider of the RUSH programming for VEC simulators. It's obvious that the terrorists knew they were targeting a symbol of our way of life and something that is cherished by this nation."

A fireman grabbed her by the arm, yelling something that was cut off as she switched off her microphone. For a few moments of confusion, they shouted silently and Susan Sparks face drained of color. Her lips clearly mouthed "Jesus fucking Christ!" before she swung back to the camera, her microphone blaring back into life.

"John, there are more – there's been another detonation – a suitcase bomb, the area is being evacuated, we are getting out of here!"

The image blackened abruptly and the news anchor returned, his face tense, struggling for professionalism.

"Susan Sparks is now being moved to a place of safety and we will hear more from her once she is out of immediate danger. I'm told we now have Bill Stone reporting from Los Angeles – Bill?"

The camera fixed on Bill was shaking back and forth with the movement of the fire truck he sat in. Other evacuees, their faces terrified, huddled behind him.

"We are in the process of being evacuated, John," he said, his voice shaking. "The authorities have determined said that the explosions are being carried out by small, but powerful devices, referred to as suitcase bombs. They are very small compared to the bombs most of us know about and the residual particle fall-out should be limited, but emergency services are taking no chances in getting people to safety." He took a deep breath, his eyes flashing as he listened to the instructions from his headphone.

"Yes," he said, "Similar to New York City, the ground zero here in Los Angeles was the Bush Building, located in Hollywood and is the headquarters of Eve Enterprises, the providers of PURE programming. Now we know ground zero for both terrorist attacks were the headquarters of VEC program companies, this appears to be a direct message from our enemies, who are attacking our freedoms, our values, and are attempting to destroy something that symbolized our Western way of life."

The image cut to helicopter shots of the scene: a gash in the grid of skyscrapers, the bustle of people like ants scurrying away and a steady flow of vehicles outwards from the center of the city. A few moved against the flow, disgorging white blobs. The news anchor was stumbling through the story as disjointed information came into the studio. "The white figures you see there are emergency services personnel in protective suits. No one can tell us yet what the residual contaminants, if any, down there are, but they are taking no chances while they hunt for survivors. For those who've just joined us – we have just had reports of two or more detonations..." He began to repeat the essential facts again.

Dawn and Marianne looked at each other's pale faces and found their hands clasped tightly together.

"Ray's in New York." Dawn's whisper was so high-pitched that it was almost a squeal. "Marianne..." Her brimming eyes were like saucers.

"It's okay, it's okay," said Marianne wildly, "he wouldn't be in that building, they said that's the RUSH building, he wouldn't be there..."

In their hearts, they began to list the people they knew in New York, trying desperately to think of reasons why they wouldn't be anywhere near the Upper East Side. Dawn scrambled in her bag for her cell phone and, with trembling fingers, scrolled down to Ray's name. It rang five times and then went to voicemail. She pressed redial, again and again, listening to it cut each time to Ray's deep voice saying, "Hi, this is Raymond Sky – please leave a message and I'll get back to you."

"Ray," said Dawn on the fifth attempt, "It's me, for God's sake phone me, I need to know you're okay…"

She hung up and looked at Marianne. "Why hasn't he called? He'll know I'm worried – Marianne, why isn't he *calling?*"

Tears were rolling down Marianne's face as she pulled Dawn into her arms. "He'll call. He'll call, sweetie." She murmured, "The networks will be fucked, everyone will be trying to phone home."

"I'll try again," said Dawn, shaking.

"No – don't, honey – the emergency services need the networks, we can't clog them up."

Dawn nodded and put her phone on her lap, staring at it. They sat in silence, their fingers digging into each other's hands. Marianne looked again at the screen, where the channel was interspersing helicopter footage with shots of evacuees and casualties. Across the bottom of the screen, a scrolling red banner carried the main information. The news anchor was being handed pieces of paper on air, which he seized and scanned before passing on the new details. Every few minutes, the core facts were repeated, with the initial shots of the blast sites repeatedly assaulting their senses. Dawn was crying silently. Marianne felt her heart twisted tight and hard and small inside her as she pushed her fears down each time they rose. She couldn't think about it. She couldn't give into the screaming terror of her imagination – if there was anything to hear, they would hear. There was no reason for Ray to be in that building. He would phone; he would be fine. The cell phone networks were busy. She mustn't work herself up into a frenzy. Someone had to be strong for Dawn. Her thoughts went round and round in this loop, keeping hysteria at bay. After an hour, she went to the liquor cabinet and poured two brandies.

"This is not a drink, this is medicine," she said steadily to Dawn.

Dawn nodded, swiping at the tears streaming down her face, and gulped it down. The fiery liquor burned her throat and she coughed violently.

"Now listen to me," said Marianne and repeated to Dawn everything she had been telling herself. She knocked back her own brandy and set the glass down with unsteady hands. Dawn mimicked Marianne and gulped the rest of hers, face squinching against the sharp attack on her tongue and throat.

"They keep showing that woman's face," said Dawn shakily, looking away from the screen at sunshine outside. "She looks so... scared."

"I know," said Marianne, her mouth twisting back a sob.

Dawn stood and walked away to the window, pulling up the blind. The storm had not yet broken and the air was heavy with the metallic tang that came before lightning. The streets were eerily quiet. Everyone would be inside, glued to their TVs in horror and macabre fascination. She thought of the friends and relatives of the woman, seeing her terror exposed again and again. Why didn't they show her escaping the chaos, or being rescued?

Her cell phone rang and her stomach turned to ice as she lunged for it, scrutinizing the little screen for Ray's name – "Private number" it said. With dread and hope warring against each other in her heart, she pressed the call answer button.

"Hello?" She had to say it twice before any sound came out.

"Dawn? It's Thomas Goodman – from NASA."

"Where's Ray?" yelped Dawn. "Put Ray on the phone – let me speak to him!"

She was staring in Marianne's eyes as she spoke, her own huge with fear.

"Dawn – where are you? Is anyone with you?"

Thomas's voice was shaky.

"Yes, Marianne's here. Just tell me what happened, tell me he's okay!" Dawn yelled.

"Dawn...I'm so sorry. I've got – terrible news..."

Marianne watched Dawn's face freeze in a terrible grimace. Then she screamed, collapsing to the ground as the shrieks tore out of her throat. Marianne leapt across the room, gathering Dawn into her embrace with one arm while she took the phone with the other.

"Thomas, it's Marianne," she said shrilly. Dawn was writhing in her arms, weeping and yelling "No" and "Ray." Her fingernails tore at the carpet.

"I'm sorry, Marianne," said Thomas. His voice was choked. "Ray's been – killed..."

Marianne began to cry, quietly at first, then louder as the gulping sobs forced their way up through her. "What happened?" she moaned, the words distorted.

"New York," said Thomas. "His meeting was in that building – him and Jack..."

When Thomas hung up, he looked at the CIA agent through a film of tears.

"You fucking bastards," he said.

Les walked into the room, his eyes swollen, carrying a tray of ultra-sweet coffees.

"I'm very sorry," said the agent. "But this mission has to remain top-secret – if it wasn't for the terrorist attacks, we'd still have had to give a cover story."

"I've just *lied* to his baby sister about how her brother died," Thomas ground out.

The agent was lowering his head when a crash made both men spin round. Les had dropped the tray, the coffee spraying onto the sides of the desks.

"You...lied to *Dawn*..." He moved toward Thomas, his face contorted with grief. Quick as a snake, the agent dashed forward and grabbed his arm to stop him. Les struggled against the man's grip. Looking into Thomas's eyes, he implored, "Why? Why would you lie to Dawn, Thomas?" Les's mind frantically attempted to sort out the rationale as his emotions became more heated. "Ray's her fucking *life*! Why did you call her? Why didn't you let me speak to – How could you tell her on the *phone*, Thomas?"

Unable to get free from the agent's iron grip, his anger subsided and he stopped struggling. The agent released him and indicated a chair.

"Everyone's in shock, I understand that," he said. He stood at the center of the room, his bearing displaying an authority that his quiet suit belied. He looked around at all the engineers and technicians, his gaze meeting and subduing each one of them. "And I respect the grief you must be feeling for your colleagues. But this flight remains a top-secret mission and we cannot allow that to be compromised. Nobody contacts anybody without my permission and my presence – *nobody*," he emphasized, fixing Les with his eyes. "And nobody leaves this base until there's been a complete debriefing. Is that clear?"

The NASA team nodded.

"Good. Now let's clear that up and get everyone something to eat and drink. We're going to ask you all to stay here overnight as originally planned and hold the debriefing tomorrow when everyone is rested. In the meantime, I'm afraid I'm going to have to ask for your phones."

After two more large brandies and a mug of hot milk heavily dosed with nutmeg, Marianne managed to persuade Dawn to lie down. Her hysteria had given way, eventually, to a catatonic obedience. She'd now escaped into the merciful oblivion of deep sleep. Alone in the living room, the TV still on with the sound down low, Marianne had the opportunity at last to give way to her own grief. Nothing came. She knew there was a monsoon of tears inside her, but it was still sealed under the enforced calm she'd had to maintain all afternoon and evening. She'd cried with Dawn, true – to have been so strong that she hid all her own grief would have done more harm than good. Nevertheless, she'd reined it in, allowing tears to escape but refusing to be struck down by anguish.

In every tragedy, there had to be someone to pour drinks, to make tea or coffee, to cook food (because even people in despair needed to eat), to run baths and to make up beds. She watched the firemen, the paramedics and the hospital staff holding it together, though some of them must surely have as great a reason for sorrow as she did. She was the emergency personnel for this little slice of the tragedy. She thought of Thomas, having to phone Dawn with that news, and wondered what phone calls she might have to make. Neither Ray nor Dawn had ever mentioned any other family. Was the girl really so alone in the world; not even aunts and uncles or cousins to turn to? *She has me*, thought Marianne, with the ferocity of an Amazonian warrior. This was her chance to cry, while Dawn lay inert and dreamless, but still the iron calm held. She began to tidy the living room and put the dishes in the dishwasher. Dawn's uneaten omelet was wrapped in cling film and placed in the fridge. Too soon, it was all tidy, so she put a load of laundry in and began to dust. She couldn't vacuum – she didn't want to wake Dawn.

In the immaculate room, she poured herself another drink and sat down in front of the TV again. The disaster was still on repeat; the fresh details increasingly arbitrary. The news anchor had been changed abruptly an hour before, off schedule. Perhaps his marathon of black news had been too much for him, or he'd received some personally devastating news. Marianne hoped he was just resting. A woman had taken his place, dressed in black.

"The federal government has confirmed ground zero of both areas of detonation were the two VEC programming providers, RUSH and PURE," she was saying. "With these targets being the most cherished entertainment source of this country, the administration has immediately contracted out replacement programming to the Abyssus corporation, which will resume service as soon as possible."

Marianne stared at the TV, dumbstruck. *VECs*, she thought. *All these people care about is whether or not they'll get their VEC programs. So many people have died – Ray has died – and all they're concerned about is being able to jerk off in virtual reality. Why is this a way of life worth saving? If these are our priorities, we deserve to die. Ray did not deserve to die.*

Rage, instead of grief, welled up in her. She wanted to smash her glass into the television screen, but the shattering impact might wake Dawn. So would screaming. She didn't know how to break down by degrees, stopping before the chaos of misery overwhelmed her. Instead, she switched off the TV and began to scrub the bathroom.

I'm cold as ice, she thought, wiping down the back of the toilet. *Not cold – frozen. I don't dare melt. I don't know how to. When will the storm break inside me?*
As the sun began to rise, she checked on Dawn who lay flung across the bed, breathing deeply. A teaspoonful of nutmeg could knock someone out for up to ten hours. She put a note on the bedside table, in case she woke, and let herself out of the house quietly. She bought rescue remedy and milk, both transactions peculiarly difficult. She dreaded someone mentioning the news and kept her eyes averted, letting the black circles under them speak for themselves. She withdrew more money and went into the liquor store. She may need more provisions for the long hours ahead. Her eyes, sore from lack of sleep, kept filming over as she moved between the isles in despair.

"Can I help you?" said the clerk gently.

She shook her head mutely, a tear spilling down her cheek. He withdrew tactfully. She wished he'd pressed further so that she'd be forced to crack open. She was determined not to break down in the store. Her eyes roamed the metal shelves, unseeing and unsure of what she needed. Vodka? Rum? Would an audience with the Captain bring the needed relief? Her insides tremored violently. Turning a corner, her eyes fell on several rows of VEC programs that lined the shelves for the next five isles. Rage welled up inside her, barely checked by her self-imposed fortitude. It's because of the nation's addiction to escape that she now wandered in a stupor while Dawn faced the black days ahead; a massive hole in her life that Ray once filled. No matter Marianne's grief, Dawn's would be ten times greater.

She resisted the urge to topple each carefully stocked shelf unit, to rage against the very thing that had stolen so many hours of precious life from every person, relationship and career. Something that had stolen Ray...her light. Dawn's light. Ray.

Blinking back tears, her eyes fell upon a colorful box covered in images of the world's goddesses – from Christian to Hindu to Celtic – they all gazed back at her with serene, airbrushed beauty. The bold letters beckoned one to "Speak with the Goddess." Unthinking, Marianne reached for the box and headed to the counter. She definitely wanted to speak with the Goddess and give her a piece of her mind. She absently handed the clerk her credit card, who simply said, "I'm so sorry."

She must not have been as composed as she thought. In startled silence, she began to cry, blinking furiously, striving for composure.

Upon returning home, she found Dawn still asleep. Marianne put her purchases on the counter, in easy reach for when Dawn finally awoke. The VEC program remained in her hand. She poured herself a drink and moved toward the console as if in a trance.

Marianne, dressed in a flowing red garment lined with gold threads, approached the ornate doors of the hall. Inside, the goddesses awaited her. Hushed tones greeted her entrance, as every eye turned toward her. Wisdom was a palpable energy in this room. Wisdom and love. Marianne wanted answers.

Summoning up all the rage, anguish and pain she felt, Marianne stormed through the teeming crowd of beautiful femininity that boasted varying sizes, shapes and ages, making her way toward the center platform. She knew that she would find what she was looking for there. Mother Mary, gentle eyes filled with compassion and tears crossed her path, arms outstretched. Marianne pushed past her with a cry and kept moving. She didn't want comfort. She wanted the truth.

"Who among you is willing to face me right now? Which one of you is prepared to take me on?" She stormed; face reddened and chords sticking out in her neck. She raised a fist in the air, muscles taught and furious, ready to fight. "Who is woman enough to face my wrath?"

Athena started to move toward her when a dark hand halted her progress. The tall, armor-clad goddess retreated back and a slender, scantily clad form moved to confront Marianne. Her beautiful face, steeped with the ferocity of countless ages and battles glared, red-eyed, down at Marianne as she moved to the front of the platform. Her hair, black and untamed, jutted from her scalp like crazy daggers and whispered in the breeze of her movements. She placed the lower of her four pairs of arms on slender hips that bore a grisly skirt made of human limbs. Around her neck languished a garland upon which hung 108 heads of men who defied her. Each one wailed silently, staring from their place atop her firm, naked breasts; ever-repentant of the deeds that affixed them there. Marianne stopped just short of the razor-sharp sword another dark arm held outstretched toward her. Eyes following the gleaming line of certain doom, she held her ground as she took in the fierce, often dreaded countenance of Kali.

"Who dares challenge my authority?" Kali's voice, fearsome and resonant, echoed through the now silent chamber. "Speak, woman. What is it you seek?"

Marianne jutted her jaw forward in defiant rage. Her fists formed tight globes at her sides and she glared into the fiery eyes of raw, unfettered justice. "I am your daughter, and I demand to know why. Why has this horrible event taken place? Why have you allowed such a beautiful, sweet soul to be taken from us? We are your children, your daughters, Dawn and I...and we loved him so. Why? Why, when he was finally awakening to the Truth did you allow him to be destroyed? Tell me!"

Marianne expected the chamber walls to come tumbling down around her in a roar of fury after her tirade, but all that met her demands was a loathsome chuckle. Kali fixed Marianne with a terrifying grin that turned her blood to ice water; and still she stood her ground. "I have no more fear of you, dark mother! I defy you to justify this horrible act, this terrible loss that has hurt so many. I have been your faithful daughter. I have paid you and your sisters homage with my work and with my heart. What have I received in return? Pain? Anguish? A heart broken into pieces time and time again? Is this the terrible cost of knowing you? Don't stand there mocking my pain! Tell me now!" Tears sprang from her eyes despite her best efforts to hold them at bay. They coursed down her cheeks and fell to the marble floor, forming streams at her feet from which new life forms emerged.

"Silence!" Bellowed the Dark Mother, and everything paused. She glared at Marianne, who stood alone; the only one in the room who faced, firm and strong, her potent rage. Kali's glowing crimson eyes flowed with scorn as she spoke, her voice low and resonant, "You silly girl. You, who profess to have such a grasp of your spiritual nature, and yet are so blinded by ego and the trappings of your earthly home that the Truth that lives in your soul remains unseen. You stand here like a child, stomping your foot and raising your fists, demanding answers. You refuse comfort and safety in lieu of the satisfaction of besting me?

"You are still so deep in the throes of Maya that you cannot face the truth that you seek. Yet if you faced yourself, shed all of your foolish, simpering weaknesses and peered at what resides in your own heart, you will find that this man you speak of, this Ray as you know him, is not at all destroyed but has become as Shiva has become below my feet. He is the antithesis of your suffering; the harbinger of what is to come. You are not yet ready to see the Light in its full glory as long as you hold fast to this foolish resistance you call suffering. Go back, splendid daughter of mine, go comfort the Dawn and move forth into becoming the woman I created you to be. Only then can you embrace the Truth of what is."

Marianne opened her mouth to protest, and was met with a sound that shook the very Earth to its core. "GO!" Kali bellowed as the doors to the chamber flew open and Marianne was sucked through them and out, into the chasm of anguish, back along the path of stars to where she sat on the couch in her own living room.

"Return only when you are ready to take your place amongst us." She heard, just before she ripped the headset from her ears and fell into a sobbing heap on the floor. She lay there, curled up and shivering against the terrible visage that she had just beheld, unable to shove it away into a safe compartment in her mind.

In the West Wing of the White House, no one had slept. Everyone was dressed in sober black, ready to express their condolences and outrage yet again to the television crews. The President's face, always a mask of statesman-like gravity, was deeply solemn. Helen, ever the organizer, was striding up and down corridors, coordinating the confused and largely helpless activity. After Warren's press briefing, she'd seized him by the wrist, her nails digging in.

"We have *no evidence* that this is terrorist activity!" she hissed.

He wrenched her hand away with superior muscular force and sneered, "Of course it's fucking terrorist activity; they just blew two buildings to smithereens!"

"You are encouraging hysteria!"

"Go play with your dolls," he retorted, striding after the President.

She flipped her phone headset back on and began speaking to the Secretary of Homeland Security. "No, I don't care what the hell the VP says – there is no evidence yet for declaring this a terrorist act. No, I am *not* standing in the way of the NRP! Obviously we want every resource we can get on this." She paused, listening. "We don't need to – we'll declare it an Incident of National Significance, that'll give you powers to initiate the NRP – okay, John. There's a lot of pressure on all of us. You go ahead with that and good luck."

The National Response Plan would now kick in, with extra help diverted from surrounding areas to the two places of impact.

In the Oval Office, the President was watching the dawn seep over the garden. Warren stood in the center of the room.

"You know as well as I do that this is the time," he said.

The President turned to face him. "But what you're proposing will kill hundreds – thousands – of innocent people," he said helplessly.

"And the people in Los Angeles and New York weren't innocent?" barked Warren.

The President sighed deeply, walked over to his desk and sat down. The Vice-President followed to stand on the other side.

"Like I've said many times before, you and I both know we are eventually going to go to war with these extremist fucks and by God, right now you have the means and the reason to wipe them off the face of the planet!"

The President picked up his briefings and shuffled through them, as if reading. Warren slammed his fist on the desk. "Goddamn it, Robert, you have to wake up and avenge the death of our citizens!"

Startled and a little fearful, Robert Priest looked up at the Vice-President. "But what you're suggesting will be considered evil by most of the world."

"Screw the rest of the world!" snapped Warren. "This is not the moment for turning the other cheek – not when your own citizens get killed. This is the moment for righteous indignation and the wrath of God. This country holds the biggest damn stick on the planet and if we don't choose to use it, we are pathetic and weak and *deserve* to get hit again! And you, Mr. President, will have to live with the consequences of more innocent Americans dying due to your lack of action and your lack of guts."

Torn and frightened, the President looked away from Warren's blazing gaze to the papers on his desk. A phrase caught his eye: "Anticipated dead: 6000."

"Okay," he said.

"Okay what?" said Warren harshly.

"Let's get rid of this evil once and for all. Let's go to war."

14

Dawn moved through the silent, sunlit house, lifting things and touching them. It was Monday morning – Ray would've been at work by now, anyway. The thought of it was oddly comforting. After that first overwhelming outpouring of grief, she felt numb and empty. Marianne had understood when Dawn said she needed to spend some time at home, with her and Ray's things around her. Through her own deadened sensibilities, Dawn also realized that Marianne needed to be alone for a while, to let her own grief take precedence. When she'd walked into the living room to find Marianne crumpled up on the floor like that, she'd felt the other woman's sorrow like a sword through her heart. It had been more painful still to see Marianne wipe her face and try to recover her strength, more concerned for Dawn's suffering than her own. Dawn felt nothing now.

She put some coffee on to percolate. The components of such a task still had life and purpose in them – the bag of coffee, ready to be turned into a drink, the tap that still poured water when she switched it on, the coffee pot that gurgled into life with its little red light shining. She sat at the table and watched the deepening liquid leaping up into the pot's little glass bulb. Drained of any emotion, she felt as if her mind were photographic paper, imprinting the world around her. The sights, sounds and aroma of coffee being brewed seemed intensely pertinent. The line of sunlight across the table and the shadow of her arm held profound meaning, but what it was she didn't know. Being in the house at all felt like a brief hiatus, a short visit. What did she do now – with the next hour, this day, this week, for life?

To spare herself from a total break with reality, she had to divide time into manageable units. For the next five minutes, she would watch the coffee percolate. Then, she would drink the coffee with cream and sugar. After that – she couldn't think too far ahead, not all at once. She pulled back from the thought of going into Ray's room. His things had no right to exist without him.

The coffee pot's process was complete. She drank the first cup at the table, methodically. As she was refilling it, the doorbell rang. Mad hope leapt inside her.

A stranger in a suit, with a wire coming out of his ear, was outside the door when she opened it.

"Ms. Sky?"

Dawn nodded blankly.

"My name is Agent Brown." He flashed his CIA badge and she blinked. "I'm very sorry about your brother, Ms. Sky. He was a fine astronaut."

"Did you know him?" asked Dawn. The agent shook his head. "Well, he's not just a fine astronaut, he's a fine brother too," she said with a flicker of anger. She couldn't use past tense yet, but the present tense felt equally strange.

"I'm very sorry to intrude during this time of grief," said the agent, "but your brother was involved in some very important NASA work and we believe that he may have left some sensitive data here, which we need to check for."

Dawn stood aside, letting him enter the house. She led the way down the corridor to Ray's room.

"That's his room," she said. "I'll be in the kitchen." Pointless rage ran through her that this stranger should enter Ray's room before she could bear to. It was as if Ray's presence still hovered there, and the agent might disturb it. She returned to the sunny kitchen and set about drinking the second cup of coffee while rattles and rustles betrayed the agent's search. She heard him move from Ray's bedroom to the living room, rifling through their belongings. After a while, he came into the kitchen.

"I'm sorry to trouble you," he said. He kept apologizing, but what was the point of saying sorry for something he was going to do anyway? "Could you tell me where you keep your VEC?"

"We don't have one," said Dawn, her eyes on the coffee pot. It was half-full, which in the glass tube of the level indicator meant the line came up a third of the way. Usually, she and Ray shared a pot in the morning and that's what it looked like when she'd poured them a mug each.

"Are you sure?" said the agent.

"I think I'd notice!" snapped Dawn. "And if you knew my brother at all, you'd know he hates VECs!" There it was again: the present tense. When did one switch over to using past tense? "I'm sorry," she said after a pause. "Would you like a cup of coffee?"

"That'd be great, thanks," he said. "Do you mind if I check the rest of the house? We have to be sure that any sensitive data is contained."

Dawn shrugged. Whether she minded was immaterial – he would, anyway. She wondered what he was looking for and whether he suspected that Ray's sister would sell state secrets. She heard Ray's laptop whir into life as she poured the agent some coffee. That left the pot at an unprecedented level: three cups out. She dumped out the rest of her own chilling coffee and refilled it.

By the time he came back, she'd finished hers. He lifted the mug.

"It's probably cold," said Dawn, starting to feel jittery and sick from too much caffeine. "You can microwave it, but I put cream in already."

"That's fine, thanks," he said, gulping it down. "As far as I can tell, everything's clear so I'll get out your way now."

She saw him out and locked the door behind him. Leaning against the inside of the front door, she looked down the corridor. The agent had interrupted her plan and now she didn't know what to do next. She walked into the living room and noted where each item was situated. Her hand hovered over the music system and withdrew. Disturbing the currents of silence with artificial sounds and moods seemed wrong. She walked outside to the back yard and sat on the lawn for a long time, staring at the grass. It needed cutting and, she realized that she didn't know how to work the lawnmower. Les might know – he knew everything – or she could look it up on the internet. The shadows began to slope the other way, the brilliance draining out of the afternoon sun. She was nauseous from last night's brandy, too much coffee and nothing to eat, but the idea of putting food in her mouth and chewing was repellent to her.

My brother is dead, she thought carefully to herself. The words were devoid of meaning. She tried saying it aloud.

"My brother is dead." They still had no impact and it felt alien speaking to the empty air. She sighed and stood up, her knees aching from so long in one position. Maybe she'd sit in the kitchen again for a bit.

The Director of the CIA, possibly not for much longer, stood in the corridor between the offices of the Vice-President and the Chief of Staff. The two doors opposed each other and he glanced between them. After a few moments' hesitation, he knocked.

"Come in," called Helen. He opened the door. She was sitting at her desk, her fingers speeding across the keyboard, a pile of papers in front of her. Her eyes were sharp and alert, despite the dark rings underneath them. He held up a hand quickly to stop her from speaking and put his finger to his lips. From his pocket, he drew out a small pad of paper on which there were words written in felt-tip: "Say this naturally: 'Jane – I was just about to come find you. Shall we go to your office?'"

Bewildered, Helen repeated the words. Steven indicated that she should stand and walk towards the door. She obeyed. He shut it briskly, twisted the lock and again motioned for absolute silence. On cat-feet, he began to walk around the room. From his pocket he took a handful of small, hollow half-spheres that shone like metal. He fastened one of these behind a picture next to her desk and another under her table close to the door.

"Okay," he said in a low voice when he'd finished, "that will block all transmissions – it'll just sound like the silence of an empty room."

"What the hell is going – are you talking about *bugs*?" Helen interrupted herself.

"Keep your voice down," said Steven. "I can block sound transmission to the bugs, but not through doors." He gestured with his thumb towards her door, the opposite of which lay the Vice-President's office.

"How did you know they were there?" said Helen, the answer coming clear even as she spoke.

Steven smiled ruefully. "I'm the bug-man honey, Head of the Bugs, that's me. Luckily we only have sound in this room, no visuals."

"Why the hell am I being bugged? Who ordered this?" Helen voiced her outrage in a low whisper, though she wanted to yell.

"Who do you think? Don't take it personally, everyone's bugged these days. All in the name of national security, you know. Hell, it's incredible what you can get away with if you invoke national security statues."

"But we have sweeps…" she began.

He looked at her as if she were mad. "Who do you think conducts the sweeps?"

"Why – are – you – here?" said Helen slowly, her rage distinct.

He reached into his pocket. For a terrifying moment, she thought he was going to produce a gun, but he pulled out the small silver disc of a VEC program instead, sheathed in protective plastic. He held it up between his forefinger and thumb.

"What's this?" she asked.

"You know – I've done a lot of shit for this country,"

said Steven, "Purely out of blind loyalty and the belief that this country will always do the right thing."

"And you tell me this why?" Helen's eyes were hypnotized by the disc moving back and forth between the agent's fingers.

"Because the VP has lost it," said Steven. He sat down on one of the stiff-backed chairs around the table. Helen didn't keep armchairs and deep sofas in her office – they put women in skirts at a serious disadvantage. It was hard to argue policy when you had to manage how high your skirt rode up your legs.

"In what capacity has he lost it?" she asked cautiously, sitting opposite him.

"He's fucking playing God now."

Helen raised her eyebrows and Steven tossed the VEC program across the table to her.

"And what's this?" she asked, picking it up.

"First let's be clear about this," he said. "It does not exist. It's been destroyed, under my personal supervision. I have not given it to you and we have not had this conversation."

"Fine," said Helen, impatient with his spook-talk.

"Sordid and shameful as my job may have become, I'm not yet prepared to lose it. I have personal responsibilities – obligations – I have a duty to my…"

"Wife and kids," she interrupted sardonically. "I get it. In what way is Warren playing God?"

Steven shook his head. "I might yet resign myself to losing my job," he said, "but I'd like to keep my life."

She was about to snap at him for being melodramatic, when the truth struck her. He wasn't some paranoid civilian convinced the CIA would want him dead. He headed the CIA and instructed its agents. He knew exactly what he was talking about.

"There are very few possible sources for a leak like this," he went on, "and I'd be a prime suspect. I'll have to leave that to your own deductive intelligence. Whatever conclusions you come to will be far enough from the exact truth to clear me of suspicion. And on the subject of people's lives – I'd keep that VEC you're holding pretty well-hidden. I don't want to sound inappropriate, but put that in your bra or your underwear, not in a pocket or your bag. And if you decide it's too dangerous to hold onto, destroy it and get rid of the pieces. Not in your trash. Dropping the pieces down a deep drain is a good way. Unlike the way they show in the films, we don't spend much time in the sewage drains."

His manner was absolutely serious.

"So what the hell is on the VEC?" she asked, shaken.

"Honestly?" said Steven. "It's Raymond Sky's brain activity from his last mission. And – I think – the real God." Helen sat at her desk for a long time after Director Black had removed his little shells and left the room. She'd tried putting the program in her bra, but with her small breasts the square was too obvious. Reluctantly, she'd slipped it into her panties, where it now pressed uncomfortably against her bottom. She didn't keep a VEC headset in her office. She could check one out from the multi-media room, but that was too risky. In any case, she didn't relish the thought of immersing all of her senses in a VEC world while a megalomaniac like Warren Christian sat on the other side of the corridor. *My position is public and my death would be hard to explain,* she reasoned, incredulous that she was even entertaining these lines of thought. She'd never fallen for the TV and film glamour of politics like so many around her. She believed that a good administration was ultimately just that, administration: often tedious but incredibly important administrative work that needed to be done well if the country was to be run properly. Cloak-and-dagger dramas had no part in it, beyond people's paranoia and the petty office politics they conjured up for themselves. Evil masterminds stroking cats were the stuff of fantasy. Everyone, ultimately, was just a person, subject to the same checks and balances as everyone else. The CIA Director had left her wondering whether this egalitarian, no-nonsense view was naïve.

She shook herself out of her revelry and buzzed her secretary to ask for a cup of coffee. Sleeplessness played tricks with the mind. Director Black had refused to accuse Warren of anything directly, and was sure she could work it out herself. The need to make notes, list things, organize information, was powerful – but now she didn't dare write anything down. She began to doodle instead, the scratch of the pencil against the paper helping her thoughts flow. She paused. The pencil lead snapped. Icy rage barreled her out of her seat and across the corridor into Warren's room.

"What the *hell* are you doing from this office?" she yelled.

Warren looked up from his work, took off his reading glasses and rose from his chair.

"Did you have anything to do with the attacks in New York and LA?" Her eyes betrayed the fury her body stiffened against. Warren just glanced calmly at her and strode past her to the door. She spun. "Don't you *dare* walk out on me, Warren Christian! Did you have anything to do with the deaths of Sky and Firestone?"

Warren reached the door, closed it and locked it from the inside. He turned to face Helen.

"Little girl," he said, "I would shut the *fuck* up right now if I were you or I'll shut you up myself!"

The color drained from her face as she saw his eyes.

"Oh my God…" she whispered. He was standing between her and the door. "You've gone mad, haven't you? All this power you've absorbed over all these years… It's driven you mad."

Warren laughed scornfully. "Oh – the limits of the petty mind," he said. "A pen-pushing little girl like you, what can you conceive of? You'd like to think I was mad, wouldn't you? The idea that someone perfectly sane can have power and choose to use it – your little head just explodes at the thought. *I am the most sane person in this entire administration.* I'm the only one not hiding behind anything, inventing stupid little values and clinging to a rut. I'm the *only one* who can look rationally at the whole goddamned situation."

Helen stared at him. *He's just a man*, she thought. She walked briskly towards the door. "You know what," she said, "I don't know why I'm talking to you anyway. The person I need to speak to is the President."

Warren's hand shot out and grabbed her wrist as she reached for the lock. "Go ahead," he said, "but Robert has been my puppet for so long, I can convince him to shit on his desk in the Oval Office and make him believe it's a good idea."

She met his gaze defiantly, determined to show no fear. "Maybe you're right," she said, realizing belatedly that he was. How had she been so blind? She'd watched this foul piece of shit play the President's strings in every meeting and still refused to believe it. "Maybe Robert is just your puppet. Maybe my next stop should be the press room." She tried again to step around him, but he grabbed her and shoved her against the wall. His hand pressed hard against her windpipe. *Pure physical violence*, she thought with futile rage, *After all our equality and systems this is what it comes down to: he's stronger than me.*

"In this very moment, little girl, you have the choice of living or dying." She struggled against him, but he pinned her easily in place. "You have to choose to be with me, and the side of good, or against me, which puts you on the side of evil. And you're witnessing what I do to the side of evil."

He dropped her. Gasping, she staggered for her footing and massaged her throat. Options whirled through her head – pressing charges, going to the press, trying to convince the President that his right-hand man was pure evil – but none of them ruled out what Steven had implicitly warned her about.

Warren could have her killed.

"Take your time," said Warren, unlocking the door. Her eyes swept the floor anxiously as her hand flew to her bottom – the program was still there. Thank God for sensible underwear.

He ushered her out, saying "I do recommend that you choose wisely."

There was no answer when Les rang the doorbell. The living room light was on, the curtains open and he could see an empty mug lying on the table. He walked around to the yard and found the back door open. He knocked on it gently.

"Dawn?" he called. "It's Les." No response.

Feeling like an intruder, he stepped into the kitchen. It smelled of burnt coffee – he saw the coffee pot left on and switched it off. "Dawn?" he called again. He didn't want to scare her. He walked through the house, checking each room, repeating her name and his own. He opened the door to what could only be Ray's room. She was curled on the bed, asleep, her arms clutching a heap of sweaters. He sat down next to her and touched her face gently.

"Dawn?"

"Ray?" she mumbled, turning. Her eyes fluttered open.

"No – it's Les," he said, pained, as she saw him. She looked around her at the room and down at the armful of clothes she was holding.

"Ray's dead," she said, the knowledge sweeping back in with consciousness.

"I know." His mouth worked helplessly and he stroked her hair.

"They smell like him," she said, gesturing at the clothes. Les nodded. "But if I keep holding them, they'll start smelling like me. I don't know how…"

He couldn't bear her desperate attempt to speak, to make sense, and held his arms out to her. She curled up inside them, nestling like a child, tears wetting his neck. "I can't cry," she whispered. "Tears keep coming out of my eyes, but I can't cry properly." He held her tighter.

After a while, she pulled away. "I don't know what to do now," she said, puzzled. "Time keeps going on and I don't know how to fill it. All I want to do is sleep, but then when I wake up it all comes back." She picked up his hand, playing with his fingers as she spoke. "I try to think what I would do normally and I can't figure it out. I know I would usually clean and cook and shop, but it doesn't make sense if no one lives here. Except me," she added, as an afterthought, "but I don't want to eat anymore."

"When did you last eat?" asked Les, gently.

Dawn thought about it, frowning. Marianne had given her supper and breakfast, gently urging her to try something, but she'd eaten neither. They'd missed lunch, watching the news. In another lifetime, they'd eaten a stack of waffles for brunch.

"Yesterday, at about ten – ten in the morning," she said.

"Come with me to the kitchen," he said. "I'm going to make you something."

Still holding one of Ray's sweaters bundled up to her heart, she let herself be led by the hand, back to the chair where she'd spent most of the day. The sunlight had vanished from the room and all but faded from the sky. *Thus ends the first day*, she thought, surprised by her own coherence. A cardboard box stood on the table and from it Les took out a bottle of red wine.

"It's a restorative," he said in reply to her quizzical look. "In England they drink tea, in America they drink coffee – in Italy, wine."

He poured her a glass and began opening the cupboards. He seemed to instinctively know where everything was kept.

"Not too much until you've eaten," he cautioned, as she took a sip.

He didn't try to talk much, of which she was glad.

Through the rise and fall of the mist in her eyes, she watched him put an eggplant under the grill and start mixing olive oil and lemon juice in a bowl. He reached absentmindedly for the garlic string that wasn't there and smiled wryly at her.

"The cupboard above the stove," she said. He found the bulb, peeled a clove and mashed it with salt. From the fridge, he took two tomatoes and chopped them swiftly.

"Isn't the eggplant burning?" she asked. It was nice to sit here and watch him move around so self-assured, to only think about ordinary things like food burning.

"It's supposed to," he said.

She nodded unquestioningly and took another sip of wine. It stung her empty stomach, but he was right – it was restoring some of her strength and calm. When the eggplant was blackened and crispy all around, he sliced off the charred skin, tore it into chunks and began to mix it with the dressing and tomato. He used his hands and she watched the golden oily mixture slide down his fingers. He rinsed them off and slid the dish in front of her with a fork.

"I figured you might not want something too chewy," he said. She took a mouthful and her saliva glands cramped with the flavor. She was hungry, after all. "Thank you," she said, when she finished. His stomach lurched with love and pain. He would pick up her grief and carry it if he could, but all he could do was cook her some food – and still, she thanked him.

"It'll tide you over till supper," he said. "I think you should come eat with us." He didn't dare give his reasons, in this house, for wanting her out of there. She needed to know things that he wouldn't risk saying in those rooms. It was just caution, but one didn't mess around with risks one couldn't calculate. To his relief, she agreed without demur. She seemed to have given up independent volition along with the hope of seeing her brother again.

"What's in the box?" she asked as he lifted it to carry to the car.

"Ray's things from work," said Les. "They were going to send a courier – I wanted to bring them myself."

"Thank you," she said again quietly. He felt another pang in his heart.

Oriana met her at the front door with an enveloping embrace. They sat in the kitchen, the box between them, where Oriana began to cook. If all she had to do was watch people cook, thought Dawn, life would not be so hard to continue. The homeliness and quiet order of it was soothing. Les switched on a soft lamp, lit a candle on the table and switched off the overhead light. On the table, he placed a bowl of olives, some breadsticks and wine-glasses.

"Don't worry about spoiling your appetite," said Oriana over her shoulder, "this'll take a couple of hours."

Dawn nibbled an olive's juicy flesh and took a small sip of wine, emotionally clinging to these simple things.

"Les – what was Ray doing in the RUSH building?" she said.

Les glanced at his mother. "Anyone come around, Mamma?" he asked.

She shook her head. "And I've been in all day," she added.

Les took a deep breath. He had to start slowly, in case he spun Dawn back into shock and hysteria. "We had a mission," he began, "a top-secret one. No-one was allowed to tell anyone – we're still not allowed, but my first loyalties aren't with the government."

He told Dawn everything – the VEC program he'd created, what Ray had said about it, the push to get another speed-of-light flight, the key players' belief that they would somehow be speaking to God, the absolute secrecy, the explosion and the prohibitions the CIA had placed on them.

"So that's what they were looking for," said Dawn slowly. "Ray's VEC…" She shook herself, struggling to imagine her brother using a VEC or believing in God.

"Who?" asked Les, sharply.

"An agent came to the house, talking about sensitive data. He looked everywhere. He asked where our VEC machine was. I gave him a cup of coffee."

"Did he find anything?"

Dawn shook her head. Les reached into the cardboard box and pulled out a small silver disc.

"They were snooping all over NASA," he said. "I'm pretty sure this is what they were looking for."

"You hid it from the agents?" said Dawn, wide-eyed.

"No, I let them find it – I just got a copy first. They spent about five hours on my computer, checking copies and removing stuff and left with all my back-up tapes."

"But can't they tell – if you've made a copy…?"

Les laughed shortly. "Computers are programmed by people," he said. "I'm people."

Supper was eaten by candlelight under the velvety black of a humid August night. Dawn kept returning to Les's story, checking details. She was grateful for the numb weariness that still cushioned her from her loss and grateful too for their natural behavior.

"The explosion," she insisted, "was it quick?"

"Instantaneous – he would have felt nothing."

"And he was definitely… blown apart? He couldn't be floating out there – in his suit?" She was terrified by the thought of him hovering in black cold space, watching his oxygen levels sink and the distant planet slowly turning.

"The satellites are very sensitive," said Les. "All the debris was small – we would've picked up if they'd been there, still."

Later, she found herself weak with laughter over Les's description of the agents strip-searching his computer and she clapped her mouth over her giggles.

"Am I drunk?" she asked Oriana. "Why am I laughing?"

Shame shot through her that she could betray Ray by laughing so soon after his death, by drinking when he hated alcohol.

"No, of course not," soothed Oriana. She shrugged. "It's normal, Dawn – when people die, we cry and we laugh and we're still alive and we have to deal with that."

Nevertheless, Dawn was sobered by her fears. Her laughter vanished as quickly as it had come and her eyes were again filled with an apparently inexhaustible supply of tears.

"The funeral," she said hesitantly. The thought was sickening – part of the reality of death breaking into this strange interlude. They had no body to bury or cremate. But there had to be a funeral, didn't there? "I don't know how to organize a funeral."

Oriana sighed sadly. "One of those things in life we only ever learn the hard way," she said. "I learned how when my mother died. We'll sort it out together. But time enough for that tomorrow. You need to sleep." She lifted the stack of dishes and carried them to the kitchen.

"Do you want to stay over?" asked Les gently.

Dawn bobbed her head, assenting, studying the tablecloth.

"Would you prefer to sleep in the living room? Or…"

"Your bed." She completed his sentence, raising her head to meet his gaze. "If you don't mind. I'd like to be held."

"Of course."

"Would your mother…"

"Mind? No. I think she'd be more surprised if you slept in the living room, to be honest."

His bed was narrow, his room plainly furnished, a high stack of books on his bedside table. She stood uncertainly in the middle of the room while he switched on the lamp and pulled out a t-shirt for her to sleep in.

"I'll get some water while you change," he said, closing the door behind him.

The feel of his t-shirt on her bare skin was peculiarly intimate. Sitting up in bed, waiting for him to come back, she looked at the book titles – they were in English, French and Italian. Of the English books, only one was a novel. A tap came at the door.

"Come in," she said shyly, touched that he knocked to enter his own bedroom. He put two glasses of water on the table and sat down on the bed. He leaned forward, kissed her gently, then pulled back.

"I'm not going to – you know – or anything," he said awkwardly.

"I know. I didn't mean – I just wanted – company." She felt clumsily and as embarrassed as him.

"I know."

He changed in the dark and slipped into bed next to her. As his warm, thin arms pulled her to him, she began to cry properly for the first time.

As usual, Thomas arrived home late. Instead of letting himself quietly into a dark and silent house, however, the lights were on and Cathy was still up, both their suppers keeping warm in the oven. Since the unexpected confrontation over the VECs, she'd started waiting up for him – then, instead of her waking early to fix his breakfast, he brought hers to her in bed. It reminded him of the first years of their marriage. The sleepy confusion when she first opened her eyes, then the spreading smile as she saw her coffee on the bedside table was all the reward he needed. The other rewards, however, were countless. Sitting up together after supper and sharing their favorite VEC programs was sexier than he had imagined possible. More and more often, they were bypassing the VEC altogether.

Tonight, he was painfully grateful for the new routine.

He badly needed the warmth of her real arms around him, her words of comfort and the deep understanding that had grown between them over the shared years. When he whispered brokenly into her neck, "I feel like I've killed them both," she knew him well enough not to argue that it was nonsense. She just held him tighter; realizing that he did feel like that and he did know it wasn't true. *To think I almost lost her*, he reflected, *without even realizing...* And he clutched her more fiercely.

Marianne opened the front door in her dressing-gown, blinking in the morning sunshine, expecting to see Dawn. A familiar-looking woman stood there in a smart suit.

"Marianne Summers?"

Marianne nodded, trying to place the face in front of her.

"I'm Helen Cross."

"Yes – of course," said Marianne, abruptly connecting the face to the TV images.

"May I come in?"

"Of course." Marianne stepped aside and followed her through to the living room. She caught a glimpse of her swollen face and puffy eyes in the mirror. The blinds were still drawn and used tissues were strewn across the table around an empty, sticky glass. "Sorry about the mess," she muttered, drawing up the blinds and opening the windows. "It's been a rough couple of days. And I have to say, you're the last person on earth I would expect to see knocking at my door." As she spoke, she gathered up the mess and straightened the cushions.

"A few days ago, I would have totally agreed with you," said Helen.

It was strange seeing someone so well-known in her living room, walking and talking, looking – as the saying went – exactly like her photographs.

"What's changed since a few days ago?" said Marianne.

"Apart from – for me – everything." She sat down abruptly, sheltering her welling eyes behind her hand.

Helen slipped her hand into her bra. After the discomfort of sitting on a VEC program all day, she'd decided there was merit to padded bras after all. She held out the disc to Marianne, saying, "This."

Marianne took it, turning it over. "What's this?"

"It's a VEC program based on the brain activity of Raymond Sky from his last speed-of-light mission."

Marianne dropped it, a wave of nausea surging over her. She clapped her hand to her mouth, breathing deeply. "Sorry…" she said. "It's just a shock – I knew him…"

"I'm sorry," said Helen, sitting down. That explained the state of both the room and the woman. "I had no idea."

Fumbling, Marianne picked up the disc again. "Then why are you giving it to me?"

"Because of what's on it."

"What's that?"

"The simulation indicates he interacted with God, on his mission – something you predicted would happen. That's why I came to you. I didn't know you were personally acquainted."

Marianne sat staring at the disc. She looked up at Helen, her eyes hard. "Ray said he had no memory of the mission – nothing at all."

"That's true," agreed Helen. "I was there for the President's briefing. Then very recently, he came back saying his memory had come back to him. It struck me as strange at the time. Obviously he didn't want to mention the VEC."

"Why didn't he tell me?" whispered Marianne to herself. He'd been going to, she realized. Last night, they were going to meet up – instead of her sitting on the sofa streaming with tears, self-medicating on brandy, and wailing her way through mourning his death. What a hell of a date. It leant a whole new world of pain to being stood-up. "Okay, let me get this straight," she said, abruptly. "You, the administration, are giving me, who I'm sure you thought was a nut-case, Ray's simulation of a chat with God?"

"Yes. Although not exactly on the record."

"Why?"

"You don't seem so much of a nut-case anymore," said Helen.

Marianne looked at her sharply. Helen had appeared on TV more times than she could count, but actually she didn't look exactly like her photographs. She looked worn-out, shattered with exhaustion and tense.

"You look like hell," said Marianne. "Sorry – I mean, I do too." She waved a hand at her messed-up face and dressing-gown. "Can I get you some coffee or anything?"

Helen nodded. "It's been a difficult few days," she admitted cautiously.

As the coffee brewed, Marianne kept returning to the disc. "Does anyone in the administration know you're giving me this?"

"No."

"Then why?"

Helen compressed her lips, unsure how much information to pass on. The woman needed to know how dangerous having that disc was, but to tell her anything further might put her in still more danger.

"Based on that simulation," she said warily, "God is not some fire-and-brimstone God, as the administration would like us all to believe. If I understand it correctly – it was a very strange experience and hard to verbalize – it is a loving God – not even that – just love, itself, capital L."

"Which only makes me more curious. If the administration wants a big vengeful God to beat up their enemies with, why are you giving me this? Surely it's against your own interests?" She poured the coffee and handed Helen a mug, taking a deep scalding sip of her own. Waves of grief kept rolling through her, despite the thin veneer of calm.

"Because I believe this is something that needs to be shared with the world and you're the only person I could think of who could do it. And because I'm starting to find out the administration's best interests and the world's best interests are not the same."

Marianne snorted.

"Okay," said Helen wearily. "Maybe everyone on the whole planet knew that except me. But I have to warn you – I'm going against both mine and your interests, giving you that disc. I don't want to add to the danger by telling you too much. But let me explain how dangerous that little program could be."

15

Dawn opened her eyes and Les's peaceful face filled her vision. *I'm in Les's bed*, she thought, *and Ray's dead.* In the night, their limbs had completely entangled. She lay, feeling the sorrow seep back into her heart, taking comfort from the warm arms and legs wrapped around her. Replaying the events of the day before in her head, she cautiously realigned herself with this new reality. She had a VEC program of Ray's experience. For whatever reason, the CIA wanted it. To her, it was a part of her brother, and therefore more precious than gold. Les opened his eyes.

"Hi there," he said.

"Hello." She smiled. How strange and sweet, to be greeting someone in bed.

His hand brushed her thigh, and then tapped it. "Is this your leg, or has mine gone to sleep?"

She giggled, in spite of the constant presence of profound loss that she felt. "It's mine."

They lay still, looking at each other for a few minutes, and then Les spoke ruefully. "I'm truly in heaven, but I have to go to work. It's funny...I didn't think people had jobs in heaven."

She touched his face lightly and they unraveled their limbs.

Morning coffees at Les's house were tiny and powerful. He swallowed his in a gulp, turned to leave, then swung back to touch Dawn's hair and put his lips gently to hers. She blushed, glancing shyly at his mother, but Oriana behaved as if it were the most normal thing in the world.

"I'm going shopping," she said, "So you'll be on your own for a couple of hours. Stay as long as you want – make yourself at home."

Left alone, Dawn made herself a larger, weaker coffee and took it out to the back porch with the cardboard box of Ray's things. The morning sun was still low, glittering brightly off every blade of grass and sculpted bush. The jasmine had recently bloomed, heaping the air with its sweet fragrance, and the formal flower beds were massed with flowers. She inhaled deeply, exhaled, and began to unpack the box. At the top was a VEC machine and headset – at one time, its presence would have floored her. She rifled through several notepads, full of calculations and notations about physics and engineering. She laid them reverently aside, like a mystical codex she couldn't begin to understand, but treasured nonetheless. She took out a handful of pens, pencil stubs and a digipen, arranging them in a neat line by size. She recognized a framed photo of her and Ray in San Francisco. A stack of other photos were unframed, stuck together with the blue tac that must have pinned them to the wall around his desk. She was in all of them, at various ages. That solid proof of love destroyed her vision for a while. When she recovered herself, she looked in the box again. All that remained was the small silver disc of the VEC program. She put the box on the ground and switched on the VEC machine: its battery was full. She slid the program into the slot and put the headset on. *He's gone*, she thought, *and all I have is this little part of his mind.* She pressed play.

When Helen Cross left, Marianne showered and scrubbed herself thoroughly. She dressed, opened all the windows and cleaned her entire apartment. She needed to impose order amidst the chaos of her feelings. She also needed to delay the act of putting the program in the VEC machine. It was her last fragment of Ray, and she wanted to savor its existence; to treasure it and not use it up too fast. *This is what I wanted since the day we met,* she thought as she dusted her bedroom, *to be inside his thoughts – to understand him from the inside.* She began to make the bed, shaking the pillows back into shape and throwing the duvet into the air so that it arced like a sail before falling lightly into place. She looked at it, a knot in the pit of her stomach. *But I also wanted the rest. The whole of him. A living Ray. A constant fountain of new thoughts and new ideas. A physical Ray; to touch and hold passionately close.*

Marianne's combed hair still trailed drips of moisture down her back as she sat cross-legged on the living room floor. Fresh morning air swept through the house from the open windows as she pulled the VEC headset into place and pressed play.

Love descended upon Dawn. It wrapped her in its soft, warm light. It reached its golden tendrils into every part of her being. She had always known it, she realized. It had enveloped her with its protective shining net from the first moment Ray had picked her up as a newborn baby. He cradled her tenderly; looking up at the great big grown-ups who he knew weren't grown-up enough to look after such a priceless treasure. Infant memories of safety flooded through her. She remembered the sure arms of the Safe One reaching down through her helpless fear of a crashing giant that smelled sour and wrong. The Safe One, who lifted her up and took her to a good place where everything was soft green, bright and sweet-smelling. At night, she'd haul herself up on the bars of the cot, feeling lonely and afraid, and tried to call the Safe One. Her babble of undifferentiated syllables; her wails and wet cheeks were rewarded. He came in; smaller and yet better than the Others. He'd murmur, "~ ~ ~ here, Dawn, ~ ~ ~ Ray, ~ ~ ~," and pick her up. Those arms guaranteed her safety, like an angel with a flaming sword, defending her. The long periods when he wasn't there stretched grey and endless – then she would hear the voice her little ears yearned for. She would struggle to sit up, or she would pull herself up, then later crawl, and then stagger. She wreathed herself in smiles when he appeared, even if her cheeks were still wet from some forgotten complaint. The brightness that filled her world at the sight of his face surrounded her now. It was everywhere, whichever way she turned, and would never leave her. There was no frightening or half asleep giant just out of sight – there was only a steady flood of love and safety. It flooded her like a mighty ocean rising to cover the world, and she was gleefully tossed and tumbled by its currents; shrieking with giggles and delight. She felt the benevolent laughter of the Huge Being as it played with her, as happy as she was in this state of joy.

Is this heaven? She thought.

The Huge Being lifted her up and swirled her around like a spinning top until she was giddy with love. *At your level of spiritual evolution, my little one, this would be heaven.*

Now Dawn walked through the world; her long white dress fluttering around her ankles and her veil trailing behind her. Through jungles and cities she glided, with Ray at her left side, holding her arm. From the basket they both held, she took handfuls of flowers which she scattered around them. She knew that all the wounded people on their path could touch the flowers and be healed. Those who struggled against the black morass of despair could feel sweet hope rising in their hearts again. Their lives became transformed into something that held beauty; a life that was worth living, after all. The hard-hearted softened, and then turned to others to express compassion. Lilies, marigolds, tulips, morning glories, chrysanthemums, cornflowers, jasmine and daisies all fell from the inexhaustible basket, leaving a carpet of bright, colorful beauty and peace across the world. The couple reached a villa of golden stone that stood tranquil among groves of trees beneath a blanket of bright sunshine. Les was standing on the steps, waiting for her. He took her right hand, while her left still clasped Ray's arm. She looked around them at the peaceful countryside.

"Where am I?" she asked.

"This is your heaven," said Ray.

She looked from his face to Les's and back again. Both shone with Love.

"Yes," she murmured, "it is. But is it real?"

"Do you feel the love?" asked Ray.

Her face beamed with joy. "Yes."

"Then it's real." Ray leaned over and kissed her cheek as Les pressed her right hand between his arm and his body. "Dawn," said Ray, turning to go, "protect the birth of enlightenment."

Peace descended upon Marianne: the peace of deep sleep, of meditation, of knowing oneself to be as much loved as loving. Her heart that had once poured out passionate, anxious care for her clients, her lovers, and the world was now refilled with pure, calm Love. She floated in it, feeling herself drift with the swell of the waves. Her eyes fluttered open to the expanse of blue sky above her and closed again contentedly. The ocean could carry her where it would; all places were safe. When she felt herself beginning to sink into the water, she smiled in her soul. She knew that Love would immerse her completely. She drifted down through the golden waters and felt herself ripple outwards into them.

Just as you are, whispered the loving force that infused her. *No more trying.*

This is heaven, she answered.

At this stage in your development, you can call it heaven.

Deep below the shimmering surface, Marianne sank steadily, light as a leaf, sensing at last the enormity of the good will that surrounded her. All her life she had fought for it, hunted for it, striven to earn it – but she needn't have tried so hard, it was everywhere. There was so much. The little self that had begged so hard for this was now a forgotten shell from another time. Instead, the glowing golden kernel of her being simply accepted the Truth. With a rush of love and gratitude towards the being who was this place, she felt herself dissolve and melt, becoming another shining mote in the ocean of light.

Marianne lay curled on her side on a four-poster bed; its fine, embroidered canopy billowing and rippling in the sea breeze. It stood on a dais, which floated on the water. Crimson and gold drapery hung around each polished column of wood, a gorgeous contrast against the bright blue sky. The ocean stretched out, blue as the heavens, as far as the eye could see. Far away on the horizon, she could see the tiny speck of a figure walking towards her. She lifted herself onto one elbow, stretching her legs out lazily, watching his slow and sure approach. Her hands stroked her silken gown absentmindedly, feeling the watery fabric slide over her skin. When he reached her, the sun was setting to one side and the moon rising on the other. She sat on the side of the bed, her legs dangling over the edge, and saw his feet standing firmly on the glistening water's surface.

"Look at me," he said gently.

She lifted her face and met his steady blue-eyed gaze.

"No more fraidy-cat?" he whispered.

She blushed and shook her head, but a wild trembling in her stomach belied her words. He stepped up to the dais and lifted her hand to his lips, kissing her fingers tenderly. With his right hand, he touched her bare shoulder lightly, untying the bow of her nightgown strap. The fabric fell loose on one side, exposing the upper swell of her breast. He sat next to her and drew her face closer. His lips parted hers as his hand reached to the other bow, gently tugging it loose. Her heart hammered wildly as the silk slid down to pool around her waist. He held her in one arm, his deep kiss assuring her, as his other hand began to roam over her bare skin.

"Ray," she said against his mouth, despite her quickening pulse, "I am scared."

"I know. I know you well. But you're safe."

She laid her head on his shoulder, surrendering to his exploring hands and kisses. When he lowered her onto the bed, naked, the moon turned her skin to silver while his touches turned her veins to gold. Lost in the sea of desire, she didn't try to be anything. She let his Love slide into her as his body did, opening herself to both, and crying tears of joy. He rocked inside her, filling her repeatedly with love and warm flesh, kissing her passionately as she sobbed.

Hours, days, or light-years later, they lay clasped together, their huge, dilated eyes filling each other's world.

"I love you," he said. "Marianne...?"

"Yes?" she murmured.

"Nurture the birth of enlightenment."

The sun was high in the sky; calling up the day's swollen clouds from the marshes and ocean, when Dawn called Marianne's cell phone. She answered on the first ring.

"Dawn! Where are you? I've been trying to call you!"

"I was in the VEC – I'm at Les's house – where are you?"

"Outside your house – I have to see you. I have to speak to you." Marianne's voice was almost hysterical, bubbling with what could have either been joy or tears.

"Me too – I'll come – no, wait, come here." Dawn remembered Les's fears that her and Ray's house might be bugged. "Wait a sec, I'll give you the address." She ran into the house, adjusting to the dark after the brightness outside, looking for an envelope to check the house number.

"Dawn – the most amazing thing..." Marianne broke down, laughing through her tears. "It's fine – I'm fine – it's just – oh my God." She cried harder, still smiling.

"Can you drive?" asked Dawn, anxiously.

"Drive?" squealed Marianne. 'Right now, I can fly... I can't explain on the phone. And actually," she chuckled, "No, I probably shouldn't drive."

"I don't know if I should, either," said Dawn. She felt light-headed and faint, and caught herself on the cool wall. "I'm all..." Her words trailed off, unable to formulate an explanation.

"Of course – I know," Marianne's voice was suddenly serious. "I'm sorry, you must be so – I'm just overwhelmed."

"No," said Dawn hastily, "I feel all floaty. I'm *happy*. Okay, Cocoa Beach is halfway between us – let's meet there."

Through their mutual giddiness, they managed to fix on a place. Dawn dashed off a note for Oriana, sent Les a text message and walked out into a brand-new world lush with greenery and swollen with promise.

Marianne and Dawn floated upright in the sea, their toes just touching the sand as the light swells lifted them up and deposited them softly back onto the seabed. The beach was crowded with vacationers but out here, away from the other swimmers, they could talk freely. The long walk had calmed them both and made them remember the apparent dangers of owning the program. Meeting and finding they both had the same program had made them hysterical all over again, but now they waved back and forth in the water like seaweed, tranquil.

"Is it real?" asked Dawn.

"It's a simulation of Ray's experience – but ours were so different... How can both have simulated what he went through?"

"Les says we don't actually know how VECs work – what exactly they capture. We think it's just a straightforward sensory experience, but maybe that's because we've only tried to record straightforward experiences before."

Their arms fluttered through the seawater, which kept them standing upright. Dawn thought of Les's explanation; that experiments could only answer the questions they posed. No one would think to ask if the VEC could replicate a spiritual epiphany. Without understanding spirituality as a whole, how could it be tested? "The change in Ray was real," added Dawn.

Marianne nodded. Outside the perfection of that VEC experience, his death came back to them.

"And the danger is apparently real – Helen Cross was very explicit about that. I just don't get why the government would want to suppress something like this!"

"I do," said Dawn unexpectedly. "It makes perfect sense. They've been gearing people up for a war for a long time. All the rhetoric is in place."

"But why would they want a war?" Marianne was bewildered.

Dawn ducked underwater to wet her hair again and to cool her face. "A dozen reasons," she said, when she surfaced. "Resources being the most obvious – oil, it's been about oil for decades now. That and empire-building – not like the old colonialists, this is the construction of an economic empire. Power. To foster a solid national identity – nothing does that like killing foreigners. And also to increase the government's popularity."

"That's insane!" said Marianne. "How would a war make them popular?"

Dawn shrugged. She lay on her back, letting the salty water and the small skimming movements of her hands support her. Above them, the sky was dense with heavy clouds, turning the light greenish-yellow. "Governments are popular in war-time," she said. "Maybe it's something to do with bonding together – or feeling like your government's protecting you against some threat – I don't know. But look at history. It always happens."

The first fat drop of rain hit her forehead.

"Time to get out."

The beach had already emptied as they reached their bags and dashed, soaking wet, for shelter from the rain. In the overhang of a bar's balcony, they toweled themselves off and pulled their summer dresses over their still-damp and salty skin. Their bikinis made dark patches of damp through the fabric. Marianne glanced through the glass doors of the bar. It was densely packed with people, all gazing upwards in the same direction.

"Is there a big game on?"

Dawn turned and ducked to bring the TV screen into her line of vision. "That's not a game," she said, her skin chilling. "Come on."

As they entered, the footage of troops marching in formation gave way to the President's face, speaking from the press room in the White House. He was flanked by two flags, each topped with the fierce eagle that had once symbolized the might of Rome.

"My fellow Americans," he said. "Following the horrifying and tragic loss of life executed against our fellow citizens in New York City and Los Angeles, I have just authorized a massive military action against the perpetrators. We now have reliable intelligence that the terror attacks were carried out by many citizens of Iran, with the full knowledge and support of their government. The direct strike of this nation against the heart of our country constitutes a declaration of war. A declaration of war that we must answer with overwhelming force, if we want to prevent more attacks, more suffering and more innocent American and Israeli deaths.

"As I speak, our military forces are being mobilized to enter the region of the world that hates our freedoms, despises our morals and threatens with violence against our way of life. As your President, I, along with my closest advisors, have come to the conclusion that Iran, with its threat of utilizing its recently developed nuclear weapons, has become a cancer to world civilization and therefore must be removed. We have attempted less invasive tactics in the past, including using reason and goodwill to persuade this country to shift its malicious intent away from us…to no avail. We can ill afford another lengthy war with Iran, such as the one we experience with Iraq early in the 21st Century.

"Therefore, as a surgeon removes an organ infested with cancer to save the rest of the human body, so I believe it is time to remove the cancer of hatred and intolerance that exists in this vicious society. Doing so will save the rest of the world from any impending nuclear attacks, and will enable us all to live in peace and tranquility." He paused a moment to drink from a glass of water.

"I know the defensive action we have embarked upon will have widespread collateral damage," he went on, "and I do not take its consequences lightly. However, the administration has come to the conclusion that one powerful, decisive strike against Iran will ultimately save more lives through the elimination of one terrorist society and its evil plot to kill innocent civilians. In doing so, we will send a message to both Iraq and Saudi Arabia that to continue to threaten the world's freedoms will surely result in the same fate befalling them as well."

The crowd in the bar stood absolutely hushed, staring intently up at the screen. Dawn's four-year habit of clocking and analyzing his phrases, along with the words he chose, kicked into high gear. Filled with fear and revulsion, she knew that this was beyond an academic exercise of interpretation. "Remove the cancer," "collateral damage," "one powerful, decisive strike." Despite the gravity of his manner, he seemed to be anxiously defending something more than retaliation.

"We can expect much of the world to disagree with our actions at first. Countries we have helped to keep safe now and in the past, or that have not been targeted as we have, cannot be expected to understand the full dangers of allowing such rogue societies to continue on as they have. As the sole target of these purveyors of evil, and as the superpower that works to preserve the balance of peace on this planet, it is up to us to make the tough decisions and cleanse the world of the evil that threatens us all."

Dawn's face was white, her mind whirring. The dangerous language of "good" and "evil" was a dominant force in the Presidential Address. This was not the preservation of safety; it was a moral crusade that he expected the whole world to condemn. The UN would ask questions about retaliation, but they would be nothing the US couldn't block or ignore. What were they planning that every other country would denounce?

After a strategic pause, he continued. "So tonight, as you get on your knees to pray, please ask God for the continued strength, vision and courage necessary to finally eliminate the evil that plagues His kingdom." Again, a brief pause and then: "And may God bless America."

He left the stand without taking questions. The screen filled with heroic depictions of organized troops mobilizing against an unseen enemy. Their clean uniforms, scrubbed faces and shiny airplanes belied the horror that would follow. From the sky, their uniforms might not even get dirty. Overcome with revulsion, Dawn fought her way out of the bar and stood outside, her back to the glass, watching the torrent of rain splatter down against the beach.

"I was right, Ray," she whispered, squeezing her eyes shut. Yet her knowledge had changed nothing. Now the activists would swing into motion, belatedly fighting against the tide of opinion, after the jets had already left the ground.

Marianne followed her out. "Why would Iran sponsor terrorism?" she asked. "I thought they'd been fighting so hard to stamp it out – I thought it was hitting them harder than anyone."

Dawn gaped at her. "Don't tell me you bought that

shit?" she replied. "What government in its right mind would attack this psychopathic nation? And then bomb the *entertainment* industry, of all things?"

Marianne lowered her eyes and leaned against the glass next to Dawn.

"What's going to happen now?" she asked, her voice small and frightened.

Dawn closed her eyes; the President's language finally fell into place in her mind. "Something evil," she said quietly.

After all the hard work Dawn had put into her coursework and all the anxiety about her results, collecting her grades was a bit of an anti-climax. She noted, without surprise, that Geoff was top of the class and she had a B. That final exam had cost her dearly – yet in the end, what did it matter?

Professor Jennings passed her in the corridor and asked for a quiet word. Dawn followed her indifferently to her office.

"I won't pretend I wasn't disappointed," the professor began.

"Likewise," said Dawn. "By the exam questions, I mean – not the grade. I expected that."

Alice Jennings had obviously been expecting tears and despair. Dawn's blandness irritated her. She took a seat behind her desk and regarded Dawn with a stern face.

"Dawn, it is not accepted policy to answer a different question than the one presented…"

"I answered the one that was presented," interrupted Dawn.

"You did not *answer* it, you *dismissed* it in a paragraph!" snapped the professor.

"You always told us the work we did was important," said Dawn, "and then gave us the most trivial question possible while there was one so much more important to consider, to examine…"

She could see the fury rising in her professor's face. Once, that would have made her quake with fear, but now she just added it to a long list of suddenly insignificant things.

"You know, Professor Jennings," she said coldly, "It's laughable that I have to diminish my thought process to earn grades from you. I played the game with my last few essays for class – but when it came to the exam, I just couldn't stand it anymore. If we're not exploring things of real importance, what's the point of this course? And this…" She held up the piece of paper with her grade on it. "This is meaningless to me. If this is what I get for following the true course aims, so be it. It's just paper."

She turned her back on the still-sputtering professor and closed the door softly on her old career plans.

Ray's memorial was held at Dawn's home. Jack Firestone's had been held at Arlington, attended by the President, and broadcast nationwide. Dawn refused any media presence as resolutely as she had refused any formalities and military honors. She was amazed by her own ability to hold out against such powerful people. She followed her gut instinct on what was truest to Ray's memory, respectfully refused to budge, and found they acceded to her will.

There were no remains that required burial or cremation, and no religious observances seemed appropriate. Les and his mother cooked for the attendees. Dawn made all the terrible phone calls to old friends with Les holding her hand. She found that along the available networks, people picked up her burden and helped her carry it, volunteering to contact others and offering help. Through the links between people, the sadness spread and was eased. Marianne helped Dawn arrange the house with flowers and greenery. They tried to make a memory board depicting Ray's life, but aside from his certificates and photos, they didn't know what else to add. The life that had generated these few material things was gone, leaving them empty and meaningless. Dawn finally broke down and locked herself in Ray's room. When she emerged, Marianne had put up a single large photo of Ray – not in uniform – and arranged candles and flowers around it.

"Just him," she said. "That's what we miss."

"Thanks," replied Dawn, and allowed a wan smile among tears.

In the sultry afternoon, people began to arrive – Ray's colleagues, his old college friends, and Dawn's own schoolmates came to offer support.

"I'm so sorry," they all said on arrival, but life went on and soon they vacillated towards the people they knew, falling into conversations about other things. Dawn heard the snatches of talk around her and pressed her face against Les's chest to hide her rage. *What else did I expect?*

Thomas arrived with Cathy, their hands tightly clasped and their faces full of sorrow.

"It looks beautiful, Dawn," said Thomas, indicating their surroundings.

"Thanks." she said.

Cathy hugged her, and said softly in her ear, "You poor girl."

Their obvious grief and sympathy eased her churning emotions and she was able to turn with more understanding to the next tongue-tied arrival who didn't know what to say except, "I'm so sorry."

When everyone had arrived, she stood up to speak. A sudden hush ran around the room, bubbles of conversation popping as people turned their attention to her. Hesitantly, she cleared her throat.

"I don't remember my father's funeral, really," she began. "All I remember about my mother's funeral is Ray picking me up and telling me he'd keep me safe. When Thomas told me he was dead, I thought I'd lost my last safe place in the world. But that's not true. Ray taught me everything, including how to make the world a safe place for myself. Ray took me from six years old to the cusp of independence, and one of the last things he said to me was in approval of that independence. What I have lost is my father, my mother and my brother, all rolled into one."

She saw people's eyes fill with tears and realized that they did care, they did grieve alongside her, exactly as she needed them to. Thomas and Cathy stood, arms wrapped around each other, their heads leaning together in shared grief. It made her voice shakier, but gave her the courage to continue.

"There is no way to explain to you what Ray meant to me. He taught me to read, to dance, to work hard, to live according to my principles, and to realize my dreams. He tucked me in at night, helped me with my homework, took me on holidays, and told me about guys… How many brothers in this world have to be the one who tells their kid sister about the birds and the bees?"

There were a few hushed chuckles.

"Ray took on the job of looking after me…well, to be honest, from the moment I was born. Our parents – had their problems. He looked after me. And no one, *no one* could have wished for better." Her eyes filmed over and she had to blink hard before she could see her notes to continue. "It's very hard to describe someone you know so well. And everyone here knew Ray, too. But I would like to thank him for much.

"Apart from everything I've already said – Ray, I want to thank you for being so loyal. So loving. So principled and absolutely honest. So considerate and caring. So ambitious, because through your example, you taught me how to hold onto a dream. In the last few months of his life, Ray became so gentle, too – so compassionate – so understanding. So –

and this is a word that he would have once hated, but now he'd understand – spiritual. I lost you just as you got perfect, Ray." Her voice cracked, sliding over different pitches. She sniffed, fighting back tears, as her mouth worked.

"He's left me with friends too," she continued. "Especially Marianne – who I know he loved, heart and soul." Marianne, already weepy, covered her face with her hands as her shoulders began to shake. "And Les – who he respected so much and valued so highly. There's a Ray-shaped hole in my life that will never go away. But he got me this far, got me to the point where I could make it without him, even if it feels as if I sometimes can't. What he gave me is the most beautiful thing in the world, and I owe it to him to take it the rest of the way. Ray – I love you. I miss you. So much."

Her faltering control broke and she stepped away from the center of the room, her head lowered and her eyes blinded, towards Les's waiting arms.

Over the following week, people across the country were glued to their TV screens, their laptops, and the data-streams on their cell phones. They all saw images of Iranians lying peacefully where they had dropped in the streets, hills and countryside. They witnessed a multitude of fresh-faced American troops swiftly moving in to secure the borders and oil wells, as corporate-run restoration crews began their grisly clean-up detail. They all heard voice-overs as they watched the images, announcing how fuel prices were already plummeting and how the attack had eliminated the threat of nuclear war from the Middle East, saving countless American lives. What they didn't see were the plumes of black smoke a half mile wide in several directions as distant massive cremations of the dead commenced.

Ambassadorial staff members of the Allied Nations in Iran had been airlifted to safety in the early morning hours prior to the insidious attack. Now, U.S. embassies around the world were under siege, barricaded against angry mobs waving placards and demanding answers outside. Europe witnessed a massive uprising of people converging on government buildings and media broadcast centers alike, vowing to boycott and picket every American building or shop. MacDonald's restaurants across the world stood closed, in fear of backlash from confused and angry citizens. Riot police patrolled the streets, wary of any sudden onslaught by European residents from Middle Eastern descent who sought retaliation.

The Prime Minister of the United Kingdom, in an effort to reinforce its alliance, held a press conference at 10 Downing Street, in which he condemned the insidious actions of the United States, but pleaded with his countrymen and women to ride it out and wait for any possible wisdom of the U.S. actions to take form.

"For a long time we considered ourselves partners with the States," he said. "We hoped that our steadying influence would help them use their enormous power for the betterment of the world. In the spirit of this intention, we can only hope that the recent actions of the United States, while seemingly atrocious, may prove to have far-reaching benefits beyond what we can now discern."

The words of other Prime Ministers and Presidents were less gentle. Vitriol was heaped on the nation and American tourists were asked not to travel abroad. Governments pleaded for calm, beseeching their citizens to show "a greater moral fiber" than that demonstrated by Americans.

In Iran, all the major cities remained perfectly intact, but briefly resembled ghost towns. People instantly dropped where they stood when the stealth planes hummed silently overhead, raining deadly cargo on their unsuspecting heads. There were no screams, no displays of furious might. The particles of invisible matter simply passed through every living organism, killing it instantly before descending deep into the Earth to be dissolved in an instant and rendered undetectable.

At the same time, American citizens watched as their neighbors and colleagues – everyone of Iranian descent or nationality – was put under house arrest. The world united in confusion over what had actually taken place. It appeared that the U.S. had effectively implemented a way to decimate an entire nation of people, and then invade the country, without the use of a military force. Good Samaritans the world over were stymied as to how they could provide disaster relief efforts. Money and aid poured in, but there was no one left standing to aid.

Not much of this was known within the United States. The administration was prepared for the reaction of "a world that has not been faced with the incredibly difficult decisions that have confronted us," as the President put it. Mirror servers had been collecting their cache for some time and the national internet firewall was raised.

"As a nation that stands for the freedom of speech," the President said during a follow-up address, "this has been a hard choice to make. The hatred for American values and American freedoms that is so rife in the world right now has given us no option. It has become a matter of national security. Just as we must protect our citizens and our national resources, so we must protect our data resources from attack. We are a nation under threat, and we must defend ourselves from that threat. We will do everything in our power to preserve the freedoms of our people and we hope that our people will understand the sacrifices they may have to make in the name of those freedoms."

With the cameras switched off, the President retreated to the small chamber behind the White House Pressroom and made his way back through the corridors to the Oval Office. He needed to reread the passage again, to feel sure the decisions he had made were the right ones. For hours he had scoured his familiar Bible the night before, desperate for guidance. Nothing in the New Testament had been helpful, as he flipped past the gospels to hunt through the sterner words of Apostle Paul. At last, Deuteronomy 13:6 yielded him the passage he sought.

He sat again at his huge carved desk, drew his NIV Bible out of the drawer and opened it at the bookmark. With a deep sigh, he reread the exonerating words: "If your very own brother, or your son or daughter, or the wife you love, or your closest friend secretly entices you, saying, 'Let us go and worship other gods' (gods that neither you nor your fathers have known, gods of the peoples around you, whether near or far, from one end of the land to the other), do not yield to him or listen to him. Show him no pity. Do not spare him or shield him. You must certainly put him to death. Your hand must be the first in putting him to death and then the hands of all the people."

With a resolute sign, President Priest lowered his face into his hands and said, "Your will be done, oh Heavenly Father…your will be done."

Oriana sat at her kitchen table with Les, Dawn and Marianne. The two identical VEC programs lay in the middle, innocuous silver rings against the wood.

"They've just killed millions of people," said Marianne shakily. "Why would they hesitate over us?"

Oriana nodded her agreement. "It's time to make our plans," she said. "I can probably be more useful to you than you realize." She smiled at the slight shock on their faces. "Where do you think Les got his brains from?" she said, ruffling his hair. He grinned and gripped Dawn's hand. "With what I know already, I hold your lives in my hand," she went on, "so I am prepared to trust you with mine also. Dawn, you said you wanted to go traveling when you finished your studies. Did you say this to your classmates, also?"

Surprised, Dawn nodded.

"Good. Tell them you're going. Marianne – your book has just been released in Europe, yes? Do you have a book-signing tour arranged?"

"I hardly think they'll want to see an American…" began Marianne.

Oriana shook her head. "Putting an American on a European stage would be like throwing a Christian to the lions right now," she sighed. "But it will die down – oh yes, sooner than any of you expect. Humans are harsher and more forgetful than any of you realize. And the States still hold the purse strings of the world. So you say you are going anyway and you will take a holiday until the furor dies down."

She stood up and took the cannelloni out of the oven, putting it on the side to settle. As she moved around the table, pouring wine, she continued. "The Italian diplomatic staff will fly out in a few days. I will arrange for you to go with them." She smiled and raised her eyebrows. "I still work for my government," she said. "You see? Now you hold my life, also. Let's eat. We will continue planning afterwards, a good meal should not be spoiled by talk of work."

Marianne's hand trembled as she took a sip of wine. Her stomach turned at the taste of alcohol and she pushed it aside. "This feels like a war council," she said.

"Call it a peace council, instead," said Dawn. Under the table, her fingers entwined with Les's.

For their last few days together, Les and Dawn barely left his bedroom. Oriana and Marianne exchanged a few knowing glances, in unspoken agreement not to disturb the young lovers. After all, they had so little time. Les was keeping his job at NASA and, with the increasing travel restrictions, no one could say when they might be able to meet again.

Behind the locked door of his bedroom, they sat fully dressed at his computer, the pieces of a dismantled VEC machine and headset arranged across the bed.

"It'll be one hell of a data-stream," said Dawn. "Are you sure the firewall won't block it?"

Les shrugged. "It's too early to say – they've only just erected it and I'm sure they'll be fine-tuning it for a long time. From what I can make out, they seem more concerned about data coming in than data going out, though. NASA generates a lot of traffic, and I'm hoping I can hide it in the midst of it. If I distribute the information in data-packets across the system…" He broke off to scribble some notes on a pad of paper.

"You'll need to set up the server on your side," he resumed when he finished. "That way my data will be coming to you. And set up the initial program – once that's done and I can get in, I can talk you through the rest, or maybe bring it to you. It depends on how exactly this is going to work." He burst out laughing, tickled by the absurd ambition of what they were planning, and pulled her to him for a long kiss. After a few minutes, their hands were reaching for the hems of each other's clothes and Dawn tore herself away.

"Much as I'd like to rip your clothes off," she said with a wobbly laugh, "We need to get this set up if we want to see each other again anytime soon. How the hell is this program going to work?"

"The dual headset co-ordinates the information so two people can enter the same program, but I don't see why the headsets should be physically connected. It's just data, and data can fly. If I can just figure out how that works…" He took a deep breath. "Okay, I'm going to work on that and not think about what you would look like naked."

Dawn giggled. "Would it help if I stripped off my clothes, so your imagination doesn't have to work on that?"

"*No!*" said Les firmly.

16

President Priest stood at the window of his office, looking out into the Rose Garden. In keeping with the holiday, it had been strung with soft orange lights and carved pumpkins around the perimeter of the lawn. In the dark, the candles glowed through the hard rind, illuminating the cut-out faces. He disapproved of Halloween. All those witches and wizards and dark things, he felt, were not in keeping with biblical Christianity. Nevertheless, it was a national festival and he'd been persuaded that there was nothing Satanic about a few pumpkins and lights. Now looking at the garish grins, he wasn't so sure.

Most of his staff had already arrived for the meeting. Neal Crossing was chatting with Reed Polman and Rich Caseman, the Political and Economic Advisor respectively, over the coffee trolley. Helen Cross sat on a chair next to the sofa, her ankles crossed, and a manila folder on her lap. The door opened and the Vice-President and Secretary of Defense came in. As they all drifted towards the central seating area, Robert took his seat.

"Alright," he said, checking his watch, "Nutshell reports, I only have a few minutes. Give me the broad picture and I'll look at the detailed reports tomorrow." He had a function to attend with his wife after the meeting, and he didn't want to be late. He glanced at Rich, indicating that he should begin.

"The economy's soaring," the man began. "The steady flow of oil from the Middle East is helping enormously. Consumer confidence is up, spending is up. Every possible index to measure the health of an economy is up." He grinned.

"Reed?"

"Your favorable ratings have risen to nearly 85%, Mr. President," He said. "The percentage of people who believe the nation is moving in the right direction is at 80%. Also, interestingly, church attendance across the nation is increasing."

"Excellent news." The President nodded at the Secretary of Defense. "Our defense situation?"

"The clean-up operation is on-going. There are a lot of rumblings, but no real threats – people know who they're dealing with now. It's all under control and the details are here in my report."

"Fine. Neal?"

The Secretary of State cleared his throat. "Obviously, this has been fairly delicate for foreign affairs, but we've made a lot of headway. The fact that the initial attacks on us were devastating has done a lot to mitigate our position with the UN. Foreign governments have made a lot of noise, but with all our economic ties, they don't want to push too hard. Behind the scenes, it's business as usual, especially now that our economy's back on track. A few African countries are still calling for complete sanctions, such as South Africa, Zimbabwe, Nigeria, but they're minor players and the others can't afford to cut themselves off from us. Oh, and firing that general did wonders. Everyone understands the additional detonations were well outside his concern." He smirked.

"Okay people," said Warren, taking over. "We've done some excellent work to make this a better world to live in."

Helen looked at him. She struggled to hide her distain for him behind a professional demeanor. "Pardon me, Mr. Vice President, but how can you say that?"

The surprised faces of everyone present all turned toward her.

"We have killed millions of people at the hands of covert arsenal," Helen continued, "because six thousand of our own citizens were killed in some alleged terrorist attack." She glared at Warren. "Our entire country has been manipulated into buying consumer goods, fearing God, adoring our country right or wrong and voting conservative, all through the use of subliminal messages embedded in their VEC programs, and now we have the nerve to sit here and pat ourselves on the back for the great work we've done. What kind sinister perspective are you operating from?"

"Helen…" began the President, but the Vice-President was already talking over him.

"From the perspective that sometimes the ends do justify the means. And please don't sit there on your high horse and say that the world is not a better place than it was three months ago."

"Please don't say the world," retorted Helen. "Say the United States, if you must, though I'm not sure I agree with that, either. And it only took several million deaths to make our citizens content – pretty cheap price, if you really think about it."

She stood and began to walk out of the circle of men. Robert caught her arm.

"Helen, Helen, Helen," he said sadly, "This was a very dangerous world and we needed to make tough decisions."

She looked down at him.

"Decisions that I'm certain the rest of the world still aren't very happy with," he continued, "but I'm equally certain that in time, historians will conclude and the world will see that it was a very necessary evil that insured the survival of our planet."

Her nose wrinkled with disgust and she pulled herself free from his grip. "With all due respect, Mr. President," she said scathingly, "If you give Warren Christian enough time, he'll likely have you convinced that shitting on your desk is a very necessary evil as well."

She flashed a glare at Warren and strode out the room, slamming the door hard behind her. The remaining members of the cabinet looked at each other in stunned silence.

Warren cleared his throat. "I suspect you may want to give some thought to selecting a new Chief of Staff, Mr. President," he said.

The stone steps leading up to the apartment were slippery in the rain, which flowed in a steady stream down the red-tiled banisters of the staircase. Marianne's umbrella was no defense against the rain that seemed to bounce up off the ground as heavily as it poured from the sky. She smiled ruefully. Her visions of Italy had never included these torrential autumn rains. Her sodden coat hung loosely around her significantly trimmed-down figure. Marianne's stomach had been delicate for months now, and the weight had fallen off dramatically as a result. She should start gaining a bit soon, however.

The curtains on the other side of the apartment door were open. Inside the small room, she could see Dawn moving briskly between packing cartons, stacking the small jewel cases of VEC programs inside. On the cover of each one was a sunburst and the title, "Ray of Light: A Journey into the Metaphysical World." Renata, their main assistant, was taping up boxes as they were filled.

She stopped in front of the computer, pressing a few keys to check details. As Marianne pushed open the door, she heard Dawn speaking instructions to Renata in Italian. Turning, she saw Marianne enter the room and her face lit up with a smile. She ran forward to hug her.

"Careful, I'm soaked!" said Marianne, laughing.

"Good news," said Dawn, beaming. "Well – good and bad. We've found distributors in London, Stockholm and Paris and the first shipments are ready to go. But I forgot it's All Saint's Day – we won't be able to go to the post office until Tuesday. How was Rome? What do the publishers think of Inner Light?"

"Fine… fine," said Marianne vaguely. She took her wet coat off and hung it on the hook, wondering how to begin.

"You really need to gain some weight," said Dawn, scrutinizing her sharply. She translated quickly for Renata.

"Is okay," smiled Renata, "I understand."

"I'm sure I will, soon." Marianne plopped down on a plain wooden chair, exhausted, and looked around at the little apartment which had been their home for the last three months. Despite the freezing rain and the untreated brick, the volcanic rock from which it had been made kept it snug. Marianne felt the warmth seep back into her veins with relief. The broad stone windowsills held plants and the occasional tall candle, fixed to the sill with its own wax. As was typical for Sorrento, their little corner of Naples, the roof was wooden with crosswise-running beams. Despite the obvious hive of activity, the place was tidy and the ceramic tiles sparkling clean. Dawn was an absolute dream of a housemate. In every respect. At times, her competence felt overwhelming. The more ill and fatigued Marianne felt, the more easily Dawn picked up the additional responsibilities. Marianne wondered how Dawn would feel about this new one.

"Dawn…?" she said hesitantly.

"Yeah?" Dawn was already putting the kettle on the stove in the kitchen-corner.

"I've figured out what nurture and protect the birth of enlightenment means."

Dawn whirled around. "What?"

Marianne fiddled in her bag and withdrew a small black-and-white photograph. It was fuzzy and taken at a bad angle. She held it out. "It means I'm pregnant."

Dawn stared from Marianne's face to the scan and back again. "How is that possible? Have you been with someone I don't know about?"

Marianne shook her head.

"Then how is this even possible?"

"I was with your brother."

Dawn blinked disbelievingly. "But that was only a VEC simulation," she protested.

"I didn't believe it, either. I missed my period and took a test, but I figured it was a phantom pregnancy – they happen, you know. But then in Rome, I went to see a doctor." She waved the scan. "Real scan, real heartbeat, real baby." She began to cry. "This is why I've been such a bear to live with and why I can't eat anything," she laughed through her tears, "and why I go all weepy every time I see a goddamned kitten. I felt the love, Dawn…it was real."

"Oh my god!" screeched Dawn, her face illuminated with delight. To Renata's bewilderment, she explained hastily what was going on in Italian.

Later, when Marianne was deeply asleep and Renata had gone home, Dawn picked up her VEC headset. She stepped through the ether and onto the warm sands of Cocoa Beach on a sparkling autumn day. She sat down, digging her bare toes into the sand, enjoying the sun on her skin and the gentle rush back and forth of the sea. After a few minutes, Les sat down next to her and took her hand.

The first time she had stepped into this world of theirs, it had been a void emptier than the outer reaches of space; only their two figures moving inside it. Just learning how to create the platform for a shared simulated environment had been difficult enough, eating up their last days together in Florida. Les studied frantically and taught Dawn each new snippet as he worked it out. They didn't even know then if it would work.

All through the long flight to Italy, Dawn felt tormented with the thought that maybe they had squandered their last precious moments together on a wild goose chase. She worried that even if Les had worked it out right, she would get something wrong. She feared that the national firewall would fall between them forever like an iron curtain. But then, stepping into the void for the first time, she saw Les materialize in the blackness, smiling broadly.

"Well done, Dawn." He said moving toward her. Since then, they'd learned how to use their own sensory input to create new environments, such as the one they now enjoyed.

"Nice décor," said Dawn.

"Thanks," Les replied. "I've sat here a lot, staring out at the Atlantic, and thinking that you're just on the other side... It makes you feel closer. But also very far away."

They smiled sadly at each other and their virtual hands interwove. She filled him in about the progress they were making with getting Ray's program out. Then she told him about Marianne's pregnancy.

"Well, it wouldn't be the first time in history," chuckled Les.

"I never bought that story, before now," said Dawn grinning. "I always thought that somehow Mary just pulled the wool over Joseph's eyes. I guess the world's full of things we don't understand."

"I've always thought so," said Les simply. "But at least we get to find things out, and make it a safer place for the little newcomer."

Dawn nodded.

They sat in peaceful silence, watching the shadows lengthen. Before them, the shimmering ocean ran back and forth ceaselessly.

ENJOY MORE TITLES
BY ALAN C. LYONS:

AVAILABLE NOW:

CROSS FIRE
THE MOTHER LODE

COMING SOON:

MORE FROM THE RAY OF LIGHT TRILOGY:

BOOK 2: CRITICAL MASS

BOOK 3: REVELATIONS

FOR MORE INFORMATION
PLEASE VISIT:

WWW.ALANLYONS.COM

www.ingramcontent.com/pod-product-compliance
Lightning Source LLC
Chambersburg PA
CBHW070322260626
47160CB00003B/922